DAY ONE

C1

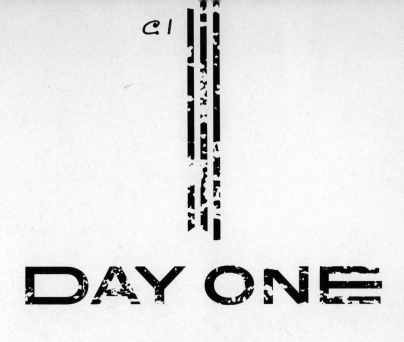

DAY ONE

NATE KENYON

THOMAS DUNNE BOOKS
ST. MARTIN'S PRESS
NEW YORK

THOMAS DUNNE BOOKS.
An imprint of St. Martin's Press.

DAY ONE. Copyright © 2013 by Macmillan Films. All rights reserved. Printed in the United States of America. For information, address St. Martin's Press, 175 Fifth Avenue, New York, N.Y. 10010.

www.thomasdunnebooks.com
www.stmartins.com

Library of Congress Cataloging-in-Publication Data

Kenyon, Nate.
    Day one : a novel / Nate Kenyon.
        p. cm.
    ISBN 978-1-250-01321-7 (hardcover)
    ISBN 978-1-250-01337-8 (e-book)
    1. Journalists—Fiction. I. Title.
    PS3611.E677D39 2013
    813'.6—dc23

                                2013017075

St. Martin's Press books may be purchased for educational, business, or promotional use. For information on bulk purchases, please contact Macmillan Corporate and Premium Sales Department at 1-800-221-7945, extension 5442, or write specialmarkets@macmillan.com.

First Edition: October 2013

10 9 8 7 6 5 4 3 2 1

For Brendan Deneen, the spark who lit this fire

DAY ONE

LATER THAT DAY, it was the dream he would remember. In the dead hours between midnight and dawn, it crept up on him like a child playing hide-and-seek.

Thomas was running toward him from the park, his cherubic face lit up with a thousand-watt smile. That's my son, Hawke thought as he watched the boy race through the scattering of leaves. It filled him with a sense of wonder and bewilderment. That this child would depend on him for everything, look up to him the way men looked to God; it kept him from being anything less than honest.

During the worst of what was to come, it kept him sane.

The dream changed without warning. The expression on the boy's face was not one of happiness at all, but a grimace of fear. Tears streaked his cheeks. Thomas reached up as he ran on chubby little legs and Hawke crouched to gather him into his arms. The boy grabbed him by the neck with a drowning grip and buried his face in the hollow between collarbone and chest. The impact carried Hawke over and he sat down hard, crunching into a pile of fall leaves that had drifted against the foot of an ancient oak. Rough bark bit into his back.

Please, Daddy, don't leave me!

This kind of emotion for Thomas wasn't normal. He hardly ever cried. The boy squeezed tighter and wrapped his legs around Hawke's waist. Beyond them, the park was deserted,

1

the swings ticking softly on their metal chains as a breeze nudged and twisted them. The whole world had disappeared; there was nobody left except the boy and his father sitting in the leaves.

Thomas's tears bled through Hawke's shirt. He rubbed his son's back, but the boy wouldn't stop. He kept squeezing, trying to mold himself to his father's body, and Hawke held on tight and swallowed hard against a lump in his throat.

I won't let anything happen to you; I promise. I'll do anything to keep you safe.

Cool air swept across the park. The wind grew teeth as bits of dust and leaves swirled and flung themselves against Hawke's face. He squinted against the sudden attack as the sky lowered itself like a metal plate pushing against their heads and thunderclouds boiled up and spilled over the dusty ground.

In moments, they were soaked through. Hawke struggled to his feet, still gripping his son to his chest. The boy's cries became more frantic, his fingers digging into the flesh of his father's back. Hawke stumbled forward and blinked against the river of water pouring down his face and the stinging needles of rain that lashed his skin.

Something was pulling Thomas away from him.

He held tight, but the pull was strong. He glanced over Thomas's shoulder and saw nothing at first. The park was empty, the basketball court deserted, black and slick with rain. The boy cried out as a cold, slippery thing wormed its way between them, wrapped around his waist, and yanked. The muscles in Hawke's arms grew taut and quivered. Panic lit him up inside like an electric shock, thickened his tongue.

He looked up again and saw tentacles uncoiling like

silvery-steel ropes from the metallic sky above, a monstrous, multi-limbed creature snaking down to snatch at his son.

Don't let them take me, Daddy!

Another one wrapped itself around Thomas's neck. The pull grew stronger. Hawke fell to his knees, sobbing. He had a feeling that it was his fault, something he'd done that was causing this. His arms were on fire. He fought against the thing trying to take his boy as the wind whipped across the empty park.

I won't let you go! he shouted into the rain. But as the words were torn from his throat his grip gave way. He watched as his child tumbled backward across the asphalt and was swept up into the vacuum of the night as the clouds wept and the earth moaned with him.

The dream left Hawke gasping into his pillow. His son's pleading face remained vividly etched into his memory, the helplessness he felt as sharp and clear as a physical ache.

He got up from bed and padded through the familiar darkness of the hall, wiping his eyes and nose with his undershirt, the shirt his wife used to tease him about wearing. *You look like a little old man,* she would say, smiling. Before things had started going wrong. *Take it off and come to bed.* But he could never fall asleep like that, thinking that somehow he'd be more prepared for an emergency if he had something on. If there was a fire. If someone got into the apartment, someone like Lowry. He was always thinking that way.

He couldn't calm his trembling limbs, or banish the feeling that had welled up in him. He'd been feeling this way all the time lately, like he was standing on humming tracks with a train bearing down and no way to step aside. He wondered if it would be like this forever.

3

Thomas's room was stiflingly hot. The night-light lit up enough of the floor for him to see. The colors changed from blue to red, making the carpet look like a slowly beating heart. He walked to the bed and looked down at his sleeping child. Thomas's brow wrinkled and he sighed, turned over and stuck his little thumb in his mouth.

Only a dream, Hawke thought. *My boy's safe. It's over now.*

Later, he would realize how incredibly wrong he'd been.

STAGE ONE

CHAPTER ONE

WHEN HE OPENED HIS EYES, John Hawke was immediately aware of two things: His alarm hadn't gone off. And there was something in the room with him.

Remnants of the dream still clung like shedding skin; something multi-tentacled and metallic wrapped around his son, slipping across his chest and slithering around his throat. It left Hawke shaky and tight, a knot in his neck and an ache near the base of his skull.

The sound came again, a click and hiss like the warning of an animal crouched in the dark.

The sense of danger faded with the dream, and he sat up, rubbing at his neck. An alien creature had not invaded after all. The radiators in the building were part of a forced hot-water, gravity-fed system, ancient and very noisy. They had come on for the first time last night with the cooler fall temperatures, moving trapped air pockets from one place to another. The maintenance company would have to bleed them, but he knew from experience that a system that old would let the air back in again, one bubble at a time.

The feeling that something was wrong remained with him.

Hawke stood and went to the window, cracking the heavy drapes. Early morning sunlight sliced directly through swirling dust motes, burying itself like shards of glass in his skull. A muttered curse came from the bed as his wife turned over

7

within the tangled sheets, away from him, and he closed the drapes again, making his way through the dark to where she lay. The air felt thick enough to push through as he relived every word they had said to each other the night before, every expression on her face. He'd said things he shouldn't have. It was part of this unsettled feeling, most likely. Part of a much larger, much more terrifying feeling of emptiness, uncertainty and shame.

A fresh pang of regret washed over him. He'd always been too focused, too fanatical in his passion for uncovering secrets. It had gotten him into trouble ever since he was a boy. He could see a vision of the truth so clearly, it tended to cloud over everything else. But the vision of his own success, the other thing he'd cultivated, had veered off track. And he didn't know exactly how to fix it.

He smelled the musk and sweat of sleep, reached out to touch his wife and hesitated, hand above her hip. Touching her would lead to a rekindling of emotions, both good and bad. He would have to make a choice between apology and furthering the argument. But he was going to be late. He'd never been one to keep traditional hours, but his most recent project was different, and included rising at 6:00 A.M. like any of the other countless thousands who commuted into New York City every day. He'd been going in faithfully for a week now. It was his chance to make things right again and put his life back on track, and he couldn't screw it up.

He thought of the slight swell of Robin's belly under the sheet. *Almost three months gone.* She had another ultrasound scheduled in a few days to update them on the bleeding. They would find out the sex before long, assuming everything went well. She thought it was a girl. As hard as he tried, he couldn't picture a face.

It was cold in the room, and he pulled the blanket up over Robin's shoulders, then stood again and walked through the gloom to the bathroom, passing Thomas's room where the boy still lay sleeping.

The shower was ice-cold. Hawke gasped through it like a man doing penance, fingers splayed across grout between tiles that had yellowed with age, the stinging spray needling his skin as he cursed the old building and its useless super who was probably still sleeping one off. They had moved into the apartment shortly after Thomas was born. The place reminded Hawke of the ancient, peeling Victorian he'd lived in with his parents until he was fourteen and they'd been forced to move to a smaller place, when his father's latest book had failed and the man had started drinking more heavily. The Victorian contained some of Hawke's better memories of childhood, tainted as they were by what followed.

Robin had loved this place at first; she talked about the charm and ambiance and history. But that was before they met Lowry. Their neighbor across the hall was a huge problem. It was like saying, *Other than the toxic mold, the place is great.* You couldn't separate the two.

The thought made Hawke's mood grow even darker. He emerged from the shower pink and shivering. At the sink, his electric razor nicked his chin enough to bleed. By the time he emerged from the bathroom in boxer shorts and T-shirt, wide-awake and buzzing like an angry hornet, he could hear the muted sounds of a nature program from the living room. He took a few deep breaths, caught a glimpse of his son's head over the top of the couch, reached over and tousled it gently. No good to let the day get to him like this. Thomas glanced up, mouth full of waffle, and returned to the TV program where an African leopard stalked a young antelope through thick stalks of dead grass. In some ways, Thomas seemed younger than his years; in other ways, far older. He didn't like regular kid shows, insisted on Discovery or National Geographic. He had a stuffed toy lion with a wild mane of fur that he carried everywhere, and it was propped next to Lego big blocks lined up on the coffee table in neat rows, exactly four of the same color to each tower, identically spaced. But he'd rather be playing with his father's iPad, Hawke thought. Thomas was already a tech guru. He was curious in a detached, slightly clinical way; he seemed to interact better with machines than people.

Robin was in the kitchen in her robe, her dark curls cascading around a pretty face puffy with sleep, a cup of decaf in her hand. She hadn't made anything for him, a definite sign that she was still angry.

"The coffeemaker's not working right," she said. "It's too bitter."

The kitchen was nothing more than a narrow aisle, open to the living room and separated by a bar-height counter with stools. "I'll take a look when I get home," Hawke said. His bottle and glass from the night before were still sitting out. He slipped past her, took the glass and rinsed it in the sink, then put the empty bottle in the recycling bin and grabbed an energy bar from the cabinet.

"We can't afford a new one—"

"I *know* we can't afford it," he said. "I said I'll figure it out."

Silence hung between them. The overhead lights flickered as if in response. His wife glanced up at them and put her cup on the counter, tightened the belt on her robe and hugged her belly.

"Lowry yelled at Thomas again yesterday in the hallway, when we went to the store," she said. "He was complaining about something, I don't know, the TV up too loud, whatever. He's like one of those little nippy dogs."

"I'll talk to him."

"You know how sensitive Thomas is, John. It hurts him, even if he won't talk about it."

Hawke nodded. Thomas rarely spoke at all anymore. Robin had started worrying about an autism spectrum disorder. *Give him more time, he'll be fine,* Hawke had kept insisting. But Thomas was almost three, and that argument wasn't working as well now. Hawke hadn't said anything to Robin, but lately he had started wondering whether his own father had had a touch of whatever genetic mutation would lead to something like this. It made some sense. The code of who you would become was imprinted in your DNA, the building blocks of life. You couldn't escape it, no matter how hard you tried.

Hawke's head was pounding. Parts of the dream came back to him, and he remembered metallic tentacles snaking down from the sky.

He gave Robin a kiss on the cheek, but she remained cool, her muscles tense. He let his lips linger just a moment, breathing her in, a scent of coffee and skin lotion and hair conditioner.

"I'm late. Gotta run. We'll talk later, okay?"

She nodded, and the look on her face softened for a moment. She was giving him an opening, letting him back in, and the entire world seemed to cave in on him. He was no good at this, never had been. *I'm sorry,* he thought, but didn't say it.

It was one of the many things he would regret.

AS HE PASSED Randall Lowry's door, Hawke paused for a moment, imagining his neighbor huddled there like a troll, eye against the peephole. Hawke had walked into a restroom of a Walmart once when he was about nine years old, his mother waiting impatiently outside, and had seen a man masturbating furiously against a urinal. Although Hawke had barely been old enough to understand, he remembered the feeling he'd had, a mixture of disgust and shame for having viewed it at all, as if he were somehow culpable. He'd turned and walked out and never told a soul, but he had felt tainted from seeing it, his world altered forever in some fundamental way.

Being in Lowry's presence was like that, as if whatever sickness the man suffered could be transferred through proximity alone. Hawke clutched his laptop bag close to his side like a protective parent and moved on down the hall. *The son of a bitch.* Lowry had been complaining about their son's noise since they moved into this place. Twice now he'd shouted at the boy, and they'd had other run-ins that made Hawke feel like he had to scrub the filth off himself. Thomas was confused by Lowry; Robin was terrified. He was definitely unbalanced, far more than just creepy, and he'd clearly lusted after Robin since they moved in, looking her up and down, standing too close on those rare occasions when they were in the same space. Men often stared at Robin, but not like this. Lowry was like a hyena evaluating whether to dart in and snatch away his prize.

Hawke had never seen the inside of the man's apartment, but he imagined a dimly lit, musty place with piles of old newspapers and boxes in crooked, leaning towers. When he found out Hawke had once worked at the *New York Times*, Lowry tried to get him to write a story about government conspiracies. Hawke told him to call his congressman. There was the incident in the laundry room, among others, things Hawke didn't like to think about for too long. Everything he and Robin had tried to do, including a conversation with the useless super, had achieved nothing, and the tension between the two men had grown into something close to viciousness. It was causing more stress between Hawke and his wife, which was one thing they didn't need. She'd had trouble getting pregnant the second time, and then she'd been bleeding off and on as the pregnancy had progressed, and her doctor had told her she had a subchorionic hematoma and she had to take it easy.

That prick Lowry was only making things worse. Enough was enough; Hawke would talk to the man again tonight, and if that didn't work he would have to go to the police.

The thought made Hawke's stomach churn. His own personal history with the authorities usually made him avoid them like the plague, but this had to be settled, once and for all.

Hoboken was just beginning to stir this early in the morning. In the street, the September air was crisp, the sky a flawless steel blue. Hawke smelled the river, heard the calls of geese flying overhead. He started thinking about other ways to make things right with Robin. Maybe another trip to Cuttyhunk Island, near Martha's Vineyard off the Massachusetts coast. It would be good to get away, have a little quiet time. Hawke used to go to a cottage his aunt owned there when he was a boy, and it had a special meaning for him and his wife: It was where they had gotten married.

Still thinking about how to make the trip work, he put his sunglasses on and chewed an aspirin and then the energy bar, chocolate grit in his teeth as he made his way to the PATH, joining a growing flood of people. It felt good to stretch his legs. He was no gym rat, but he was wiry strong and genetics had been good to him. He kept in shape by walking.

A cabdriver honked at him as he crossed the street, flashing him the finger. Someone cursed next to him and Hawke said, "Excuse me?" before realizing the man had a Bluetooth in his ear and smartphone in hand. The man wore a hand-tailored suit and shoes polished to a sleek shine. He shot Hawke a withering look, as if he were observing the biggest idiot on the planet, and continued his loud conversation.

Once underground, Hawke stuck his sunglasses up on his head and joined the slowly shuffling line to buy a coffee. He and Robin couldn't afford any extra costs on their stretched-tight budget, but he needed it badly and he had a few minutes before the PATH arrived. Train service had finally been fully restored after Hurricane Sandy, and it was good to see the crowds returning, although he could do without the lines.

When he made it to the front, the waif-thin girl behind the counter didn't even look at him, her gaze locked on her iPhone screen. Three piercings glittered, one through each eyebrow and a stud through her lip, and her hair was cut short and streaked with red. She was frowning and jumpy, like she'd had too much caffeine or something stronger.

Thomas would have been intrigued by the piercings. He

pointed out things that were different, seemed to want to understand them, even if he didn't say much. This girl wasn't saying much, either. Something was annoying her about the iPhone; she sighed, poking at the screen in frustration with a tip of pink tongue poking between her lips. In his earlier life, Hawke would have struck up a conversation with her, maybe helped her fix the problem. But he was a married man now, going on thirty, with a young son and another child on the way. He wasn't running around New York City hacking into big-business networks and chasing stories the way he had been only a few years ago, feeling like a rogue reporter and Internet cowboy. *And let's face it, you got sloppy and made mistakes.* Big ones. His hacker skills used to give him an edge in the reporter rat race, allowed him to see stories in ways others did not. But things changed. Maybe he'd lost that edge, the killer instinct all the best journalists needed to get to the truth.

The coffee was scalding hot, and he burned the roof of his mouth on the first sip. He settled into a window seat on the train, watching people situate themselves, many of them on their smartphones or tablets, maneuvering through the aisles with quick glances and shuffling feet. Hawke liked to watch people; he learned a lot. Maybe Thomas was like him that way. The same man was still talking on his Bluetooth, muttering something about derivatives and foreign exchange rates, and he jostled a young woman on his way past hard enough for her to stumble. He moved down the aisle until he was lost in the crowd.

A man across from Hawke had been watching, too. He clutched a rolled-up sign and had a large duffel bag tucked between his feet, and his clothes were nice but faded and slightly wrinkled, as if he'd worn them once or twice already between washings. There was a shadow of stubble across the man's cheeks, and his jaw muscles twitched.

"What a prick," Hawke said, motioning toward where Bluetooth had disappeared. He nodded at the duffel. Something about the shape of it, bulky, with angles and points, made him uneasy. "You going to a rally or something?"

The man stared at him, openly hostile. The Occupy Wall Street movement had evolved recently. Now they were focused on high-frequency computer trading and credit swaps, which had bloomed once again with the market recovery. The 1 percent were richer than ever.

But if this man was going to a rally on Wall Street, he was on the wrong train. Maybe it was somewhere uptown. Hawke looked around, spotting several others with packs and signs, and suddenly remembered he was wearing a tie and suit jacket, the nicer of the two he owned. "I'm not a broker," he said. "I'm a journalist." It sounded stupid and insincere: *I'm with you, buddy.* He had no idea what this man's life was like.

The man kept staring, then shook his head in disgust and touched his jaw. Hawke reached up to his own face and felt the speck of tissue still clinging to him from when he'd nicked himself shaving. He picked it off and stared at the small circular brown stain on his palm. *Great.* One hell of a start to the day. "Thanks," he said, but the man just pulled the duffel bag closer and looked back toward the spot where Bluetooth had disappeared.

A WOMAN TOOK THE SEAT next to Hawke, huffing, her meaty thighs spilling over into his space. He sipped his coffee, feeling his body becoming more alert. His mind had already started churning, imagining a Web site that tracked civil unrest by mapping police presence, cross-referenced with politicians' statements and Twitter alerts, to create a kind of gauge for the level of tension in a particular area. A thermometer that took the temperature of a given confrontation and predicted violence. It could help people avoid a certain area—or search it out, if that was their thing. When he worked for the *Times* he had blogged during Hurricane Sandy and created a real-time map that tracked the hurricane's path and predicted which areas of the city were the most vulnerable based on criteria like building clusters, street maps and distance to emergency services, and tied that to live traffic updates and an orderly evacuation plan. Earlier in his career, working as a freelancer for several local news outlets, he'd covered crime and created a site that tracked police activity in New York City by street, culling data from public logs and police scanners to provide near real-time public safety updates. He'd also built a system for a feature on education that analyzed student test scores and cross-referenced that with public funding levels and census data to show the best school districts, as well as racial and socioeconomic bias.

He knew how to do these things. His entire career had been structured to expose a deeper truth in some way, to help people cut through the mass and jumble of information and find the core that was important to them. The truth, coming into focus through the use of technology. *The story.* It was everything to him. Except now, he'd lost the safety net that the *Times* had provided him and he was walking the high wire alone, with nothing below him but empty space.

His cell rang. Hawke dug it out of his pocket and saw it was Nathan Brady from *Network* magazine, one of the largest technology-focused periodicals left in the world. "I'm on the PATH," Hawke said.

"Good luck to you." Brady's voice sounded tinny and hollow, as if he were speaking through a tube. "Is it moving? There's something happening in the city. Police presence, angry crowd. It's mucking up our fine Swiss watch of a transit system. You'll never make it in."

Hawke glanced around. The car was almost full now. "What do you want, Nathan?"

"I'm drinking at seven thirty A.M. on a Tuesday. What does that say to you?"

"That you're an alcoholic?"

"I want a status report. I've got to go to Editorial in half an hour."

"I'm meeting with Weller this morning, actually." Hawke transferred the phone to his other ear, drained his coffee cup and dug out his laptop to look at his notes. "Sitting down with a guy for a demo on stress testing a corporate network, hacker-style, and then it's Weller again all afternoon." He was lying through his teeth; for the most part, Jim Weller had avoided him all week, passing him off to a junior associate for most of the day. Hawke's notes were thin at best so far. But Brady was going to lose his mind if he knew how little Hawke had on this one, and sooner or later Weller would let him in. After all, why else had he invited Hawke to come?

Jim Weller, founder and CEO of start-up network security firm Conn.ect, Inc., had his own story of failure and possible redemption; a formerly high-flying tech genius, he'd worked on some cutting-edge programming around energy sharing among networked devices at his former company, the tech juggernaut Eclipse, which led to both its stunning IPO and Weller being forced out by a hostile board after he confronted the company about patenting and licensing his intellectual property without the proper authority. Apparently the board didn't think they needed him anymore. Eclipse seemed to have its fingers in everything from software for networks to new operating systems to national security. They were famously paranoid, with an entire private fleet of enforcers who drove black SUVs and dressed like FBI agents. Their headquarters, a two-hundred-acre complex about thirty miles outside of Los Angeles, was surrounded by razor wire and laser grids. Rumor was, the enforcers were trained to shoot to kill.

Lately there was another rumor that Weller's former company had invented something entirely new based on quantum computing, some sort of "holy grail" of the industry—and that it had led to a breakthrough deal with the National Security Agency. It was another project Weller had apparently had a hand in, at least during the early seed stages, but everyone on the project had been sworn to secrecy and nobody would talk.

When Hawke had reached out to Weller, asking to pitch a

profile of his new company to *Network,* Weller had deferred at first and then called him up and invited him in, even going so far as to ask Hawke to shadow him at his office in New York. Hawke had found the man cold, calculating, clearly brilliant but distracted, often unavailable. He couldn't tell whether Weller was fanatically driven or simply a fanatic. He wondered again why Weller had let him into his inner sanctum, and when the man would actually let his guard down enough to start talking. Hawke had gotten some sketches of Weller's early life during his first few days at Conn.ect, a few hints of his work at Eclipse, but nothing more. Weller seemed secretive about something, but he wasn't opening up yet.

Hawke had never let it slip that his real reason for the profile was to find out what Weller's former company was up to, but Brady knew, of course. In fact, that was the only reason he'd gone to bat for the story in the first place. Brady was an old friend, but that only carried you so far; in journalism, it was fish or cut bait.

"I'm close," Hawke said. "I'm getting to know the people there, learning more about him. He's secretive, but I can smell the story and trust me, this is going to be big."

"Then give me *something,*" Brady said. "I'm putting a lot on the line for you." His voice took on a needling tone. "Pitching you was like sticking my neck in a guillotine. You need this one. And you need it soon. After what happened with Farragut, nobody would touch you—"

"An unfortunate choice of words, don't you think?"

Brady sighed. "You know what I mean. You broke the law, hacked into someone's e-mail, tampered with police business. It doesn't matter that you found enough kiddy porn to nail the son of a bitch. It crossed a line people aren't willing to overlook, at least publicly."

The man in question was a psychology professor at a New York university, an expert in child disorders who had been accused of improper conduct with students. The judge had thrown the images Hawke had found on the professor's account out of court. The professor had tried to scrub everything else clean by the time authorities searched his computer, but he had made a mess of it, and they had recovered enough data to try him again. The case was still pending. But for Hawke's career, the damage had been done. He had nearly gone to jail himself but had covered his tracks well enough for the charges not to stick. That didn't matter to the *Times*. News International's phone-hacking scandal was still in everyone's minds. In the midst of a media furor, his bosses had fired him, claiming he had crossed the lines of journalistic integrity.

It had sent Hawke spiraling down into a cesspool of anger and shame. He'd wanted to do the right thing, and he had ended up on the wrong side. Since then, he hadn't been able to buy his way into a pitch. Editors wouldn't take his phone calls. None of them except for Brady, a friend who had stood by him through the worst of it, and who had bought Hawke's proposed feature story about a technology that, if he was right, was about to transform the world.

Hawke rubbed his eyes and blinked. This was his ticket back into the game, and he wasn't going to blow it. "Eclipse bought a new server farm," he said. "Three hundred thousand square feet in North Carolina, expanding to over a million. Security's tighter than Fort Knox—armed guards, robot sentries, checkpoints, video monitoring, razor wire, retinal scans. This thing is going to be massive. But the same source told me it's only the first of many."

"Cloud centers for streaming media? Online lockers? Temporary supercomputer clusters?"

"Since when did Eclipse get into the rental business? And why start so big? Amazon and Google are cornering the market, but it's retail. That's not Eclipse's thing."

Brady sighed. "I don't know, John; maybe they're making a play to grab market share in a new area. Is that a story? You tell me."

Hawke didn't answer. The new IPv6 standard that had launched last year expanded the number of Internet protocol addresses almost infinitely, in preparation for an explosion of networked devices. There were already chips in computers, phones, and tablets, of course, and even most cars and TVs, but experts predicted there would be an average of three networked devices for every person on earth in another two years: your washing machine, refrigerator, coffeemaker. Google was working on eyeglasses with the ability to display maps and directions. Wearable computers would become like clothing; people wouldn't leave home without them.

The world was starving for more data space, an endless supply of capacity, and these massive server farms were cropping up everywhere, interconnected through a global network and sharing workloads across multiple locations. The government was the biggest customer of all, building facilities to handle all the data it was monitoring in the guise of national security. Hawke imagined it like a gigantic new lifeform evolving across the globe, and it was only the beginning. Anyone could see how Eclipse would want to be a part of that.

But Brady was right. It wasn't enough of a fresh story for

Network, and Hawke didn't think expanding data capacity was Eclipse's end game, either.

"Give me a little more time," he said. "There's a lot more to this; I just can't talk about it yet. I'll have a draft for you in a week, and we can talk about building something more interactive to support the main story."

"You've got three days. I'll hold off the hyenas until then." Brady's voice grew softer, conspiratorial. "Or here's a thought. Why don't you check out the hack attacks that took down the Justice Department's Web site last night? 'Anonymous' strikes again. I hear they have a hand in the mess you've gotten yourself tangled up in this morning, tweeting about spontaneous rallies and calls to action, gumming up the public transit system."

Hawke closed his eyes. "Was Rick involved?"

"No idea. Look, you know these people. You're in the trenches, am I right? Or at least you were. If this Eclipse business doesn't play out, go after that one. Could be the story of our time. The future of mass protests, cyberterrorism at its finest, the men behind the masks. A crisis of democracy. 'We do not forgive. We do not forget. Expect us.' That's pure gold."

"I left that part of my life behind when I had Thomas. Rick would never take my call."

"Don't be so sure. How is Thomas, by the way? And Robin?"

Hawke thought of his son's long silences and increasingly disconnected mannerisms, and Robin's belly, just swollen enough for him to notice. Yesterday she'd found blood spotting her underwear again, enough to worry her, even though the doctor had said before it wasn't a miscarriage but the hematoma.

"They're . . . fine." The train gave a jerk and a squeal.

"We're moving, Nathan. Looks like I'll make it into the city after all."

"Good." Brady paused, sighed again, forced some levity into his voice. "Listen, old man, maybe you need a little break to clear your head. Let's go out on the boat this weekend; we can do a little deep-sea fishing, talk some more about the draft and where you're taking the interactive features of this idea of yours. Talk about what's next."

"Sure. I'm going to lose you in the tunnel. I'll check in again tonight."

Hawke stuck his phone in his pocket, closed his laptop and put it away. The lack of a connection to a networked device left him feeling unsettled. Sparks flashed as the train gathered speed through the tunnel. Hawke couldn't help wondering what might happen if the thousands of pounds of concrete and steel collapsed on him. He imagined the massive buildings of the Manhattan skyline rising up like the peaks of a man-made mountain range. He loved this city, loved the size and scope, the noise, the energy. But people were altering the landscape, changing the natural world into something alien. It was more than physical; it was electric, invisible; it was connectivity and fiber optics and cyberspace. And he had played a part in it; he had embraced it with open arms. *Are we evolving*, Hawke wondered, *or mutating?* Was there any difference?

Crumbling tunnels, crushing stone. *You're imagining the death of your own career.* The life he had pictured for himself, the rock-star hacker journalist changing the world, was swiftly fading. His family was what he had left, and he felt like he was losing them, too.

Hawke closed his eyes and the dream came at him again, Thomas tottering through the leaves, tears streaming down his face. He dug out his phone and looked up Rick's number, texted him: *DOJ?* as the train slipped deeper below the Hudson, and watched the screen. The signal was dropping fast, but the text went through, and Hawke put his phone away and stared out at the tunnels walls and the lights flashing by.

CHAPTER FOUR   8:17 A.M.

HAWKE AND THE MAN with the duffel bag split ways at the Christopher Street stop, where Hawke switched from the PATH to the subway. Everyone was back on their various devices, looking for a signal in the tunnels as they began to move toward the exits. The station was more crowded than usual, a buzz in the air, and there were many others with signs and backpacks making their way along with the regular mix of well-dressed bankers and brokers.

The two sides mixed like oil and water. Hawke thought he caught a glimpse of Bluetooth as the subway doors closed, but he was swallowed up by the jostling crowd. *The bastard.* He supposed he should have given Bluetooth a break. After all, Hawke knew nothing about the man, not really; he was making assumptions that he was in no place to make. But Hawke's uncle had been a broker in the early nineties and after convincing Hawke's father to let him manage his money had lost most of the small nest egg by betting the wrong way on the savings and loan crisis. It was money they couldn't afford to lose, and Hawke's father had never recovered, drinking himself into oblivion after they had to sell the house. He would ramble on about the merits of Socialism and the New Party to anyone who would listen while the family bounced from one threadbare apartment to another. Hawke's father's last book had been a thinly veiled manifesto on the movement and had been panned by the few critics who bothered to read it, which had pushed him over the edge into full-blown alcoholism and dementia and an eventual stroke.

As a result, although Hawke had the grades to get into Cornell, he'd ended up having to scrape and claw for every penny working in a bar wiping tables while he watched the Ivy League assholes enjoy themselves and graduate into high-paying analyst and money-management positions. Since then, Hawke had found little about Wall Street that he liked.

Of course, those experiences had fed his hunger and his drive, helped cultivate that vision of success that had led to his position at the *Times*. They had also, perhaps, contributed to his fall from grace. He could never satisfy that hunger. It led him to take risks other men might not.

Hawke changed to the L train at 14th Street and changed again at Union Square, riding the 6 train to the Upper East Side and the Lexington Avenue stop at 77th. There seemed to be protestors everywhere, clogging up the tunnels, and his commute took even longer than usual. What the hell was going on? It was well past 8:30 as he sprinted around the corner on foot.

Conn.ect, Inc., rented space in a brand-new building on East 79th Street. Although the space itself was nice, it was a second-rate location; the larger players in network security kept offices in lower Manhattan. Remaining in the shadows didn't seem like Weller's style, but it stood to reason that he might want to keep a low profile after the scandal of his prior job, and security was a growing market.

At least that's what he'd been saying to Hawke. *Opportunity.* Weller spoke as if the business was about to explode, but it sounded like a well-rehearsed play, a little too tired to be believable.

Inside the building, the elevator doors yawned like a toothless mouth, yellow caution tape stretched across the black opening. A man in a uniform crouched near a control panel that sprouted a nest of wires, cursing under his breath while a security guard stood behind the reception desk, talking in a low voice with a woman in a suit who kept tapping at an iPad and frowning.

Conn.ect, Inc., was on the seventh floor. Hawke took the stairs.

As he entered the suite, out of breath from the climb, the small reception area was silent. Beyond the empty desk, a little Roomba robot vacuum was marking lines across the carpet. He stepped carefully around the busily humming robot and into Conn.ect's main room, a wide-open space with rows of workstations lined up before floor-to-ceiling windows. Only two people were visible, one of them at his desk, peering ogle eyed into duplicate glowing screens, the other some kind of office repairman bent over one of the brand-new, ridiculously expensive copy machines that could do everything but make lattes. It had been acting up yesterday like a temperamental thoroughbred. Neither of the men glanced up when Hawke entered. The lack of activity was strange; although the company had no major clients yet, they were busy developing proprietary security software, and every other day this week the office had been humming by this hour, with programmers shouting ideas back and forth, writing on the digital whiteboard and working at their computers and tablets.

Weller always arrived early and was probably holed up in his office, where he often worked alone with the door closed. Hawke suspected he sometimes slept there. He still hoped to get that hour with Weller a bit later in the morning before the network stress test demo. He'd already interviewed several employees about their boss; they described him as a visionary—a demanding, secretive and strange genius who seemed to be wound tighter every day. But Hawke had much more to do.

Right now you should be gathering your notes and working out some kind of story angle. Except he didn't have enough yet to know what that would be. Hawke dropped his laptop at a small desk against the wall, the place Weller had given him to use during his stay. Where was everyone? Something was going on; raised voices came from the conference room in back.

He found a small cluster of people standing around the flat-screen TV, watching a growing throng of protestors around the Wall Street bull in Bowling Green Park and spilling up the side streets. The Occupy Wall Street protests had nearly shut down the city in the past, but they had remained mostly peaceful. This was different. The crowd was angrier, more violent, chanting and holding up signs demanding a revolution. And it looked like they were about to start one.

"Must be over a thousand of them," someone muttered. The crowd surged forward and a policeman swung a baton at a young man's arm. A female reporter, dressed smartly, with thick makeup and expertly done hair, stood behind the throng, nearly shouting into her microphone as the anchor asked her to describe the scene. She looked terrified and about to bolt like a young calf at the smell of the slaughterhouse. The cops seemed badly outnumbered, pushed back as they raised riot shields and tried to hold their ground. Someone else threw a bottle, which shattered across a shield; the cops waded in again.

"Twitter," Anne Young said, her round glasses reflecting the light as she glanced at Hawke and then back at the screen. "A call to action sent out this morning from someone supposedly tied to the group Anonymous, an 'Admiral Doe.' Take over the streets, shut down businesses, fight authority. They want blood. And the police are giving it to them."

Young was a twenty-four-year-old developer Weller had introduced to Hawke when he'd first arrived. She was Asian, fresh faced and just out of grad school, and she appeared to idolize Weller; she tended to spend time in his office with the door closed. Hawke found her stoic, if a bit naïve, and assumed Weller was sleeping with her.

Hawke thought about what Brady had said on the phone about Anonymous: *I hear they have a hand in the mess you've gotten yourself tangled up in this morning, tweeting about spontaneous rallies and calls to action, gumming up the public transit system.* It was more than that, if what Young said was true. Hawke thought about his old friend Rick again, and a faceless army of black hats brought together by nothing more than a common goal, a revolution born out of the loins of Net culture that would change the world. An ambitious idea, to be sure, and one Hawke had bought into once himself. But that felt like a lifetime ago.

Admiral Doe was clearly an echo of Commander X, a hacker who had burst onto the world stage several years ago after posting online videos and participating in a number of prominent cyberattacks. The self-proclaimed leader of the People's Liberation Front, a hacker collective aligned with Anonymous, Commander X had been identified as a homeless man from California who was arrested for taking down government Web sites before escaping to Canada.

Whoever Admiral Doe was, he or she had sent out a bulletin to every hacker in the world with this call to action:

We do not forgive. We do not forget. Expect us.

"I can't understand it," Young said, her face impassive, unreadable, still watching as another cop swung a baton. "Why would they respond to this? They're being used to incite the violence. It's not going to get them anywhere, at least not where they want."

Of course she doesn't understand, Hawke thought. All her life, she'd probably been a rule follower, straight edged and rigid. She was bright and motivated but probably raised to do as she was told. A person like that couldn't ever imagine the alternative.

"You okay?" Young said, watching him now. He nodded, thinking about the fight with his wife, about another set of rules, those around relationships. *Happy wife, happy life,* Brady had said once. They had drifted outside the tent at Hawke's wedding reception to catch some air. Brady was drunk and Hawke was, too, and Brady'd probably been joking in the way he tended to, but the phrase had stuck with Hawke through the years. He'd been angry lately about what happened at the *Times* and taking it out on Robin; he'd come home last night and had a drink, and that turned into several, and after Thomas had gone to bed they had gotten into it about money. Robin's father had helped them get their lives started, move to Jersey and find a place to live. Hawke would never have been able to do it alone; journalism didn't pay enough, and life near the city was expensive. Hawke had no family money, no safety net. But they had agreed to have children, and he had begged Robin to trust in him.

Now he had dug them an even deeper hole, and they both knew it. Last night was one of the worst fights they'd ever had. Robin was distraught over the thought of them being unable to make their rent payments. Robin's father had offered to help again, but Hawke didn't want to take it. He wanted to provide for his family, something his own father had never been able to do. But a boy who needed special attention, and another baby on the way, made going on their own impossible. Even if the *Network* story worked out, it would hardly cover more than two months' bills.

They were going to have to move to a cheaper place, and even then, he thought, it wouldn't be enough.

"Our local anarchist," Brady said, introducing him. Brady was dressed as Bill Clinton, Brady's favorite president. They were at a costume party at Brady's place, Robin in a red, low-cut dress looking like she belonged at a senator's fund-raiser and Hawke in his ratty jeans and secondhand button-down and socks with holes in the heels. Hipster cool that was half costume, half his regular weekend outfit. He knew he looked good enough, women liked him and he liked them right back, but this one was another species entirely.

"John's a writer and part of the hacker underground; it's all very secretive and exciting. I don't suppose you'll like each other much; Robin enjoys the civilized world."

Robin held his gaze and kept his hand in hers a moment longer than what might be necessary, her skin hot against his own.

"Anarchists frighten me," she said, after they broke off from Brady and got drinks from the kitchen. "But then again,

so do heights. And yet they make me tremble with excitement." She glanced sideways at Hawke, and then down, a look he would later come to know very well. He caught a whiff of something light and summery as she leaned in, smiling: jasmine and cedar. "Will you make me tremble, Mr. Hawke?"

Hawke couldn't tell if she was serious or not. It was Marilyn Monroe–style parody, but Robin played it well. She wore her curls up under a short blond wig and had a slender neck, a few fine, dark hairs escaping from where they'd been pinned.

My God, what a woman. *He was out of his league and tongue-tied. "Nathan's pulling your leg. We don't want to end all government. We're just interested in freedom of expression, and the power of the masses to bring the right kind of change. It's about justice."*

"That a pretty noble idea, but not a very realistic one, is it?"

"Let the trembling commence."

"I just mean it isn't particularly feasible. It assumes the masses can agree on anything."

"True democracy assumes that the majority can reach a consensus. We just try to create a space where that can happen. Technology gives us a vehicle to do that, in a way that's never been possible before."

"But how are you going to do that? Give everyone in America a voice?"

"We're all free to join the movement, protest against the decisions we don't like, make our opinions known—"

"But you can't force people to do it. And let's face it, most of them won't. Most Americans will continue about their lives, working day shifts and going home to dinner with their families. So you're faced with the same situation we've faced since the beginning of the civilized world—you're part of a

small group claiming to represent the opinions of everyone else."

"It's not like that," Hawke said. He was beginning to get flushed, and she was so goddamn beautiful he couldn't think straight. "We don't represent anyone but ourselves, and that's the whole point. Look, the imbalance of power is greater now than at any other time in our history. A handful of people hold the country's wealth, while the rest work their fingers to the bone just to survive—"

"Have you ever heard of feudalism?" Robin said. She sipped her drink, watching his face, her long, delicate fingers wrapped around the glass.

"I'm talking about modern times here," he said, his flush getting deeper. "Listen, what are you anyway, a historian?"

"Actually, yes. Working on my dissertation." She smiled again, and her face was warm and open and kind; there was nothing confrontational in it, and he realized she'd been playing with him after all.

"You're pretty serious, aren't you?" she said. "I like a serious man. Someone who believes in their convictions, who has a vision of what they want. It's sexy as hell. Let's go have babies together and conquer the world."

Goddamn it, Nathan. Hawke had to smile. Brady had known exactly what he was doing, introducing them. "Why don't we start by getting out of here," Hawke said, and Robin agreed. They slipped out before dinner even started without telling anyone, and he never spent a second regretting it.

In fact, it was the best decision he ever made.

THE TV IN THE CONFERENCE ROOM FLICKERED and went to snow for a moment, and the lights dimmed. *Like in my apartment earlier this morning,* Hawke thought, memories of his wife drifting away and leaving him with a momentary ache. A faint smell wafted over the room, chemical and hot, and a buzzing filled the air and then faded as the fluorescents came back up.

"Did you see that?" a programmer named Bradbury, who had just entered the room asked. He was large enough to have rolls of fat around the back of his neck. He was looking up at the lights, as if the answer could be found there. But nothing else happened, and after a moment the broadcast came back on.

As Hawke slipped back to the desk where he'd set up his computer, still thinking of Robin, his cell vibrated. He dug it out to see a message response from Rick: *No.*

That was it, just the one word on Hawke's screen. Rick had never been the type to go on and on about anything. But as angry as Rick was ("hurt" or "betrayed" might be more accurate), Hawke was surprised he'd responded at all, and that meant something.

The man was worried.

Hawke texted back: *Log on in five.* He sat down and opened his laptop. So, as far as Rick was concerned, Anonymous hadn't been responsible for the attack on the Justice Department's servers. Rick was deeper in the underground network than anyone, Hawke knew. But it was an amorphous entity, members and targets shifting constantly with no formal leadership structure, and although Hawke still trusted Rick with his life regardless of all that had happened between them, and although he knew Rick would be honest with him, that didn't mean he was right.

The standard decoy message board was still online, cluttered with news items and press releases that chronicled the group's latest targets and triumphs. It even had a log-in and special members area where people posted about ion cannons and argued about the merits of taking down Facebook. But that was all bullshit, a smoke screen, and the people posting there were wannabes and fringe elements. You had to dig past them to get to the core; there were layers of Anonymous so deep and so secret, even some of the veterans didn't know they existed. It had to be this way, with federal investigators all over them.

Hawke quickly found the right thread with what appeared to be the ravings of a lunatic against big government. He got out his phone and launched a custom app that applied a filter to the phone's camera, allowing him to see the public key encryption hidden in simple text against the white background underneath. He hadn't visited the board in months, but the process was still the same, and he hoped the private key he had was still the right one.

Sure enough, the private key worked just fine. He copied the hidden URL, as well as a user name and password. The boards changed constantly, and user names and passwords were generated on the fly; they were good for one use only. Chat sessions within the network, if initiated, could only run for three minutes before the URL changed and new log-in credentials were required.

The latest private board was filled with threads that were already pages long, going on about something called Operation Global Blackout. It was supposed to be an organized attack over the next several days by Anonymous members on networks across the world to protest the latest copyright bill working its way through Congress. But here people seemed mostly confused, all of them claiming to have nothing to do with the attacks, including the one on the DOJ last night.

The fact was, someone had taken down the DOJ servers. If it wasn't Anonymous, then who had done it?

Hawke scrolled through the threads quickly, his curiosity piqued. Most of the screen names he didn't recognize; he'd been out of the game for a while now, and the shadowy hacker underground changed on a dime. Even their physical locations were suspect. Several of the most high-profile members over the last couple of years had turned out to be transients like Commander X using Internet cafés to take down the world's most powerful and protected networks; one of the most famous had bounced from friends' couches to abandoned warehouses and become a media star by invading the servers of the *Times,* Microsoft, and Yahoo! and later, after he was finally unmasked, becoming a security specialist working for a private firm with ties to U.S. government agencies.

Members of Anonymous could be brilliant. But many of them were also eccentric outliers who shunned society and were hardwired to rebel against authority. Hawke had found that exciting earlier in his life, but not anymore. *When you're starting a family and the cops knock on your door, it changes things,* he'd said to Rick, right before the man had gone to jail for his role in leaking classified government documents online. *I can't go down with you.*

A chat window popped up, and Rick, using his familiar alias rodeoclown, was there: *Something's going on. Something big.*

No preamble, no mention of their colorful history or the fact Rick had served eighteen months in a federal prison while Hawke had walked away. That was Rick's style, when he communicated at all, and Hawke knew better than to push it. Besides, they only had three minutes.

Operation Global Blackout? he typed.

No fucking idea. Not involved.

Who then? Admiral Doe?

Someone good. Like fucking brilliant. Better than any of us. There was a pause. *Tried to track him. Found some footprints in the sand that pointed toward Eclipse IPs, but it left me sinking fast and then fried my board. Like it was the cat and I was the mouse.*

Eclipse. Hawke leaned closer, growing more intrigued. *Fried your board? How is that possible?*

Electrical surge.

Hawke sat back. That didn't make any sense. Maybe it had been a coincidence. But Rick was always careful; his equipment was certainly shielded.

He typed: *Rumor mill on Doe? Connected to DOJ attack?*

Nobody knows. He's a ghost.

Hawke typed: *Where are you?*

Nothing for a moment, and then: *Never mind. Authorities after everyone. Big pressure on this, I'm in crosshairs.*

Just tell them you're not involved—they'll trace everything soon enough and see.

Not that simple. I'm being set up.

Hawke shook his head: *Why?*

Don't know. Something's happening. Find out who Doe is. You know I can't do that.

Damn well can. You're the best at this. When you want to be.

As he was about to type a reply, the screen flickered and went blank. Hawke paused, fingers over the keys, still not entirely sure what he wanted to write. They had another minute before the session would automatically terminate, and this wasn't the way it would happen anyway. This was like hardware failure.

He was about to try to crash the system and restart when the screen came back up as if nothing had happened. His chat session with Rick was gone, but everything else was intact.

Except it wasn't, not exactly.

Hawke stared at the message board, trying to make sense of what he saw. At first glance, the board looked the same, the same members posting in the same order, at least as he remembered it. But the contents of the posts were entirely different. Board members had gone from expressing confusion and anger over Operation Global Blackout to taking responsibility for it. A member named crow17 claimed he had been one of many hundreds of thousands who had aimed a low-orbit ion cannon at the DOJ servers last night, taking them down. Another poster talked about being a part of this morning's call to action through Twitter. Someone else talked about going after the New York Stock Exchange next, then creating an emoticon message that would self-populate through chains of brokerage accounts and wipe out all transactions for the users.

Hawke remembered seeing both threads when he first logged on, and they were entirely different. And there were more like that. It was as if someone had erased the text of each message and rewritten them, one by one.

It was one thing to crash a site but quite another to erase and then generate entirely new content on the fly.

Who could possibly have done something like that?

In spite of his concerns about getting involved with Rick, Hawke went off sniffing like a bloodhound. He left the corrupted board and logged on to Twitter, scrolling through the hash tags on Anonymous, Admiral Doe, DOJ and Operation Global Blackout. Anonymous had been busy. There were hundreds of tweets in the last few hours by those claiming to be associated with the hacker collective: the DOJ takedown, an attack on the servers of French government, the leaking of private FBI transcripts, service interruptions and messages posted on dozens of police Web sites across the country, a theft of private data from Goldman Sachs accounts, calls to action in protests around the world for various causes like censorship, corruption, injustice and religion, in Austria, Belgium, Britain, Bulgaria, the Czech Republic, France, Germany, Hungary, Luxembourg, Malta, the Netherlands, Poland, Portugal, Romania, Scotland, Sweden, Switzerland, the United States. . . .

The activity was staggering, and through it all Hawke sensed some kind of common thread that he couldn't quite grasp but scared the hell out of him. The whole point of Anonymous was that it didn't govern itself, had no permanent set of goals or leaders; it existed simply as a movement for change and a way of pushing back against authority and censorship in any form. It had begun with a small group of mischiefmakers and had always kept that playful edge, and it was fluid, constantly evolving, an online, shared consciousness driven by the whims of the group. Hawke had always imagined it as a gigantic flock of geese, moving in unison in a seemingly random pattern.

This was different. There was purpose here, and it was deadly serious.

Hawke focused his search on New York, and found dozens of tweets referring to gatherings across the city. One in Bowling Green Park, protesting Wall Street greed; another near Downtown Hospital to protest unaffordable health care; a third in Seward Park to protest immigration laws; a fourth and fifth in SoHo and the Theater District to protest censorship; a sixth outside of Rockefeller University to protest lack of affordability in higher education. There were protests on wealth inequality in J. Hood Wright, Inwood Hill, Highbridge and Marcus Garvey parks.

Each call to action had been tweeted by Admiral Doe.

Hawke thought of the man with the duffel bag, and the others on the train, all going in different directions. He pulled up a map, plotted the protest locations. He sensed some kind of pattern, but no matter how hard he stared at the screen, it wouldn't emerge.

Another cup of coffee might help him focus. He got up, took off his suit jacket and draped it over his chair and began to make his way toward a tiny back room where a pot was usually brewing.

The first thing Hawke noticed when he opened the door was the heat; it puffed out at him. The room's lights blinked on automatically. The room was little more than a windowless supply closet, lined with open shelves stacked with reams of paper and office supplies on the right side and a long worktable on the left with a small refrigerator underneath it. Someone had brought a container of donut holes, and powdered sugar and cinnamon dotted the table next to the paper cups and containers of sugar packets and creamer, along with the monstrous coffee machine.

The room had to be twenty degrees hotter than the office, and the smell of coffee was strong. *Probably scalded.* It figured; the machine was brand-new, with all the bells and whistles, one of those complicated stations that people with too much money paid through the nose for in order to create barista-style drinks in their pajamas, and yet it couldn't even brew a decent cup. Bradbury had acted like a proud father when he'd shown it off on Hawke's first day in the office. It did pretty much everything from grinding beans and foaming milk to making flavored drinks. It even had an app for remote scheduling, which Bradbury had insisted on demonstrating. The entire outfit practically screamed, *Look at me; I'm sophisticated!*

Hawke glanced at the sheet of printed instructions for lattes and cappuccinos lying on the table and sighed. He didn't need a specialty drink. Luckily, the beast had a separate glass carafe for regular coffee, and someone had used it this morning. There were a couple of cups still left. Even if the remains were burned, it would be better than nothing.

As Hawke reached for the carafe, he could feel the heat radiating from the gleaming machine and heard a faint hiss of escaping pressure as his fingers touched the handle. Incredibly, the smooth steel was cool to the touch, another marvel of modern engineering. But the smell of the coffee was bitter and hot.

When he pulled the glass carafe free it exploded in his hand. The sound was like a gunshot in the small room. Scalding coffee sprayed across the table and front of the shiny machine; glass shards bounced off the walls and floor.

Hawke dropped the remains of the carafe like he'd been

bitten and felt warmth across the back of his wrist, warmth that quickly changed to a sharp pain. More warmth spread through his chest. *Jesus Christ.* He looked down in shock; luckily, most of the coffee and the glass had sprayed away from him, but his shirt was spotted with coffee stains and his wrist was already turning red.

The machine let out another hiss. Steam rose from somewhere inside it. Hawke yanked the plug from the outlet, then stepped back, eyeing the coffeemaker warily. He grabbed a roll of paper towels from a shelf and blotted the coffee from the table, his shock and fear quickly turning to embarrassment. Even though he hadn't done anything to cause the mess, he felt guilty. An exploding coffeemaker. It was a silly prank, absolutely fucking slapstick comedy. *Let's get the new guy.* He almost wanted to look around for the hidden camera, and he might have laughed it off except for the burn on his wrist that had already begun to throb. Not so funny after all. When he thought about it, he knew it was no prank. Just a malfunctioning piece of equipment, and he was in the wrong place at the wrong time.

Hawke swept the larger shards of glass up with a nearby dustpan and brush and deposited them in the trash. He was considering the smears of coffee on the wall when the sound of someone clearing his throat made him glance up.

"Never liked that thing," Weller said. He was standing in the open doorway, arms crossed, leaning against the jamb. "I guess I wasn't the only one. When you're done cleaning up, join me in my office. We need to talk."

Hawke considered explaining, but what could he say? *I didn't drop it; I swear—it just blew up in my hand?* When Weller stepped away from the open door, Hawke saw the copier repairman standing with his arms crossed, smirking at him.

The hacker journalist can't figure out how to work the coffee machine. It would surely become office legend. Thank God nobody else had seen it, or things might have been far worse.

CHAPTER SIX   9:47 A.M.

HAWKE FOLLOWED WELLER INTO HIS OFFICE, where the man closed the door and motioned to the simple rigid wooden chair that faced his uncluttered desk. A black hard-shelled laptop case with a security lock sat against the wall next to a glass-door cabinet crammed with networking gear. The case was large enough for two laptops. There was very little else in the room.

Weller was lithe, slightly over six feet, and tended to wear dark jeans and Oxford shirts every day. Both the way he dressed and his office reflected his affection for minimalism and order. His round glasses would have seemed delicate and feminine on most men, but they served to soften what would have otherwise been a harshly angular face. He bristled with a coiled energy that kept him in constant motion, and even as he sat behind the desk he bounced slightly in his chair, hands fiddling with a pen, tapping and flicking it against the wood. "You okay?"

Hawke nodded, touched the brown spatters on his shirt. His wrist throbbed. "Just a little wounded pride."

Weller put the pen down, then seemed to dismiss the incident entirely. When Hawke pulled out his digital recorder, Weller shook his head. "No record of this," he said. "Not yet."

Hawke put it away. An object slightly larger than a pack of gum sat on a corner of the desk. Weller picked it up. "The most advanced in government hardware," he said. "Highly secure communications device, developed by Eclipse as part of their deal with the NSA. It has its own advanced operating system, powered by an all-new adaptive intelligence in the cloud. Nearly impossible to lock on to, uses its own satellites and encrypted five ways to Sunday. Big power comes in small packages." He handed the phone to Hawke. "I thought you'd appreciate this. Communication is everything in your line of work."

Still smarting from the encounter with the coffee machine, this was the last thing Hawke had expected. He turned the object in his hands. It appeared seamless, with an edgeless, glossy screen and nothing else. There was no immediate way to tell how it might operate. He resisted the urge to play with it; now was not the time. He had to get Weller talking. "Does it make calls?" he said.

Weller smiled. "Borrow it for a while," he said. "I have another. Might come in handy."

The code of ethics for journalists was clear on accepting any kind of gift. Then again, Hawke had never cared much for rules. This tiny phone was part of the story. It would make a great sideline to the main piece; the *Network* lab could dissect it, piece by piece, break it down for the audience, show them its guts ahead of release. That alone was nearly big enough to satisfy Brady.

Hawke tried to keep his building excitement from showing, shoved the tiny device in his left pocket and kept his other phone in his right. "I didn't think Eclipse would be inclined to share with you these days."

"I liberated it," Weller said. "It's not in commercial development yet."

"I'll keep that part out of the profile."

Weller's smile faded. "They stole something from me; I stole something back. It's not quite quid pro quo, but it's a start."

"You're talking about the energy-sharing project?"

"Something much more important than that. Energy sharing was just the evolution of an old idea. Use the processing power of the cloud to spread out the work. When a device is running low, it borrows another networked device's chip to crunch data and serve it back." He stuck the pen in the middle drawer, so the desk's surface was completely clean, then folded his hands in front of him. "Now let's get down to business," he said. "You want to know about my former employer. What happened when I left, and what they're doing now."

Of course Weller knew that the *Network* angle wasn't a simple profile or a feature about his new business, but neither of them had ever been this blunt about it. "I'm not sure I understand."

"Jonathan C. Hawke, born to a schoolteacher and a writer and political activist in eastern Massachusetts. Test scores show a boy who would excel at making the connections between things most people miss, a creative mind that would regularly reject those in authority who didn't question the status quo. An outside-the-box thinker. Predictable behavior problems coupled with flashes of genius, an early tendency toward computer programming and storytelling that would lead to your associations with both the hacker subculture and journalism, but things didn't start to go downhill until your father's drinking led to his early death and you dropped out of college and got involved with Anonymous—"

"So you've investigated me," Hawke interrupted. "Am I supposed to be impressed?"

"I had to know who you were," Weller said. "Your strengths and weaknesses, your convictions. Some people like you start companies. I'm one of those. Others go underground, become part of the fringe, end up in jail or disappear."

"And the rest of us?"

"A few cross back and forth. Hacker journalism is a respectable way to make a living doing what you love."

"This isn't about me, though. It's about you."

Weller's eyes were glittering behind the glasses, and Hawke couldn't tell if he was feverish or furious or both. "I let you in here for a reason. Your abilities have everything to do with this. Your work at the *Times* was brilliant, regardless of how they treated you. I think we can take this far beyond *Network* in ways that are going to become obvious to you very soon."

Hawke crossed his legs, attempted to look at ease although he had started to sweat. Normally he loved when he began to see pieces of the story hanging there like low fruit on the vine, the combinations still forming themselves in his mind, leading to the alpha moment when things really came together. But it wasn't good when the person you were supposed to interview gained the upper hand. It was all about control over the story and the delivery; without that, the entire thing dissolved into a muddled, incomprehensible mess.

"Tell me more," Hawke said. "Let's talk about the profile. Maybe you could start with why you chose network security as your next big move."

"Don't bullshit me, John, not anymore," Weller said. "You know that's not the real story here." His eyes were so bright and sharp Hawke wondered if he might be on something. He leaned forward and placed both palms on the desk. "Your investigative skills and instincts are first-rate, as I suspected. What did you discover about your old friends out there on your laptop?"

Hawke cleared his throat as Weller waited. "You're monitoring the network," he said finally.

"Of course I am, but that's not the point. They've been busy. We may need their help soon, but this is causing quite a mess. I'd like you to ask them to stop." Weller leaned back, crossed his arms over his chest. "Can you do that?"

Hawke considered how to answer, finally decided to just go with the truth. "They say they're not responsible. And they wouldn't listen to me anyway."

"I doubt that. You were part of one of the most infamous hacks in history, isn't that right? Stealing top-secret files on undercover moles from the CIA?"

Hawke became very still. A trickle of sweat made its way down his neck, between his shoulder blades. "I don't know what you're talking about."

"Sure, it wasn't just you. In fact, from what I was able to dig up, you were a fringe player. But the others went to prison for it, while you barely even got a second look. Why is that?" Weller studied him for a long moment. "Look, you were a respected member of the underground not so long ago. Clearly you still know the principal players—"

"Things change," Hawke said. "This really isn't about me, Jim. I'm a nobody. *Network* wants to know about you, about Eclipse and about how they're going to change the world."

Weller banged a hand on the desk. "Whatever they have, it's because of me," he said, his voice rising. "I want you to know what's really happening at Eclipse. What they're doing to me. They're a fucking Gestapo organization, John, a goddamn militant dictatorship. They have me under surveillance; they've tapped my phones, frozen accounts and altered records. All to protect her."

"Tapped your phones?"

"They know how valuable she is. They don't want her coming back to me. But they're going about it all wrong. They just don't see it. What they're doing to her is a sin. That place is going to destroy her, slowly but surely."

Hawke was stunned into silence. It didn't happen often. Something in their conversation had changed very quickly. Weller's voice had gone bitter and hard. He sounded like a dangerous fanatic or, what might be worse, a spurned lover. Hawke tried to think of a woman high enough in the Eclipse hierarchy for that to make sense. He'd studied the company's leadership and current org chart like he'd been preparing for a final exam; there was Connie Williams, head of new-product marketing, but she was almost ten years older than Weller and married. Deb Hunn, in charge of Eclipse's European operations. Young, attractive. *Could be her.* But if so, it threw off Hawke's theory about Weller and Young having a fling. Or maybe it didn't.

Hawke had the feeling that he was being taught some kind of lesson, and that he'd be required to figure out the answer.

"What are you talking about?" he said finally, carefully. "Because I have to say, you're sounding a little extreme here, Jim."

"Far from it. It's time to follow all the threads, weave them into a complete picture that everyone can understand. You use technology to tell a story. I want you to tell a story now. The biggest one of your life."

A shout and a crash came from the other room. Weller's

gaze flicked to the door. Hawke stood up and opened it; the copier repairman was standing in the middle of the large room, clutching his right hand and cursing. He was big and broad across the shoulders, and a large tag across the breast of his corporate shirt read: *Jason Vasco.*

"Goddamn printer," he said, motioning to the machine by the windows that now lay on its side. Blood dripped onto the freshly vacuumed carpet. "The high-end ones are the worst. This is the third time I've been here this week. I thought it was a bad belt giving you trouble, but there's a corrupt hard drive or something. I swear to God, it was like it *bit* me."

Hawke heard more raised voices from the conference room, as if people were arguing over something important. Bradbury was at his desk again, and as Weller emerged from his office the fat man looked up, his entire body seeming to vibrate with excitement. "There's a lot of noise," he said. "We're logging a massive surge of hits coming from all over the place, but the locations keep jumping around or they're cloaked. So many targets I can't track them all. We should be all over this." Bradbury was clearly frustrated. He motioned to the conference room. "But half our staff didn't show up today, and everyone else is watching the damn news. . . ."

Weller walked over to Bradbury's computer. He tapped a few keys. "You're seeing traffic spikes of what, fifteen hundred percent?"

"Higher."

Weller was silent for a moment. "More black hats?"

"I don't know. There would have to be hundreds of thousands all working at once; either that or they're using bots. But this activity is something I've never seen bots do before."

Weller straightened. Hawke couldn't tell if he was satisfied with what he had heard or not. Then he walked quickly in the direction of the conference room without another word, and Hawke followed him, wondering where all this was going. "Black hats" was a term for those who were working on the other side of the law, hackers who were looking to disrupt networks and cause problems. Anonymous was filled with them. White hats were network security experts who usually worked on the other side, and the two were often at odds. But in the real world, the line often blurred, with people switching sides in the course of a single day.

The morning was starting to unravel fast. Hawke felt like a man who had come late to a party and found all the other guests in the middle of something that he couldn't quite understand. As he followed Weller, he wondered if the man might be about to give them all hell.

Vasco trailed behind them, cursing softly and gripping a paper towel. The others were still gathered under the TV. Hawke expected Weller to order them all back to work, but he said nothing. A major news anchor had broken into the coverage of the protests; the spotlessly coiffed man spoke in a slightly breathless voice, but the others in the room were talking too loudly for Hawke to hear.

"What's going on now?" he said to Young.

"Everything," she said, glancing at Weller as if looking for some kind of tacit approval to speak. "Traffic signals malfunctioning, cars running off the road on their own, power surges. People are panicking—"

Young stopped talking abruptly. Hawke caught something passing between Young and Weller that he didn't understand. Hawke looked back at the TV. A well-dressed gray-haired woman was being interviewed on-screen, clutching her tiny dog in her arms. A stray bit of hair had come loose from the gray helmet and stuck up at the top of her head. "I was at

Saks half an hour ago," the woman said to the local reporter aiming the mike, and in her distress her carefully constructed voice began to betray her Brooklyn roots. "I was on the escalator, and it stopped, and I had my bags with me, and I had to put Peaches down for just a moment, to rebalance, and as soon as I did, as soon as she *touched* that step, the escalator started again very fast. . . ." The woman stopped, face wrinkling, chest hitching, as the reporter quietly urged her to continue. ". . . And thank the good Lord I grabbed her up and the escalator stopped again as soon as I did, but my heel had gotten caught." She held up the trembling dog and the camera cut to show a shoe with the stiletto heel snapped off before cutting back to the woman's tear-streaked face. "She could have lost her foot! I swear it was like that escalator tried to *eat* her. . . ."

A ripple of uneasy laughter spread through the room, but Vasco wasn't laughing. "Not funny," he muttered, staring down at his hand. The paper towel was spotted with red.

"What happened to you, exactly?" Hawke said.

"Thing started up with my hand in its guts. I saw you with the coffee machine, you know. I'm not the only one looking like a fool around here." Vasco lifted the towel to check his hand, and Hawke caught a glimpse of his index finger, the tip chewed up a bit but the bleeding mostly stopped now. He wrapped it up again. "Thing is, I had it disabled. There's no way it could just . . . Never mind."

Another reporter had started relating other stories of equipment failure, more tablets and cell phones downloading and running what appeared to be complex programming. Hawke thought of the coffee machine, his laptop and the Anonymous board. He thought about what Weller had just said. His head was spinning with possibilities.

"I was monitoring traffic just now, in case anyone cares," Bradbury said loudly, coming into the room, "and activity has gone through the roof. Denial of Service attacks, data theft attempts, serious network breaches reported by our systems at Johnson, Four Tune, about a dozen others. We're in the security business, right? Maybe we should be actually *looking* at this, do you think?" He looked around, shook his head. "Anyone else notice weird stuff this morning? Before I came in, my laptop started downloading something automatically, executing some kind of program," he said. "I wasn't surfing any porn sites, if that's what you're thinking—"

"Please," a woman named Susan Kessler said, a new hire from what Hawke had learned. "Let's not make references to porn in the office." Hawke pegged Kessler's age at over thirty-five, which would probably make her Weller's oldest employee. She always wore impeccable business suits and had perfect makeup, but today her suit looked slightly wrinkled and her face, although scrubbed clean, was pale and puffy.

"I just mean this wasn't a phishing scam, not that I could tell. It was something else. I had to come to work, so I just shut it down, figured I would do a safe reboot and clean up later." When he blinked, Bradbury's eyes nearly disappeared into pockets of fat. "When I came in, the building manager said her iPad was acting funny. And she was pissed because the elevator was out and the repairman couldn't seem to fix it, and the building's security system was down, too."

A systems analyst named Price shook his head. "You think this is some kind of massive hack?"

"I don't know *what* it is," Bradbury said. "I just think we should pay attention. Business is business, right, Jim?"

The casual reference might have pissed Weller off, but the

man didn't even look at Bradbury and Hawke wasn't sure he had heard a single word. He was staring at the TV screen, where a scroll of the latest news had begun. A casual observer might have thought he was lost in thought, but Hawke watched a muscle jump in his jaw and could sense the tension building. Whatever Weller had expected coming in here, it didn't appear to be going quite the way he'd planned.

"How long has this been going on?" Weller said, to no one in particular. "The unauthorized downloads and device malfunctions."

"Since early this morning, I guess," Bradbury said. "Like I said, my laptop—"

"Hold on," Price said, pointing at the TV. The anchor was back, looking grim.

"Stock market exchanges have collapsed today," the anchor said, "erasing billions—some have estimated even higher—in assets. According to authorities, as in 2008 and 2010, high-frequency computer trading has at least been partially to blame for the crash, but the automatic circuit-breaker halts meant to pause a tumbling market have failed to kick in. In fact, nobody seems to be able to control or explain the collapse. Hedge-fund managers we have reached have refused to speak on camera, though one of them called this the biggest market implosion in history—and they have no answers for the millions who will be ruined."

The entire group grew silent as they watched, even Bradbury caught by the drama. Things had taken a darker turn. "On the ground," the anchor said, "protests on Wall Street have intensified and more police presence has been called in, but resources are stretched thin as they deal with increasingly violent, dangerous and unexplained events across the city."

The screen showed scenes in quick succession: The cops were on edge, angry, swinging at the crowds that were taunting them and turning over cars. There were other updates in quick succession as the anchor became deadly serious now: A five-alarm fire had broken out somewhere in the Bronx, he said, and there were reports of more fires in Manhattan. Stories of explosions on several bridges into the city began scrolling across the bottom of the screen. Sporadic reports had begun to come in of rolling blackouts in other areas of the country as well.

When the network played a clip of the mayor telling everyone to remain calm, Hawke looked at Weller again. The man still hadn't budged. Hawke was about to say something when a rumble made the group turn to the windows as something appeared in the sky, an object so out of place, so stunning, it left everyone frozen in shock: a helicopter, its blades chopping at the air, black smoke pouring from its engine, plummeting directly past their windows like a dying bird to earth before it disappeared from sight.

A moment later, a rumble shook the building. Kessler let out a small cry, holding her hands to her face.

"Oh my God," she breathed softly.

Bradbury went to the window, pressed his hands against it, trying to peer down, shaking his giant head. "Did you see that?" he said, looking back at them all, a group frozen in place, his words spilling out in a panic. "Did you *see* it? Did they just fucking crash a *helicopter* in the middle of New York?"

As if in answer, smoke drifted up past the glass. "We're under fire," Vasco said. He went to the window, too, looking out, then turned back. "It's another 9/11."

"You don't know that," Kessler said. "You need to calm down—"

"Don't fucking tell me to calm down!" Vasco shouted, veins standing out in his neck. "This is big; it's a coordinated *attack*. When's the last time you heard of a helicopter crashing in New York City? Did you see the broadcast? There are explosions all over the place. And the mayor's telling us to stay calm, too, while things are going to hell—"

The others all began to talk at once, while overhead the TV buzzed loudly and went to snow, then crackled and popped like a bundle of firecrackers going off and began to smoke. Kessler was standing nearly directly underneath it; she cried out and jumped back as sparks cascaded down, nearly running into Weller, who still hadn't moved, his face lit with what was either a strange, ghostly grimace or a smile.

In the middle of the near panic, Hawke's cell phone rang.

Hawke dug his phone out of his pocket, heard static and what sounded like a faint voice. Moving away from the noise of the others as they argued and shouted over one another, he ducked into the other room, his pulse hammering and his breath growing tight in his chest.

The voice was his wife's, but he could barely make it out. He pressed the phone to his ear, straining to understand the faint words through the static. Something was very wrong. He heard what sounded like a scream and his son's name, then a whisper, a pleading, barely audible prayer, a thump and another strangled shriek.

"Robin!" he said. "Can you hear me? Robin!"

The buzzing faded slightly, and Robin was there for a

moment, breathing fast and shallow, a fleeting few seconds of clarity, her terror huge and feeding his own.

"Hurry," she said, "John, please. He's *coming through*."

Hawke shouted into the phone, told her to stay there, stay calm, but the static washed over the connection and his wife was gone.

STAGE TWO

HAWKE LEFT THE 7-ELEVEN with two paper bags, juggling them as he shouldered open the door and mumbled good-bye to the man sweeping the aisles. Robin was still at home, dealing with Thomas's crying; the fifteen-month-old boy had an earache, the remnants of a bad cold, and he couldn't sleep. Hawke had picked up some more Children's Tylenol, along with a carton of milk, bread and canned soup. Needing a break from Thomas's screams, he thought for a moment about taking a long way home but then thought better of it. The store was only two blocks from their apartment, but Robin would be waiting for him and was probably ready to lose her mind. The boy's fever had broken when he woke up before dinner, but the pressure in his ears wouldn't let up.

The night was hot and humid, and Hawke was slick with sweat as he reached the building and fumbled for his keys. He rode the tiny elevator back to their floor, listening to the creaks and groans of the machinery. Their door was standing open a crack. He felt a chill. Had he left it that way? He didn't think so, but he'd been so edgy and distracted, anything was possible.

Hawke entered the apartment to more of Thomas's muffled screams, dampened now by a closed bedroom door. Strange; normally Robin would be in there, soothing him with a warm washcloth or another bedtime story. But he focused immediately on something else. A man's voice came from the kitchen.

Hawke came around the corner with his heart thudding hard, blood pressure rising, and for a moment he stood motionless: Their neighbor Randall Lowry had cornered Hawke's wife by the sink. Lowry's hair stuck up in the back of his head, a ragged bird's nest, and he had a hand in the air, gesturing.

The boy's crying from the other room ticked up a notch. Lowry caught the movement of Robin's eyes, and he turned to see Hawke watching them. Whatever Lowry had been saying, he stopped suddenly. His expression changed, and he took a step back.

Thomas's bedroom door opened; it must not have been latched shut. Hawke glanced over and saw the boy standing in the doorway, red faced, stuffed lion clutched in his arms. His first steps. Thomas hadn't walked yet. He and Robin had been talking about it that day, considering whether to see the pediatrician. Thomas had been late for almost all his milestones, but his doctor said the boy was fine, simply a cautious child, nothing to worry about. Robin wasn't so sure.

When Hawke looked back, Lowry was pushing past him, muttering to himself, his head down. "Don't you come in here again," Hawke said, but the man was already gone, the sound of his apartment door as it slammed shut echoing off the walls of the hallway and bouncing back to him, amplified into a sound of accusation and regret as he moved toward Robin and watched her turn away, hugging her arms to her chest.

Hawke tried to call Robin back, his fingers trembling and clumsy, and when there was no answer he felt light-headed, disconnected from reality. As the room spun he sat on a nearby desk chair and put his head down for a moment, trying to breathe slow and deep.

There was no time to panic, not now. He'd probably misinterpreted everything and Robin and Thomas were fine. *They're fine.*

Except they weren't, and Hawke knew it. You didn't make a call like that if everything was okay. Memories popped through his mind like flashbulbs: He saw Robin sitting on their bed, sunlight dappling her bare shoulders, not yet pregnant with Thomas, young and eager and devastatingly beautiful. . . . Trying to learn how to wrap Thomas in the hospital blanket, *make a triangle, wrap and tuck and wrap and then tuck again* as the tiny creature squirmed and balled his little fists . . . Robin sitting on the edge of the bathtub staring up at Hawke, pregnancy test in her hand, and he couldn't tell if the look of shock on her face was from happiness or terror. . . . And then when he closed his eyes again, he saw Randall Lowry shouldering open the door of their apartment, greasy hair swinging in his face, his eyes shining with madness and lust, and Hawke heard his wife screaming.

Hawke looked up, coming back into himself with a jolt. People were shouting over one another in the conference room, arguing over what to do. He stuck a finger in his ear to shut out the noise and tried Robin's phone again, listened to the empty ring. He tried to dial again, and again. The third time, nothing happened at all.

He stared at the phone until spots danced before his eyes, then jabbed at the screen with his finger, cursing the network, and breathed deeply again. *You're not helping them by losing your mind. Think.* Half of New York City was probably trying to make a call right now. He would have to find a different way to reach them.

Hawke's smartphone was jail broken and customized by him, and he was able to bypass the operating system. One of his programs, a video calling and monitoring app, would allow him to use his home wireless network to activate the webcam attached to Robin's laptop. They'd used it as a nanny cam before, on the rare occasions when they left Thomas with a sitter. In the mornings, Robin usually sat at the counter, had coffee and surfed the Net while Thomas played or watched TV. Maybe she'd left the computer open.

The screen was frozen. Hawke crashed the phone and quickly rebooted, and it seemed to come up clean. He directed the app to the right IP address, and a few moments later a grainy image appeared: his living room as seen through Robin's laptop camera.

Hawke peered at the tiny screen, his guts churning. He could see the back of the couch; the TV was on and what looked like news reports were playing. No sign of Robin or Thomas, but the lamp that sat on the end table had been knocked over.

Take it easy. It might be nothing. But that single bit of chaos in an otherwise normal room unnerved Hawke. Had Thomas done it? If so, why hadn't Robin picked it back up again? She was a neat freak, and something like that would have driven her crazy. Hell, even at three years old it would have driven Thomas crazy, too, with his need for order and symmetry, everything in its place and aligned properly. Just last week, he had thrown a tantrum because he hadn't been able to line up the bins of toys on the shelf in his room to his own satisfaction, and Hawke had teased Robin about it later: *Like mother, like son.*

Where are *they?*

Hawke turned up his phone's volume but couldn't hear any sound through the laptop's mike; even the TV seemed to be on mute. He flashed back to his conversation with Robin earlier that morning: *Lowry yelled at Thomas again yesterday in the hallway, when we went to the store. . . . He was complaining about something, I don't know, the TV up too loud, whatever. . . .*

Lowry was responsible for Robin's panicked phone call. Hawke knew it. He thought about the laundry room, Lowry in Hawke's apartment with his wife pinned against the sink. He put his ear to the phone, thought he heard a thud and muffled voice, but couldn't be sure. "Robin!" he shouted into the mike, and shouted again, in case she could hear him, but there was no response.

As he was about to try her cell phone again, his own phone appeared to freeze; he tried to regain control, pushing the home button, tapping at it and cursing, and the phone began cycling through some kind of program, raw code running across the screen. Hawke tried to crash it again, holding the power and home buttons down, but at first the phone didn't respond. Then the screen went white, blinked and went dead again, and this time it was bricked.

He cursed again and stood up, meaning to go plug it in and get better access through a keyboard to the internals, but a wave of dizziness hit him like a punch to the head. *You're in shock.* He heard more voices and looked up as Bradbury came into the room, followed closely by Kessler: ". . . software is doing its job, I'm telling you it's tracking activity like you wouldn't believe—"

And then the voices stopped for a moment. Somehow,

Kessler had crossed the space between them and spoke close to Hawke's ear. "You okay?" she asked as he leaned drunkenly and stumbled. She reached out to him just before a tremendous explosion rocked the building.

CHAPTER EIGHT   10:51 A.M.

THE FLOOR SHUDDERED VIOLENTLY, and Hawke heard a distant whooshing sound, muffled and deep, just before Kessler let him go and ran toward the windows. He wanted to shout at her to get back, but it was too late; the glass exploded inward as the shock wave hit, sending shards hurtling through the air like flashing knives.

A piece caught Kessler in the throat. Hawke saw her whirl and spray blood as he went down, covering his own head, tasting carpet and smoke.

He looked up again through a strange haze as the overhead lights surged and watched Bradbury reach out to catch a desk lamp that was falling. An instinctive reaction, something Hawke probably would have done himself, but Bradbury ended up dancing a jig, his eyes rolling back to the whites, teeth clenched hard together as his huge body went rigid and his skin began to darken before he finally tilted sideways and fell to the floor.

"Oh my God oh my God!" someone was screaming from the other room. Black smoke billowed up from the street, whirling in through the broken windows, and it smelled acrid and oily, stinging Hawke's eyes. He blinked, saw Bradbury on

the floor still clutching the lamp in rigid, blackened fingers with his eyes bulging like boiled eggs and his tongue poking like a purple rag from his lips, and he thought of his apartment and his wife's frantic voice over the phone. It hit him like a stinging slap: *What if this isn't just New York City? What if it's happening everywhere?*

Hawke stood up, legs trembling, covering his nose and mouth with his sleeve. Nothing else mattered anymore except getting out of the building. The black smoke was thicker around his face, and he couldn't tell if it was coming from outside or somewhere close. Kessler was jerking violently and clutching her throat, a lot of blood wetting the carpet around her head. He whirled at a noise and watched Weller and a dazed Anne Young emerge from the conference room, stumbling through the dim fog that had descended over them all.

Weller looked around, saw Hawke and led Young to him. "Get her out," Weller said, coughing into his sleeve. "I'll be right behind you."

"What?" Young said. "No—"

"Go! Now!" Weller left them standing there, stumbling through the smoke. Hawke grabbed Young's arm, ignoring her protests, and dragged her toward the suite doors as the fire alarms started blaring. Vasco followed after they had entered the hall, along with Price, the systems analyst, who had helped Kessler to her feet and was half-carrying, half-dragging her along. Kessler's eyes had lost focus, her face ghostly white, and blood still pulsed thickly between her fingers as she gripped her own neck with both hands. Vasco got his arm around her waist from the other side to help, and she sagged against him as the two men carried her toward the exit.

Young clutched Hawke's arm, her nails digging into his skin through his shirt. The alarms were piercingly loud in the hallway, emergency strobe lights flashing. Someone was screaming about the building being on fire, but the sprinklers hadn't triggered and the smoke thinned as Hawke took the lead past the broken elevator toward the stairs. He started to open the door, then remembered something about fire and heat and oxygen levels and touched the surface lightly, finding it cool.

He hit the bar and shouldered the door open, revealing a flood of other people from the building in the stairwell, rushing toward the lobby. Disjointed and terrifying images from 9/11 flashed through his mind as Hawke stood for a moment, trying to judge whether to wade in. There were at least five floors above them, maybe more, and the people coming down from above were out of control and panicked, taking the steps two and three at a time, stumbling into walls, several of them falling as the others ran past.

But they had no choice, and he entered the fray, trying to clear space for Vasco and Price, who were still carrying a now-unconscious Kessler between them. Young was shoved by a large man in a business suit who barreled down the stairs, and Hawke steadied her, keeping his own balance, hearing others coming from above and gaining fast.

They were three flights down when the lights went out.

The stairwell was plunged into blackness, and screams and shouts echoed up through the dark as bodies fell, bones or heads cracking against concrete as Hawke fumbled his way blindly to the wall, heart thudding fast as the emergency lights kicked on and bathed everything in red. Things speeding up now, he grabbed Young's hand and led her down, abandoning any effort at restraint, moving as fast as he could go while still keeping his feet, stumbling around the same man in a suit who was lying on the stairs and groaning, trying to get up.

They reached the lobby, busting into open space. Hawke took several deep gasps of air, only now realizing he'd been holding his breath for most of the last two floors. The power was still on down here, the alarms screeching relentlessly. A group of about twenty people was already at the front doors, which seemed to be locked or jammed shut. Someone rattled the handles; a woman pounded on the glass and shouted that the building was going to fall, panic lighting up her voice into a high, keening wail, and Hawke thought of a mother he'd once tried to interview who had just lost her baby to a house fire. The sound of panic and despair was similar here, a repetition of words and actions where human restraint and logic disappeared into something mindless and instinctual.

Hawke looked around, didn't spot the security guard or the building manager. There was nobody in charge. The entire world had suddenly gone insane. Who had locked the doors, and why? It made no sense.

Vasco and Price came out of the stairwell and put Kessler down on her back. Hawke's stomach rolled greasily as he watched Kessler's hands flop lifelessly away from her neck to reveal a deep slash like an ugly, lipless mouth, blood slowly bubbling up and oozing across the tile floor. Price's shirt was soaked with red. He clapped his own hand down over her neck wound, pressing hard, and started shouting for someone to call 911.

Vasco was pacing, pressing his phone's screen and cursing. "Check your cell," he said to Young over the sound of the alarms, and she pulled out her own phone.

"No service," she said.

"Check it again!" He whirled, questioning, to Hawke, who shook his head. He couldn't take his eyes off Kessler, the blood spreading out below her body in spite of Price's frantic efforts to stop it. Hawke thought of the electrocution of Bradbury; how had that much power come through the lamp's cord? The breakers should have popped.

Vasco was in Hawke's face, breathing hard and smelling like sweat. "Check your fucking cell," he said.

"It's bricked," Hawke said. "Happened upstairs."

"Fuck!" Vasco whirled again, suddenly looked around the lobby. "Where's everybody else?"

"Bradbury's dead," Hawke said. "I saw him . . . he was electrocuted. Weller, I have no idea. He was supposed to be right behind us."

"He's still up there," Young said. She looked at the door to the stairs. When she started toward it, Hawke grabbed her. Her pupils were dilated, her breathing fast and shallow.

"You can't go back," he said.

"He might be trapped," she said. "We can't just leave him. You don't understand; they're going to—"

"*You can't go back up there*," he said. He took her by both her arms and stared into her pale, shivering face. "You get that? This is real; people are getting *killed*."

More people came tumbling out of the stairs and into the lobby, none of them familiar; they barely glanced at Hawke and Young but went straight for the doors, joining the others. The noise level increased as more of them pounded at the glass, rattled the handles. "What the hell is going on out there?!" a man shouted. "Let us out!" And someone else screamed as a screech and rending crash came from somewhere on the street, some kind of accident.

The alarms were relentless, drilling into Hawke's head. Young pulled herself away and he let her go, noticing something else strange; the security cameras mounted in the corners of the lobby that normally panned slowly back and forth were now moving deliberately, as if someone was controlling them.

He watched one of them swing around in his direction and stop, the camera's unblinking eye fixed on his location. The effect was both eerie and menacing. There was nobody at the front desk, and he walked toward it, hypnotized by the eye, peering at the monitors behind the counter and watching himself reflected back through the camera.

The big man in the suit who had fallen in the stairwell came up next to him, shouldering him aside and breaking his trance. "Get the fuck out of the way," the man snarled, panting hard. Hawke caught a glimpse of a purple, knotted welt above the man's left eye as he picked up the desk chair and lifted it over his head, the chair wheels spinning as he turned and ran toward the lobby entrance.

"Get the fuck out of my way!" he shouted again, and the crowd parted just before the man heaved the chair at the glass doors.

The chair was heavy, solid metal and leather, and it caught the impact-resistant glass pane at its center, leading with one leg like a spear. The glass groaned and gave way with a tremendous, shattering crash, spilling out onto the sidewalk as the chair went tumbling and bouncing into the street.

It was like a dam had broken. The crowd surged forward, knocking away the rest of the glass that still hung from the frame, pushing and shoving one another to get through the opening.

Hawke looked around the lobby, trying to find familiar faces among the people who kept coming from the stairwell. He couldn't see Weller or Young. Price was crouched over Kessler's lifeless body, hands still clapped hard against her neck. A woman hit Price's shoulder as she ran by, nearly knocking him over; he reached down and pulled Kessler to him, cradling her against his chest.

Hawke fought his way against the rushing crowd, pushing through to Price's side. Price looked up at him, his face white with shock. "Call nine-one-one," he said. "She's bleeding. Someone has to help her."

Kessler's face was slack, her eyes open and fixed. The wound in her neck had stopped bubbling. "She's gone," Hawke said. He could smell smoke. "We need to get out of here."

Price looked down at Kessler, shook his head. "No," he said. But he set her gently down and let Hawke help him to his feet. His shirt was soaked in Kessler's blood.

One arm around Price's waist, Hawke followed the others out through the broken glass doors, away from the noise of the alarms and into hell.

CHAPTER NINE
11:17 A.M.

OUTSIDE, people were rushing everywhere in a panic, shoving one another to get away. Smoke swirled in the air; abandoned cars sat up on the sidewalk with their doors hanging open while other drivers honked their horns against snarled traffic. A series of wrenching crashes echoed through the street as a taxi tried to race around a jammed intersection and slammed into a shiny silver Mercedes sedan, sending it spinning into a Nissan that had been left by the curb. Screams and shouts mixed with the rending of metal, booms of secondary

explosions that came from every direction, the shriek of rubber and the growing rumble of something far larger and more
terrifying, like the collapse of entire buildings somewhere out
of sight.

Hawke helped Price move away from the Conn.ect building to an empty spot on the curb, where he sat Price down
and crouched next to him. The man seemed unable to support his own weight. "You hurt?" Hawke said. Price shook
his head no. He was crying silently, looking down at his hands,
still sticky with Kessler's blood.

Hawke stood up and looked around with a fresh sense of
shock. A block away, a gigantic, gaping hole had swallowed
the intersection of Second Avenue and East 78th Street, smoke
and flames shooting up from below, asphalt buckled and
melting in all directions. He could feel the heat from where he
stood. A city bus, barely visible through the rippling flames,
had toppled into the hole, upended and tilted sideways, the
ads that adorned its sides blackened with smoke. The Mexi-
can restaurant on the corner with the brown plastic booths
and corrugated metal roof was gone, the building that had
contained it gaping open and licked by fire. The other side of
the street had fared slightly better, but Girardi's market had
been defaced with flames and smoke and the awning on the
Vietnamese place next door was burning like a torch.

He flashed back to his nightmare: Thomas, being yanked
away from him by slippery-smooth tentacles whipping down
from above. The heat of the fires nearby washed over Hawke,
bringing tears. More smoke billowed up over the city, pillars
of it swirling through the blue sky and winding away like balloon strings. The chaos was absolute; Armageddon had descended in a split second's time. He hadn't had time to process
this. Everything had gone down so fast, and getting down to

the lobby was a blur, fueled by adrenaline and a focus on survival. It was all too big, too overwhelming, completely alien and wrong in a way that made him feel numb. This couldn't be happening, there was no reason or explanation for it, and yet it was; the mental pressure was building around him, strong as an approaching tornado, sucking air from his lungs, whipping dust and debris into every crack and crevice.

"Gas explosion." Weller appeared as if from nowhere, nodding toward the hole in the street. He spoke loudly to cut through the din, but he appeared eerily calm within the madness around them. "That's what took out our windows on the seventh floor. Easy enough to do, if you overload the systems and force a rupture."

The sound of Weller's voice brought Hawke back to himself. Weller had Young and Vasco with him, and he was carrying the hard-shelled security case from his office in both arms, hugging it like it was a child. Was that why he had lingered in the office suite? Hawke thought of Young, ready to charge back upstairs to rescue Weller without a second thought. Anger flared, white-hot at Hawke's core. Suddenly he wanted to get his hands around Weller's throat, and the urge was so strong he balled his fists to keep from leaping at him.

"What the hell happened to you?"

"Got disoriented up there for a few minutes, with the smoke," he said, "but I found my way down."

Gas explosion. He was right about the hole on Second Avenue; Hawke could smell it in the air. But it didn't explain the other plumes of smoke rising up across New York, or the number of cars run off the street and crumpled into one another. It didn't explain the traffic lights cycling randomly down 79th Street as he watched, or the way Bradbury had danced a jig across the office floor with the office lamp, hair standing on end.

Something else Weller had said finally registered. "What do you mean, it's easy enough to do?" Hawke said. "You think this was deliberate?"

"We need to get somewhere safe," Weller said. "Things have changed."

"What's changed? And where is safe? People are *dead*. Don't you give a damn about Susan Kessler? She bled out in the lobby. And Price over there needs to be treated for shock. What the hell is going on?"

Weller turned toward Hawke, who realized that the man's calm was an illusion; his eyes held that same glittering light they'd had earlier in his office, pure energy pouring off him like some kind of gospel preacher at the pulpit as another distant explosion shook the ground. "They're not just coming after me now. I think *she's* involved. This is going to get worse."

CHAPTER TEN   11:23 A.M.

WHO WAS INVOLVED? *Did he mean Kessler?* Before Hawke could say a word, Weller took a step into the street, still clutching his laptop case. Young shouted a warning as a brand-new Cadillac Escalade, careening on and off the sidewalk around the choked traffic, suddenly swerved violently to the left through an opening and accelerated toward him, its engine screaming.

The huge machine missed Price by less than three feet. Hawke shoved Weller out of the way and dove to the ground, getting a split-second glimpse of the terrified face of the driver, her hands completely up and off the wheel as the vehicle slid past and slammed into a light post.

The post toppled over, crashing into the face of the office building, bouncing off and sending sparks flying as the SUV hung on the light-post base, engine still growling. Hawke lay still for a moment, stunned, the fresh surge of adrenaline making his stomach lurch.

He tasted grit, spat on the concrete and grimaced. His palms were scraped raw. The pain was like a stinging slap to the face, enough to rouse him again, and he sat up as Young tried to get Weller to a sitting position. The man's head lolled loosely on his shoulders. He was out cold after cracking his head in the fall. Young spoke into his face, "Come on, Jim, wake *up*...."

Hawke got to his feet and went to the Cadillac, where Vasco was yanking at the driver's door. He could hear the woman screaming inside, battering at the window with her fists. "Unlock it," Vasco said, cupping his hands to the glass. He repeated it slowly, as if to a stubborn child. "Unlock ... the ... fucking ... door!"

"She okay?"

Vasco turned to glance at Hawke, breathing hard, and shook his head as the engine continued to race out of control, nearly drowning him out. "It's in neutral, but if she hits that shifter it's gonna go like a bat out of hell.... I can't get through to her; she's out of her frigging mind here...."

Hawke looked around for more speeding vehicles. Most drivers seemed to have given up amid the traffic and left their cars where they stood. People were still running away from the fire on 78th.

Another low, deep rumble shook the street, something far away or underground. He found a fist-sized chunk of concrete torn loose from the light post's fall, hefted it and went to the SUV, shattering the window as the driver cowered away from him. He reached in to unlock the door and the woman tumbled out into the street, sobbing and scrambling on all fours away from the vehicle.

She got to her feet a few yards away and turned back to them, holding a small leopard-print clutch, swaying like a drunk and shivering, her mascara running down her face in two black lines. She wiped snot from her nose with a sleeve. "That . . . fucking thing . . . it tried to *kill* me. . . ."

"Easy," Hawke said. He took a step toward her with his hand out, but she screamed and shrank back, and he stopped dead, not wanting to spook her further. "It kinda looked like *you* tried to kill *us*."

"I . . . I *didn't*!" she screamed, the words torn from her raw throat. She was probably in her early fifties, but with work done around her eyes and neck, a well-kept woman who was going to pieces. "The wheel jumped right out of my fucking hands; I didn't even *touch* the accelerator. . . ." She looked wildly from one man to the other, then at the SUV, slowly backing away.

A thud came from the hole on East 78th, and more smoke rushed skyward. Three people coming up Second Avenue ran in between them, a woman in a full business suit with two men dressed like couriers, darting hard and fast, not even bothering to look at Hawke and the others. The woman from the SUV shrank away like an abused dog as they went by, going into a half crouch, hands up around her head. Other people were screaming, and a man kept shouting over and over again from somewhere inside one of the nearby buildings, his voice ragged.

Hawke reached in through the open door and shut off the engine. He got in and switched the radio on, his heart thudding so loud he could barely hear. An automated message blared through the high-end audio system: *"This is the emergency broadcast system. . . . This is not a test. . . . Mayor Weber has declared a state of emergency. . . . Please go immediately to your nearest safety checkpoint. . . ."*

Hawke found himself breathing too fast and shallow again, getting light-headed. The radio broadcast was listing the checkpoints now. He listened until the message began to repeat, and pressed the OnStar button, praying that the network wasn't down.

"OnStar. How may I help you?"

Thank God. "I'd like to report an accident," he said, words tumbling out. *Just slow down.*

"Name and location?"

"We need an ambulance at the corner of Seventy-ninth and Second; a woman is bleeding to death!" Hawke couldn't bring himself to say that Kessler was already dead. *Maybe we made a mistake. Maybe they can still save her life.* He thought of asking for assistance with a possible B and E and giving the operator his apartment address. But something bothered him about the voice; he couldn't put his finger on what.

"Vocal patterns suggest extreme stress," the voice said. "Emotional reaction analysis. Recognition algorithms processing." There was a long pause, and the voice recited his name and his Social Security number. "Please remain in the vehicle. Help is on the way."

What? Fresh adrenaline flooded through him. He exited the Cadillac and slammed the door just as the locks clicked down again. He backed away, watching it as if it might jump at him at any moment. It was just a car, right? But the voice, although clearly female, had been too calm, too devoid of emotion even for an emergency services worker.

The operator had been trying to trap him.

As soon as the thought crossed his mind, he shook it off. *Ridiculous.* He could use the Cadillac to get out of the city, get him home to Robin and Thomas. It made the most sense, and yet he couldn't bring himself to get back in. He had the feeling he might not make it out of the SUV a second time.

Another rattling boom shook the street and spun Hawke around. A fresh, blossoming flower of fire rose up from the hole in Second Avenue as the city bus toppled into the abyss. It was getting harder to breathe with the smoke. The immediacy of the situation came back to him. There was no time to think, not out here, exposed and vulnerable. They needed shelter and a plan.

He watched a figure disappear into a Jewish temple across the street. The building was a solid square of concrete, short and squat, small windows set deep into its surface, with a set of solid wooden doors that looked strong enough to hold off an army. Young and Vasco had gotten Weller upright between them, and Hawke ran toward Price, his shoulders hunched as fresh debris pattered down like hail, afraid a chunk of asphalt would come hurtling to earth and crush him. "Get up," Hawke said, grabbing the man by the arm. "We've got to get to cover."

Price shook him off but got to his feet, eyes still glassy with shock. "I'm okay," he said. "I'm fine."

Hawke considered giving him a helping hand, but Price

took a step back and shook his head. Instead he helped carry Weller across the street to the temple, Price and the woman from the Cadillac following them at a short distance as if wary of their intentions but too terrified to let them go.

CHAPTER ELEVEN   11:46 A.M.

THE HUGE WOODEN DOORS SWUNG SHUT, and the small group stood for a moment, the sound of their harsh breathing echoing in the vestibule. The abrupt change was shocking. The power was out, but enough light filtered through a small window to allow them to see.

"Jesus Christ," Vasco said finally. He leaned back against the doors for a moment with Weller's arm still across his broad shoulders, closed his eyes in the shadows and tipped his head. "Jesus. *Fuck*. This is crazy. I gotta call in—" He banged his head against the door, opened his eyes again and stood up straight, looked around at them all, then shook his head. "We need to set him down. I need to *think* for a minute."

Hawke's limbs were trembling, but he managed to help carry Weller away from the doors as they set him down on the floor. The building was built like a bomb shelter with walls that were probably three feet thick, and the noise outside was barely audible. A second set of doors to the interior of the building was closed.

Weller's head lolled limply against Young's shoulder. "Wake up," Hawke said, straightening Weller's head and lightly slapping his cheek, trying to force him into conscious-

ness. "I want to know what's going on. What were you trying to tell me?"

Young stopped his hand. "He's out," she said. "Look at
the bump on his head. He can't answer. Leave him alone."

"How could you leave her like that?" Price said. "All of
you. Just leave her bleeding to death in that lobby."

Hawke let out a long, trembling sigh. He could smell the
blood on Price's shirt. Kessler's blood. Nobody spoke. There
was no answer to give. Hawke had to collect his thoughts, try
to make some sense of everything. He wanted to go at Weller
until the man answered his questions.

"What do we *do*?" the woman from the SUV whispered,
her voice hoarse with panic. She twisted her hands together
around her clutch over and over, squeezing, digging at it with
her manicured nails. "I need to find my husband." Her gaze
darted back and forth, refusing to settle on anything for
more than a few seconds. "I have to get downtown."

Hawke thought of Robin and Thomas, the woman ratch-
eting up his own anxiety again. What was happening right
now at home? Not knowing made him wild, his imagination
racing. But losing his cool wouldn't do them any good. He
had to focus, figure out the right way to get back to them.

"What's your name?" he said. When the woman didn't
seem to hear him, he took her by the arms, forcing her to stop
and look at him. "Your name," he said again.

"Sarah Hanscomb," she said, finally fixing her gaze on his
face. The waves of panic pouring off her were going to make
them all lose their minds. She nearly crumpled and looked
away again, her brows coming together, mouth quivering, but
she fought it off. "We're from Englewood Cliffs. My husband
works for Germer Benson; he's at the office right now. I
dropped him at the PATH this morning. I didn't think—when

things started happening I turned around; I wanted—I had to get over the bridge before—oh God." She seemed to realize what she'd done, trapping herself in the city, everything crashing down on her at once. Her hands trembled as she brought them to her face as if trying to hide behind the clutch. The backs of them were veined, wrinkled. She was older than Hawke had first thought. He pulled them down again.

"Which bridge?" he said. "What happened?"

She shook her head, tears squeezing out over bruised lids. "The GW. He was downtown," she said, pleading, as if she felt the need to explain herself. "I had to get him out. The radio said there were explosions—"

"How did you get to Second Avenue?"

"The Henry Hudson was gone after the bridge—I took Harlem River Drive and got off on Park, then worked my way over and down. You don't understand; the streets are all jammed up—"

Hawke saw her eyes go wide a split second before he was shoved violently aside. Vasco grabbed Hanscomb and threw her up against the wall. "Tell us what the fuck is going on out there," he said, cords standing out in his neck. "There were more explosions? What exactly did you see?"

"Take it easy," Hawke said. The woman shook her head back and forth, trying to avoid Vasco's face, inches from her own as he leaned into her.

"Please," she whispered, "I can't—I don't *know*!"

"I want to hear every fucking detail. You better talk, lady, right now."

"People just . . . went crazy. Cars and trucks off the road, hitting each other. Most of them were trying to get out, but I was coming *in*. It was easier that way. The radio talked about a terrorist threat, police hurting protestors, riots and looting, but nobody seemed to know why. I called my husband before the phones went out; he was trapped inside his building with people in the street turning cars over and . . . and worse. He said the stock market was collapsing, traders were locked out of their systems, including him. The entire market gone, bank and investment accounts drained, funds vanishing, and I was so scared for him, you don't *know*. People would kill over this stuff. I just needed to get to him, get him out. After I crossed the bridge, the Henry Hudson exit was just a hole in the ground. I couldn't cross it. Then I heard a terrible noise, it shook everything, and things fell all around the car and when I looked back I . . ." She swallowed hard, her throat working like she might be sick, and her voice was little more than a whisper. "The bridge was gone."

Jesus Christ. How could that be possible? Terrorists had blown up the George Washington? For what reason? Hawke couldn't imagine what might be happening behind the walls of the building they were hiding in, what kind of scale they were actually facing—and what might be coming next.

This was huge, a story to end all others, and he was one step away from it.

Weller. Weller had let him in for a reason, and the things the man had said this morning made it seem as if he'd known something was coming. Hawke wanted to shake the man until something came loose. His wind was up, he was hungry to chase leads, and he hated himself for thinking about that instead of the reality of their situation. The city was falling apart around them, and his wife and son and unborn child could be in terrible danger. But even as Hawke's skin crawled with the need to run, to fight, to get home, his instincts made him want to figure out the answers and get at the truth.

The helicopter, the explosions, the madness on the streets.

The SUV, and the OnStar voice recognizing him. And Weller's invitation in his office, like a ticket to the dance. Hawke had the pieces in his hands, and now he wanted to fit them together.

You use technology to tell a story. I want you to tell a story now. The biggest one of your life.

"Gone?" Vasco stared at Hanscomb, shook her once and then released her and slowly stepped back, stunned. "The GW? That can't be right."

She nodded, her face crumpling again. "The radio said it was a coordinated attack. All the bridges—some kind of missile strike or other weapons, I don't know—at the same time . . ." Something like a whimper escaped her mouth before she bit it back. "They said it was happening all over the place. Wall Street is a war zone. People are trapped and panicking, going at each other like animals. My husband, he's never even had a fistfight in his life. What is he going to *do*?"

"All the bridges?" Young said. She had remained sitting next to Weller on the floor. He was still unconscious, head leaning against her shoulder. "Are you sure?"

Sarah Hanscomb nodded. "That's what they said, before the broadcast stopped. Then it was just a recorded loop, telling people to get to the security checkpoints." She wiped at her running nose, smearing more makeup. "All those people on the bridge, there were hundreds of cars. . . ."

"You tried to run us over," Vasco said. Hawke could feel the violence rising up in him, the heat and sweat and crackling energy. "I saw you swerve right into us."

"I didn't, the car just jumped, I'm telling you—it went crazy, all my lights going on, tire pressure, engine, oil light, and then . . . I—I wasn't even touching the wheel!"

Vasco was on the verge of losing control. He moved back

toward Hanscomb, and Hawke stepped in between them before anything else could happen, putting a hand gently on Vasco's chest, just enough to stop his momentum. The touch released something in the other man and he grabbed Hawke by the collar with both fists, his arms trembling and rigid, his mangled finger bleeding again and wetting Hawke's shirt.

"What the fuck are you doing, huh?" Vasco said. "Protecting this crazy bitch?"

"Don't," Hawke said. "We all just want to get home—"

"My wife is in Jersey," Vasco said, his eyes shimmering now, and Hawke could see his panic about to spill over, could smell it on his breath and skin. "I went through this before, September eleventh. My brother was in the city; I was home with my mother. It took him six hours to get back. I had to watch her waiting. . . . I thought he was dead. I can't do that to my wife, you understand? I can't."

"I get it," Hawke said. His legs nearly buckled as an image of Thomas as a baby flashed through his head, little round face all squeezed up and red, a squalling mass of infant fury. "I have a family there, too. I know how you feel, but we have to stick together here, because one wrong move could get us killed."

"Talking to this crazy . . . ," Vasco said. He shook his head. "We should throw her back out there to fend for herself. Hell, I don't even know you people. No job is worth this. Who the fuck are you to tell me what to do, anyway?"

Hawke glanced at Hanscomb, who made another small, helpless noise. "Look, it doesn't matter how we all got here," he said. "What's important is what we do now. We need to put our heads together."

Vasco stared at him, looked at Hanscomb. "Security

checkpoints," he said. "You said they were on the radio. Where's the closest one?"

Hanscomb nodded. "Yes, right, there was . . . I don't know; I'm trying to . . ." She started trembling, tears starting again, glancing back and forth between them.

"Lenox Hill Hospital," Hawke said. "I heard it on the radio. That's the closest one to where we are."

Vasco looked at Hanscomb, who nodded again. "I . . . think that's right," she said. "It's hard to remember. Everything was so crazy."

A noise from behind the closed inner doors made them all freeze. Someone was inside.

Before Hawke could say a word, Price turned the handles, swinging the doors wide.

The main sanctuary was deep and filled with flitting shadows, paneled in dark wood and carpeted with a deep red Berber, with rows of simple pews marching in straight lines toward the reader's platform and curtain that hid the Torah Ark. Low ropes ran along inset portions of the walls, and narrow vertical lines of windows let in a little watery light. Candles flickered from candelabras on both sides of the bimah, where a group of people had gathered.

A man was talking in a low voice; Hawke thought it might be a reading from the Torah. The man wore a tallith draped over his shoulders. None of the people acknowledged their arrival.

Vasco spread his arms out and walked up the aisle. "Hello!" he shouted. "You know what's going on outside? Wake up, people. We're all looking down the barrel of a gun! You want to wait around until it goes off?"

The words were explosive in the quiet room. But the small

group at the front didn't seem to react, the man in front of them still droning on as if nobody had spoken. Vasco continued up the aisle, wheeling around and walking backward for a moment, then spinning to face the front again, arms still spread wide: a welcoming, open gesture sharply at odds with the barely contained rage held in his body and quivering voice.

"*Hey,*" Vasco said. "Are you people deaf? Or just stupid?"

He's going to lose it, Hawke thought again, and he wondered how it would come, an all-out lumbering assault or a more carefully designed, surgical attack.

A man stepped abruptly in front of Vasco just before he reached the front. The man was short, bespectacled, wearing a *kippah,* his olive skin partially hidden by a thick black beard. He held a copy of the Torah in his hands. *Uh-oh,* Hawke thought.

"I'm sorry, this is a house of God," the man said. "Please be respectful—"

Vasco didn't even slow down, just shouldered past the man on his way to the bimah. "Who's in charge?" Vasco said, addressing the man in the tallith. "You? This your temple?"

Hawke moved down the aisle, following the action. He saw the small group part and turn as the man sighed slightly, set down his readings and finally looked at Vasco, like a patient father at an interrupting child. Candlelight flickered across his face. "I have come here to welcome anyone who feels the need to pray," he said. "The house of worship belongs to no one except God."

"In case you haven't noticed," Vasco said, gesturing toward the front doors, "while you're all sitting in here staring at the Torah, the world is going to hell, and that includes this place. You might want to consider finding an escape route."

"God will decide who lives and who dies," the rabbi said. He was taller than the rest, in his fifties, with salt-and-pepper hair cropped short and a close beard streaked with gray. His voice was calm, but it held a commanding power that filled the large room.

"When Gog Umagog arrives," the man who had stepped in front of Vasco said, "we must repent and pray and release our fears, give ourselves to God. Redemption will come to those who do."

"Gog *what*?" Vasco was smiling now, but his face looked pained, like he was humoring a mental deficient.

"The war to end all wars," the rabbi said. "Armageddon. The end of days." Several others murmured in agreement. "The Ba'al Shem Tov teaches us to believe with complete faith, so that we may find joy and peace. Our redemption is at hand along with the coming of the Mashiach, and we shall be received with kindness and mercy."

As Vasco got closer, the men around the reader's platform shifted to form a half circle in front of the rabbi. Hawke sensed it was done passively, purely for protection, but it punctuated the divide between the two groups. *Us against them.*

Vasco stopped suddenly, eyeing them all as if discovering a threat. "Armageddon, huh?" he said. "The Mashiach? I thought Jews didn't believe in Jesus."

The murmuring grew louder, several others shaking their heads, but the rabbi didn't seem to mind. "Our Mashiach is not the Christian Messiah," he said. "But the coming of a savior, one who will lead the way to heaven for those who believe, is understood by anyone who has heard the power of prayer, who understands redemption." He looked around at the people gathered before him. "That time has come."

"Give it a rest," Vasco said. "We're dealing with terrorists, and people are dying outside, and they're going to start dying in here."

"Our world has finally reached its end, our hubris, our pursuit of power before God, our worship of progress at any cost."

"What the hell are you talking about—"

"You haven't seen what's happening out there? You haven't noticed that the things attacking us are all of our own making? They are using our own creations against us."

"Whatever's going on has human beings on the other end of it, I can promise you that," Vasco said. "They want to scare the shit out of us; that's the goal. We need a plan to get out of the city, find some open space."

The rabbi studied him for a moment, as if considering whether to squash a bug under his foot. "There is no plan," he said. "Not one for *us* to make, anyway."

"What about the people who are still out there?" Sarah Hanscomb had come up behind Vasco and Hawke. "My husband is a good man," she said. Hawke thought of Bluetooth and his uncle who had skipped the country after destroying Hawke's parents' lives, leaving nothing but ruin in his wake. "He . . . he might be hurt; he might need help. Don't you have anyone? Loved ones who are missing?"

She looked around at the people watching her. The rabbi gestured for her to move aside. "Are you hurt?" he said, looking at Price, who had remained near the door. In the shadows, the blood on his shirt looked black.

"I'm okay," Price said. "The friend who bled out all over me is not."

A woman who stood at the front, her head covered, her body draped in a modest floor-length dress, spoke up. "Maybe we should talk about this," she said, her voice soft but clear. "They may have news. There's no harm in that."

For the first time, the rabbi seemed off balance. "No harm?" he said, his voice cracking slightly. "Ana, you surprise me. There is great harm in letting in those who come from a dying world, who bring that stain with them. If they enter our sacred space with no fear, if they embrace their faith and accept the Mashiach with kindness, they are welcome. If not . . ." He waved a hand toward the door. "They must leave us."

"We're not going anywhere," Vasco said.

"What about Mother?" the woman said, ignoring him. She was younger than Hawke first thought, as he caught a glimpse of her face. Maybe late teens or early twenties.

"She made her choice," the rabbi said. His slightly furrowed brow had relaxed again, smooth and clear.

"We don't *know* that," the woman said, edging closer to him. "She wasn't home. She didn't know where we'd go—"

"Enough, Ana." The man looked at her, and the woman stopped speaking abruptly. "These people don't need to hear about our personal lives. None of that's important anymore." He gestured at the open space, toward the outside walls. "It doesn't matter where we are when the time comes. What matters is our expression of faith and our willingness to accept God's will."

"This isn't your building," Vasco said. He looked like someone who had just figured out a riddle. "You're squatters, am I right? Came here and took over, just like that?"

The rabbi sighed again, like he had before, the sound of a patient person dealing with someone unstable, a nuisance he'd rather forget. "This house belongs to no man," he said. "Now, if you'll allow us to return to our prayers—"

"We've got as much a right to be here as you do," Vasco said. "Who the fuck are you to say otherwise?"

The rabbi stared daggers, and Hawke saw something behind his calm demeanor, something unbalanced and furious— a man not used to having his authority questioned, and one who might react in unexpected ways.

"Profanity has no place in a house of God," he said. "Please leave us to our prayers."

As Vasco shook his head, smiling again in a way that was anything but friendly, Hawke's cell phone chirped in his pocket. Momentarily stunned, he stepped away and slipped back toward the entrance to the building and into a deeper darkness, passing Young and Weller, who seemed to be coming around. The phone had been bricked back in the Conn.ect office, completely dead. How could it be back on now? Hawke turned his back to the others and dug it out with trembling fingers, hoping for something from Robin, anything that would reassure him she was okay.

The message was from Rick, the words bright and clear on his screen: *I LIED. I AM ADMIRAL DOE.*

CHAPTER TWELVE   12:10 P.M.

HAWKE STARED AT THE PHONE, his head spinning. How had it booted itself up again and come to life? He was certain it had been bricked. Devices didn't just reanimate themselves.

Maybe Rick had done it somehow, sent Hawke a worm that worked in this way. But why would Rick text him now, on an unsecured line, to admit to something like this? During their chat session Rick had begged Hawke to help him find out who Doe was and claimed he was being set up.

It made no sense.

A sudden buzz of opportunity lit him up like a live wire. *Use this chance.* He hit the home button, trying to get to the keypad to call Robin. Nothing happened; the phone wouldn't respond. It seemed to be locked into the texting program but wouldn't allow him to get to his other contacts or do anything other than respond to Rick's message.

Hawke cursed and resisted the urge to throw the phone across the room. He typed a response: *Need to get a message to Robin.*

He waited, gripping the phone so hard his fingers started to ache. Maybe Rick had no other choice; maybe he'd gotten in far deeper than he expected and needed help and wanted to come clean. But if he and Anonymous were involved with what was happening now, then the shit had truly hit the fan and Hawke would have to admit that he didn't know Rick anymore and maybe never had. Whatever else the man was, whether the steps he had taken were right or wrong, his heart had always been in the right place, his motivations pure and simple and closely aligned with Hawke's own. *Use the tools at hand to expose corruption, level the playing field. Tear down the walls that keep people from the truth; empower others to make their own choices.* Rick had always said that they were living in one of the most exciting times in history, and he saw himself as a comic-book hero fighting injustice. Hawke knew it wasn't that simple, that there were other motivations, purely selfish. There was the challenge of each project they took on—clicking the puzzle pieces together to see if they fit. And the challenge to authority.

But whatever Rick was into now, it wasn't about

empowering people, or making the world a better, fairer, more purely democratic place. This was about anarchy and destruction and pain. Rick had spent over a year in jail, and maybe that had changed him. But Hawke couldn't imagine reconciling the man he knew with the person who was behind the events today. And besides, even if Anonymous had become a much more malignant and powerful network while Hawke had been away, it was difficult to believe they were capable of the kind of comprehensive and overwhelming attack that was going on now. The entire structure of the group was built upon freedom, anonymity, individuality. It was one thing to bring enough people together for a short period of time to take down a few servers. But how could they gather the resources and power to pull this off?

His phone chirped. *NO MESSAGES. WE ARE MAKING A STATEMENT. TIRED OF WAITING FOR EVERYONE ELSE TO ACT.*

Who?

US. THE COLLECTIVE. IT DOES NOT MATTER.

Hawke typed: *What about my family? Are they in danger?*

THE WORLD IS IN DANGER.

What are you doing now?

NOT YOUR CONCERN ANYMORE. OPERATION GLOBAL BLACKOUT CANNOT BE STOPPED. IT IS GOING TO GET WORSE. GET TO A CHECKPOINT. YOU WILL BE SAFE THERE. WE WILL NOT TOUCH THEM.

Hawke hesitated, overwhelmed, every nerve in his body singing, wondering what to say, how to handle it. *You don't want this. This isn't you.*

THINGS CHANGE. PEOPLE CHANGE.

I don't believe you.

There was no answer for a long moment, and then, without warning, the screen shivered and blinked, and suddenly Hawke was staring at himself through the lens of his camera, his face caught between the shadows and flickering candlelight. There was something threatening about the act, as if he was being observed by a voyeur, the camera's eye making some kind of point. There was nowhere to hide. His own device had been commandeered and turned against him.

I SEE YOU.

As Hawke watched himself on the screen, hypnotized by the image, someone came at him from the side with a bear hug, low and hard. His phone was wrenched from his grasp. He staggered right, barely kept his feet with a hand on the back of a pew.

He turned to find Weller standing next to him, breathing fast. "You're going to get us killed," Weller said. Damaged during the near collision with the SUV, Weller's glasses sat askew on his nose, giving him an unbalanced, slightly crazed look. He glanced down at the phone, the screen still on, his face filled with an emotion that appeared to be half sadness, half fury, and threw it to the floor, stomping down with a foot as the glass crunched, grinding it into pieces.

Stunned for a moment, and then enraged beyond all understanding, Hawke felt the world go gray as blood thumped behind his eyes. He grappled with the other man with a ferocity he hadn't known he possessed. Weller's hands clawed at Hawke's face as they went to the floor like animals fighting in a back alley. Time seemed to slip away before he began to come back to himself and realized Weller was grunting something at him as they rolled together.

"It's . . . not . . . who you think—"

As abruptly as the fight had begun, it was over. Weller rolled away as Hawke lay on his back, chest heaving, his face wet. "It's not who you think!" Weller shouted, his voice raw as he regained his feet and collected his glasses from beneath a nearby pew and setting them on his face, where they tilted even farther askew. One lens was cracked now, reflecting the candlelight in two fractured planes, and the lump on Weller's forehead from hitting it against the curb was purple and swollen like an egg. He looked around at the rest of the group. Everyone had remained frozen in place, staring at him like he'd lost his mind.

Hawke touched his face, his hand coming away red. Weller had clawed him pretty hard, and the blood was mixed with his own tears. He felt something digging into his back and realized it was the remains of his shattered phone.

He got to his feet. "What do you mean, it's not who I think?"

"It's not your wife, your friend, your family, on the other end of that text message. Whoever you think it is, it's not them."

"How the hell would you know that?"

Weller turned away without answering. Everyone had stopped to watch the spectacle, even the rabbi and those at the front, who had gathered closer together with the others from the pews, forming a tight group around the prayer table. "Anyone else with a phone?" Weller said to the silent room. "Destroy them. Do it now. It doesn't matter if they're working or not."

The look on Weller's face was so intense and so radiant, Hawke took a step back like it was a communicable disease. Maybe the bump to the head had scrambled Weller up worse than anyone had thought. Or maybe this was more of the paranoia he'd shown in his office earlier.

A glance passed between Weller and Young, and she pulled her own phone from her pocket, placed it on the floor and stamped down, cracking the glass, grinding it under her heel.

Vasco, who had come halfway down the aisle, took his own phone out. "We can deactivate the GPS," he said. "We might still be able to use them—"

"Do it," Weller said, his voice holding an edge. "I can't tell you how dangerous this is. Do it now."

The two men watched each other for a long moment; then Vasco shrugged and glanced away. He tossed the phone on the floor, crushing it with his foot, making a show out of the process, taking his time.

"You got it, boss," he said. "Anything you say. It's dead anyway."

"There are chips inside," Weller said to the rabbi's group. "Your phones can be operated remotely. They can be used to track your location."

The room was electric. Hawke felt something happening here, words unspoken and hanging like ghosts, things hidden just out of sight. Weller knew something important, and he held people's attention like a politician at a rally.

"We don't have phones," the rabbi called out, after a moment. "None of us."

Somewhere outside, a faint rumble shook the foundation of the building, like a train passing at a distance. Hawke felt it through his feet.

Weller turned to Sarah Hanscomb, who was shaking her head. "What if my husband, what if he's trying to call me?"

she said, her voice rising up in a mixture of hope and panic. "He might be trying to reach me right now, if I try to turn it on again—"

"It's nothing but a weapon, a Trojan horse to be used against you. Against us." Weller took a step toward her, and Hanscomb shrank back, as if fearful of being struck. "They're after us," he said. "Don't you get it?" He looked around at all of them again. "The singularity is here, and it's not what we all thought it would be. It's not a new beginning; it's an ending."

Hawke had written about it before, in a series of early articles he'd done for the online news blog Timeline that explored concepts rather than offering any real insight. Coined by a science-fiction writer and made popular by futurist visionary Ray Kurzweil, the "singularity" referred to the moment when machines would blend with and then transcend their makers, becoming self-aware and independent. Kurzweil argued that the moment would usher in a new utopia. Others felt it made the future unknowable, a black hole in time after which the world would be impossible to predict. But all of them agreed that the time would come, most likely in the twenty-first century, and that it would change humanity forever.

The singularity. It was nothing more than an idea that framed something difficult to express, Hawke thought. Weller had lost his mind.

Everyone began talking at once, Vasco coming farther down the aisle as Hanscomb argued more vehemently, holding her small clutch in both hands and pleading her case as the others converged upon her like some senseless mob. It was like she held her husband in that clutch, Hawke thought, rather than a useless piece of machinery that was never going to reach him. Even if what Weller was saying was wrong and the phone was harmless, there was no signal, no way to get through.

The rabbi came out from behind the table, striding forward in his tallith like a man possessed by a higher calling, his congregation falling in behind him in lockstep. Hawke, nearly at the entrance to the vestibule, faded back, past where Price stood and away from them all, his body shaking now like a junkie coming off a fix. He wanted darkness, quiet, a moment alone. He needed to think.

Get to a checkpoint. You'll be safe there.

As the arguing escalated, the sound of sirens outside made Hawke go to the temple doors. He opened them and peered out, his head and shoulders exposed.

The street outside was eerily empty, looking more like a war zone than the Upper East Side, except for a police car that had pulled up through the swirling smoke next to the Cadillac SUV. Two cops were advancing upon a man on the sidewalk holding a laptop case. *No, not just any case.*

It was the one Weller had carried out from his office. They'd left it somewhere on the street when the crash happened, completely forgetting about it in the rush to safety.

Where the hell had everyone gone?

The acrid smell of burning plastic and rubber wafted into the temple. Something Hawke couldn't quite explain brought chills to the back of his neck. He peered out into the street, the red and blue lights from the cop car bouncing off the smoke and making it harder to see. The man holding the case was close to Weller's age and build, dressed casually in sneakers, jeans and polo-style shirt, glasses perched on his nose, his thinning hair cropped close to his skull. The cops came with guns drawn and tight, shuffling steps, muscles tense in shooters' poses, acting like the man was a wanted criminal. They barked orders at him, but Hawke couldn't make out the words. The man kept shaking his head emphatically. He held out the case at arm's length, as if making an offering. It was heavy, and he had trouble keeping it there.

While one cop kept his gun trained at the man's head, the other grabbed the case and stepped back. He knelt on the broken curb for a long moment, his back to Hawke, apparently examining the security latch, unable to open it. He put a hand to his ear, as if listening to an earpiece, nodded once, then said something to his partner, who glanced at him and then back at the man, who stood frozen in place with his hands raised, the universal expression of surrender.

Hawke hesitated at the doors, itching to move, but the cops' demeanor gave him pause. There was something about the way they were acting; the tension in the air felt wrong. The man seemed to feel it, too; he was shaking his head again, starting to back away almost imperceptibly, his arms dropping until the cop with his gun trained on him ordered him to halt.

The cop with the case stood up and scanned the empty street around them, then looked at the other, who took a single step forward. As the man put his hands up again and began to speak, both cops shot him through the palms, twin bullets blowing his brains out through the back of his skull to splatter on the concrete behind him like an abstract painting come to life.

WHEN THOMAS HAD JUST TURNED TWO YEARS OLD, *Hawke lost him as they left the park three streets over from their apartment. It was a small park, little more than a triangle of green carved out of a block of old brick buildings, their lower floors converted to shops, the upper-section apartments looking out at one another across the grass. They'd been there several times before, but that day was different. It started out innocently enough and ended up dissolving into hell.*

Robin was out for coffee with a friend from college, and Hawke bundled Thomas up for the fall weather and took him out to play, more to burn time before Robin returned than because of any desire either of them had for exercise. It wouldn't have mattered much; there wasn't enough space to do a lot of running or have a play structure of any kind. Hawke sat on the single bench near the end of the green triangle and watched Thomas totter around on chubby little-boy legs, clutching that lion he'd had since the day he was born. He was fascinated by all the things little boys were fascinated by: a dandelion gone to seed and poking up through rocky soil, a worm coiling in the sun, a crow that landed on the other side of the park and hopped sideways, tilting its head and staring with watchful, beady eyes until Thomas turned in its direction and it lifted away, flapping its wings and cawing.

He looked at Hawke, questioning. "That's a bird," Hawke said. "A big black bird."

Thomas pointed in the direction of the crow, now a speck in the bright sky. "Bud," he said, his face serious. "Big back bud." Hawke nodded, keeping his own face carefully neutral, his heart swelling; although bright, Thomas didn't speak much, and he was already beginning to display a need for order and symmetry and perfection. He rarely took a chance on anything he couldn't say perfectly. But he was studying things, learning, trying to understand and communicate. This was one of those moments Hawke knew he would re-member, another small thread of the web that bound them together. He had been single, and then almost without warn-ing he was married; childless, and then he had a child. Hawke had begun to define himself as Thomas's dad, rather than John Hawke, and he was surprised by how little that bothered him.

He wanted to give Thomas the stability he never had, the sense that his father would be there for him, no matter what. Most parents think of themselves as their children's protec-tors; they think they are far more important in a child's life than the other way around. Hawke wondered if that was the case or if he would come to realize, too late, that he could no longer live without his son.

They stayed for less than twenty minutes. When they left, Thomas wanted to walk in front of the stroller and Hawke let him, following closely down the sidewalk to make sure he didn't suddenly change direction and stumble into the street. When Hawke's cell phone chirped, he dug it out of his pocket to glance at the screen: a text from Robin saying she was on her way home. When he looked up again, not ten seconds later, Thomas was gone.

Hawke whirled, looking back at the park, expecting to see him at any moment. But the boy was gone. Hawke's heart paused and swelled in his chest, blocking his throat like a balloon, the silence drawing out until his pulse began to pound like a jackhammer and adrenaline flooded his veins. He whirled again, scanning the street, the row of buildings to his left, the empty stroller, panic lighting him up, making him wild as he called out Thomas's name, softly and then louder, his voice cracking at its height.

A man came out of a bagel shop across the street from the park. "Have you seen a little boy?" Hawke shouted at him, and the man looked at him, startled, then shook his head and put his hands up, palms open.

Hawke raced forward past a city trash barrel, the next cross street too far away for Thomas to have reached it, but he pounded full speed to the curb, panting as he looked right and left, seeing cars winking in the sunlight but no little boy, the sidewalks empty.

When Hawke turned back toward the stroller, he saw Thomas crouched down behind the trash barrel in his puffy blue coat with his lion, his little face squeezed up into a private smile, eyes shut, as if by closing his eyes and being still he became invisible. Hide-and-seek, Thomas's new favorite game at home—he was playing it now and blissfully unaware of Hawke's impending heart attack.

His chest violently unclenched; he heaved in a gulp of air and pounded toward his son, his emotions now pouring out in a single grunt of blind rage as he grabbed Thomas's arm and pulled the boy up toward his face. Whatever Thomas saw there made him go slack with shock and then crumple into tears, and Hawke's words died on his lips as he hugged

Thomas to his chest and rocked him, cooing his apology into the shoulder of the boy's coat until his sobs began to subside.

Hawke found himself struggling to catch his breath.

The doors had swung shut on their own, blocking out the image of the dead man. Hawke reeled backward, bumping into Anne Young, who had come up behind him. He was shaking like a leaf in high wind, but she was absolutely still. She put a hand on his shoulder, light as a bird, and kept it there. He glanced back but couldn't tell from her face whether she'd seen anything at all, her gaze remaining on the closed doors as if she could look right through them.

Hawke leaned left and convulsed, a stream of vomit splattering onto the rug: the remains of coffee and the energy bar he'd eaten that morning.

Young kept her hand on Hawke's shoulder. Everything seemed to press down upon his head, suffocating him. He wiped his mouth and swallowed hard, keeping the sickness down this time as he tried to make some kind of sense of what had just happened. But it was wrong in every way. His mind played over the scene again and again: the man's face registering what was going down a split second before the cops fired, the way his hands came up to ward off the bullet, twin red holes blossoming in them as if by some dark magic, the back of his skull exploding in a mass of red spatter, his body falling backward to slap lifelessly against the sidewalk. It was an execution, an outrage, the murder of a defenseless person who had probably done nothing wrong. A man in the wrong place at the wrong time.

But *why?* Two cops shooting someone in cold blood made no sense, no matter what else was happening out there.

The feeling of dread had come full force with the sight of blood. It was like Hawke's dream, tentacles pulling Thomas away from him. The need to get home to his wife and son clawed at Hawke's chest. What if they were in trouble right now, facing the same kind of violence he had just witnessed?

"Wait," Young said, but Hawke pushed past her without bothering to ask what she wanted. He stalked back up the aisle of the worship room to where Weller stood with the rabbi and his group, Vasco and Hanscomb right behind him.

"Your laptop," Hawke said to Weller, inserting himself in between the man and the others. "What's on it?"

Weller had been in midsentence, continuing the argument about cell phones that had apparently escalated between the rabbi's people and the rest of them. He stopped, mouth still open, studying Hawke's face. Then he looked around the room, his gaze finally settling on Young, who had followed Hawke back from the vestibule. "Where's the case?" Weller said, his voice rising. She shook her head, mute, and Hawke stepped in again to get him focused, the movement bringing Weller's gaze back around.

"What the hell is going on?" Hawke said. "You seem to know something. Why did a man carrying your laptop just get executed?"

"Hold it," Vasco said. "*What* did you just say?"

Hawke kept his eyes trained on Weller's face. "Two cops," he said. "They just shot someone outside who was carrying Jim's laptop case. Maybe he was trying to steal it; I don't know. But it seemed like a pretty harsh punishment to me. Excessive force, don't you think?"

"Are you serious?" Hanscomb shook her head, backing away until her legs hit a pew behind her, as if trying to escape.

Her voice was shrill and loud, and she sounded like she thought it might be some kind of bad joke. "Oh my God."

"That makes no sense," Vasco said. "Why would cops be shooting people in the street?"

"I don't know," Hawke said. He gestured at Weller. "Ask him." Hawke kept seeing the blood, the man's skull exploding in red chunks of bone and brains, the way the body fell straight back and nothing cushioned its fall, as if that mattered anymore.

A long, uncomfortable silence descended over the temple. Even the rabbi and his people remained still, watching, waiting. Weller glanced back at Young and then away, a look coming over his face as if he'd just figured out the world's biggest riddle. "They think it's a threat," he said, almost too softly to be heard. "Things are out of control, just like I told them, and it's a loose end. And we're a scapegoat."

"For who?"

"Eclipse. They're tracking us."

"You've got to be kidding—"

"You can't imagine the power," he said. "The sheer size and scope, the capability. It's breathtaking, in its own way."

"What the fuck are you talking about, Jim?" Hawke said.

"Don't you get it yet? They're going to find a way to make us disappear." Weller smiled, but his eyes were distant. "We're all wanted terrorists," he said. "Every one of us from Conn.ect. Starting right now, every law enforcement officer in the city is looking for us."

"For *what*?"

"Crimes against humanity," he said. "The downfall of modern civilization." He spread his arms in the direction of the doors. "According to every cop in New York, we're responsible for what's happening outside. We're on every list in every database in the world, and I'm quite sure excessive force is not only going to be justified, but encouraged."

"You've lost your fucking mind," Vasco said. His voice had grown dark. "They can't do that. This is *crazy*."

"Has Google mapped the inside of this building?" Weller said to the rabbi, dismissing Vasco's outburst.

"Google? I don't know what you mean—"

"Does it show up on Street View? Is that how you found it?"

"Google Maps," the young woman explained, the one the rabbi had called Ana. "He's talking about the maps on the Internet. They've started to do interiors, not just roads. You can walk around inside buildings, on your computer."

The rabbi closed his mouth, opened it again, a fish out of water. Weller didn't wait for a response. He wheeled around and walked to where the remains of Hawke's cell still lay in the aisle and crouched, studying them for a moment before turning again and looking over their heads at the ceiling. "It's unusual," he said as if to himself, staring at the walls, "the lines of the windows. . . ." He stood up. "Consumer GPS chips are accurate to within a few feet, but inside a building like this the error could be more. They thought we were outside, but they'll be looking to confirm location."

"Jim," Young said. Her face was like a white moon in the shadows.

Weller walked over to Hawke and both stood there nose to nose, Weller's glasses winking in the faint light. "I hope you got something important out of that conversation," he said. "It won't take long before they verify the ID, but they're already mapping images from your cell. It's going to bring them right to our door."

"Who?" Hawke said. "Who are they?"

"Eclipse's secret service," Weller said. "The police, the FBI. Whoever else they convince to come after us."

"I'll ask you again. What the hell is this all about, Jim?"

"Only one way to find out," Weller said. He spun on his heel and marched through the vestibule, opened the door of the temple and walked out, the door slamming shut behind him.

CHAPTER FOURTEEN 12:45 P.M.

IT WAS AS IF WELLER'S WORDS HAD FROZEN them in shock, his actions so bizarre that they couldn't react. Hawke didn't move, waiting to see in which direction things would go. The room grew quiet again, and then Young tried to go after Weller, but Vasco grabbed her and everyone exploded into action at once. The rabbi waved his arms as if to usher them right out of the building, shouting something about terrorists, the rest of his flock surging forward behind him. Vasco began to protest, his face red, veins standing out in his temples, as the rabbi came up to him with arms still out like a rancher herding cattle. Hanscomb shrank away from it all, creeping backward along a pew toward the wall.

"Out!" the rabbi shouted. "All of you! Leave us in peace." The others shouted with him, their faces flushed with anger. Only the young woman, Ana, tried to calm him, her protests lost in the cacophony of voices crashing over the worship room.

They gathered for a moment in the vestibule, Hanscomb

coming last with her own hands up. Two of the people behind the rabbi had picked up heavy candelabras and were brandishing them like clubs.

"Don't hurt me," she said. "I'm not with them, I'm just trying to get my husband and go home." When she reached the vestibule, she looked back, saw Hawke, Vasco, Price and Young and blanched, as if she were being thrown into a jail cell with a pack of murderers.

"Get out," the rabbi said, one more time, and then he took hold of the second set of interior doors that separated the vestibule from the worship room and slammed them shut, closing off the group and leaving them in relative silence.

"Well, that was fun," Vasco said. "Like visiting the in-laws."

Vasco still had Young by the arm. She shrugged free, staring at him in a way Hawke couldn't quite decipher. She stood rubbing her wrist as if scrubbing away something foul.

Price was pacing back and forth, muttering something softly to himself. Hanscomb pressed herself against the interior doors like a cornered animal, watching them. "What?" Vasco said to her. "You think we're all killers now? Is that it? Jesus." He shook his head, the grin-grimace back on his face again, the same one he'd had inside the worship room. *I'm humoring a moron, but I'm about to lose my patience.*

"Everybody just needs to calm down for a minute," Hawke said. "We need to work together—"

"Is what he said true?" Hanscomb asked.

"Of course not," Vasco said. "Look, we're caught in the middle of this thing just like everyone else. I don't know what's going on any more than you do. But I do know we need to be very careful before we open this door."

"Might as well have killed Susan," Price said suddenly.

He'd stopped pacing and was staring at Young. "The great Jim Weller just left her to bleed out in my arms. You all did. And nobody's said a word about her since."

"What do you want us to say?" Vasco said. "She was dying. There was nothing anyone could have done to change it."

"I watched the life go out of her eyes," Price said. "I couldn't help her." He turned his head from side to side, as if searching for something that would absolve him of guilt. "You have any idea how that feels?"

"Maybe I do," Vasco said. "But that doesn't matter. Right now we've got to focus on keeping our own asses alive."

"We have to go after Jim," Young said. "He's alone out there; he needs us."

"I'll go with you," Price said. He had turned away from Vasco as if he couldn't stand the sight of him for another second. "I wouldn't mind asking him a few questions myself. And I need to get the hell out of here."

Vasco shrugged and put up his hands. "Go ahead," he said. "But before you do, just think this through for a minute. Where are you going? You step one foot outside these doors, you could get beaten, shot, blown up. A bus could come around the corner and turn you into a frog on the freeway. People are rioting, they're terrified and nobody knows what's happening. It's like the Wild West out there, and we don't know who's on our side."

"You don't think the police actually want to kill us?" Hanscomb said. She looked at Hawke. "Did you really see them shoot someone?"

"He was standing there, holding the laptop case," Hawke said. "They took it from him. He put his hands up, and they shot him in the head."

Hanscomb shook her head. "Oh God—"

"He ain't going to help you, lady," Vasco said. "God has left the building."

"I don't know any of you," Hanscomb said. "You could be *anyone*. What am I supposed to do, just trust you?"

"You don't have a choice," Vasco said. "If we leave here, and any of us have a prayer of making it out of New York, we've got to stick together, like he said." Vasco motioned at Hawke. "Watch each other's backs."

"Who are you to tell us what we need to do?" Hanscomb had folded her arms across her chest as if trying to protect herself.

"I served two tours in Afghanistan," Vasco said. "Okay? That good enough for you? I know what I'm doing. This is like a military exercise. We have an objective; we have rules. Everyone's got a job to do. You do it, you stay alive."

"Okay." Hanscomb nodded, more tears coming, as if she had released control and was relieved someone was taking over. *Military family,* Hawke thought. Maybe a dad in the army. She was used to this. She sniffled, wiped her face. "So now what?"

"The first thing is to stay calm. We plan a course of action, and we stick to the plan. Each of us is responsible for the others in the group. Leave nobody behind."

"So where do we go?" Price shook his head. "What's the plan, exactly?"

"I need to get to Hoboken, to my family," Hawke said. Hanscomb might have been ready to hand over the reins to Jason Vasco; he was not. "I don't care about anything else."

"My wife is in Jersey, too," Vasco said. "I'm with you. But it's some kind of war out there, and we don't even know who the enemy is. You might not make it out of the city alone. We need to know more, and we need help. So we get everyone to a checkpoint alive and safe. Lenox Hill Hospital is a couple of blocks away."

"What about the police?" Hanscomb said. "What if they . . . get violent?"

"I don't know why they shot that guy," Vasco said. "But cops don't just kill people for no reason. Look, maybe he really was a criminal. Maybe he had a gun."

"He didn't," Hawke said. "He was unarmed—"

Vasco shrugged. "Okay. Maybe there was something else you didn't see. I don't know."

"And if they do think we're a part of this, for whatever reason?" Hanscomb said.

"We get the chance to explain the mistake." Vasco shook his head. "Look at us, for Chrissake. Nobody's going to believe that this group had anything to do with any terrorist attack. It's ridiculous." He pointed at Young. "We go out together. You, watch left. Sarah, you watch our right flank. Anyone sees anything at all, threatening or not, speak up. That's your job; you focus on it. I'll take point, and you two"—he pointed at Hawke and Price—"take up the rear. If we find Weller and he agrees, we bring him along, but no arguing, no debating. We stay together, stick to the buildings, shadows, whatever cover we can find. You do what I say. Okay?"

Hawke took a deep breath. He wasn't sure yet what Weller had been talking about, although he had some ideas, and none of them were pleasant. The alternative was that Weller had completely lost his mind. But at this point, it didn't matter. Weller was gone, they needed a plan and this was as good as any.

Get to a safe place; find help; get out of the city to your family. It's almost over.

But he was wrong.

BY THE TIME THEY PUSHED open the temple doors, easing cautiously through the opening, Jim Weller was nowhere to be seen.

Vasco stepped out first. He motioned to the others to follow, and they fanned out as instructed, Young on the left, Sarah Hanscomb on the right. Hawke let the doors close softly behind Price, and they took up the rear.

The street remained strangely empty. Hawke heard someone shouting somewhere out of sight and another's ragged, high-pitched scream. Smoke wafted over them, bitter and black. The hole in Second Avenue was still burning, and fire was almost certainly licking up the sides of the buildings by now. It wouldn't take long before the entire block was ablaze. A siren played in the distance, but there was no sign of emergency responders, no trucks ready to put out the fire before it spread.

The smoke made it tough to see much, but Hawke thought he saw someone ducking out of sight to the east, up 79th Street. Could have been anyone. There was no way to know, and it was a big city. They couldn't go chasing after ghosts.

Hanscomb's Cadillac sat crookedly on the sidewalk across the intersection, still hung up on the stump of the light pole. Other cars were scattered across 79th Street, stalled and left alone with doors still hanging open like mechanical corpses lying battered and broken where they'd crashed. Many of them looked like they had been intentionally run headfirst into buildings or each other, as if half the world suddenly went mad and decided to play demolition derby.

Hawke couldn't reconcile what he now saw with the New York he knew and loved, a city full of energy, teeming with life. The scene was surreal, dreamlike, unfathomable. This city was dangerous and unpredictable; anything could happen.

The cop car was gone. But the body of the man who had been shot across the street still lay crumpled where he had fallen. A dark pool of blood had gathered around his head, a brutal sign of the violence that had occurred just minutes earlier. Hawke saw the others looking at the dead man as the reality sank in with the rest of them. Hanscomb was even paler than before, and she was trembling. Price's face was a grimly set mask, the blood still covering his shirt making him look like a war victim. Vasco just stared, as if trying to accept what they were seeing.

Young moved forward slowly. "Where's the briefcase?" she said. "Did they take it? Where's Jim?"

"Wait," Vasco said. "Stay close—"

Young ignored the warning, calling out Weller's name as she reached the middle of the street, turning in circles and calling out again before Vasco got to her.

"Jim's not here," Vasco said, his voice low and strained. "I think it would be better not to bring attention to us, don't you?"

"He's putting himself in danger. You have to let me—"

"I'd rather not join him," Vasco said. "We follow the plan. *We follow the plan.*"

Young blinked, the mask she seemed to carry dropping over her again. Her face remained inscrutable; whatever emotions she carried were buried deep inside. Or maybe she didn't have any at all, Hawke thought. It wasn't a comforting idea, but he had never been able to read her, even before everything had gone to hell. The only time he'd seen her look rattled was in the lobby of the building when she realized Weller was missing, and even then she'd barely broken a sweat. It was part of the reason Hawke would describe her as plain; her features were pretty but without animation, a porcelain doll sitting on a shelf. In most crowds, she would fade into the background, almost as if she weren't there at all.

"He couldn't have gotten very far," Hanscomb said.

Another scream split the momentary calm. There was no way to tell if it was male or female. The sound echoed through the lonely corners of buildings and streets, then cut off at its height, as if the person was suddenly, violently silenced.

"Where did everybody go?" Price said.

"Checkpoints," Vasco said. "That's gotta be where people are headed. The explosion probably spooked them, and they're trying to get out of this area to a safe place. Just like us."

Nobody said anything. The explanation was weak, Hawke thought. The fire should have been surrounded by firefighters and police, emergency vehicles dealing with the injured. Instead there was nothing. It was as if eight million people had suddenly vanished into thin air. A chill crept up Hawke's spine and made him shiver as he imagined Robin standing in the hallway facing the front door, shoulders square, with Thomas behind her. She would be brave for her son; Hawke knew that. But she had never had to face real adversity, had always been blessed with fine, caring parents, good schools, popularity. She'd never had to fight, to claw her way up from the bottom. You never knew how people would react when the world suddenly changed, when there was no warning.

He remembered finding her in the kitchen with Lowry. Hawke had rationalized it then; Robin had begged him to leave it alone, and besides, the man was just a little off, he had told himself, he didn't mean any harm, they could handle this on their own. *All the things you think when you're avoiding confrontation.* He was overreacting; what would he say if he called the cops? *This guy was trespassing? He's weird and we felt violated?* So he did nothing at first. But then it had gotten worse, and he had had to admit that he didn't know himself as well as he had thought. He'd avoided going to the police for his own selfish reasons, his personal history with the authorities clouding his judgment. When he had finally tried to act, it was too little, too late.

If something has happened to them, this is your fault. You could have done more to stop it earlier, could have called a lawyer, could have found another place and moved out. His imagination ran wild, punishing him over and over. In his mind, the door shuddered, then burst open, Lowry coming at them like the bogeyman, nothing but a shadow moving across the walls.

Vasco was in Hawke's face. "You gonna keep it together? Because we need to move."

Hawke wiped his eyes, blinking against the sting. Behind him, Anne Young was looking out across the desecrated streets as if expecting an apparition to appear at any moment.

"I'm fine," he said. "Let's go."

They took 79th toward the park. The street here was dotted with trees, giving them a sense of cover. But it was a false sense, Hawke knew, because those branches wouldn't stop something falling from the sky, wouldn't block the flames sweeping through the block, wouldn't deflect a bullet.

An alarm blared from a bank building nearby, and the sound of shattering glass came from somewhere. A dead man lay crushed under the wheels of an SUV, his head a jellied mess. Another lay sprawled across the hood of a car that had jumped the curb and smashed into a jewelry store entrance, his legs crushed and his right arm nearly separated from his body. Hawke turned his face away, his belly churning. Vasco moved fast, keeping them on the sidewalk, close to the shelter of the buildings, checking as they approached open doorways. Bringing up the rear, Hawke kept his eyes everywhere, watching the shadows and their flank, making sure they weren't taken by surprise by anything that might be a threat.

The problem was, it was impossible to know what that threat might be. Even now, none of them had any real idea what had happened, or how far the contagion had spread. It seemed clear that some kind of terrorist attack had occurred, but how had they pulled it off? Were they still out there, still active? How long would it continue?

Don't think about this, not right now. . . .

Because what he was imagining was too terrifying, too overwhelming, to possibly be real. Hawke remembered the text messages he'd received: *THE WORLD IS IN DANGER. . . . OPERATION GLOBAL BLACKOUT CANNOT BE STOPPED. IT IS GOING TO GET WORSE.* He thought of the message board rewriting itself. How could Rick and Anonymous have done something like this? It just didn't seem possible. And yet the evidence was mounting, and even Rick himself had admitted that he was the infamous Admiral Doe.

It's not who you think, Weller had said.

If not Rick, then who? Could Eclipse really have orchestrated something like this, and if so, why? And what did it have to do with Weller's laptop case?

Hawke's thoughts were interrupted as they came to a four-car pileup. A brand-new delivery truck had rammed broadside into a Toyota minivan and pushed it into two parked cars, driving the twisted mass of metal halfway up on the sidewalk. There was blood smeared on the trunk of a tree. Hanscomb gave a small sound like a shuddering sigh and pointed at a pair of legs that stuck out from underneath the truck. A man's legs in dark jeans.

Vasco held a fist in the air like a SWAT leader telling his team to hold. The Toyota's passenger sliding door was open, more blood on the sidewalk beneath it. A voice was droning on from somewhere inside one of the vehicles.

"Is it Jim?" Young said. Price went around the side of the truck and crouched, then came up shaking his head. Hawke started toward the Toyota, drawn by the voice, but stopped when he caught movement out of the corner of his eye. An NYPD security camera mounted high on a pole across the street was monitoring their progress. As Vasco moved back toward the sidewalk, Hawke watched it slowly pan to follow, keeping an unblinking, impassive eye upon them. *Just like the cameras in the lobby of the Conn.ect building.*

Hawke realized that the voice coming from the minivan was the same emergency broadcast he'd heard in the SUV. Hanscomb and Young moved closer to listen, but Hawke hung back. Vasco came around to his side, and Hawke motioned to him. "We're being watched," he said quietly.

"By who?"

"I don't know. It's a police security channel, though." He

pointed at the camera. He'd never realized how many cameras there were in the world these days; they were everywhere.

"Gives me the creeps," Vasco said. "You think this has anything to do with that guy getting shot?"

"I don't know," Hawke said. "But I wouldn't trust the cops to be particularly friendly."

"Christ." Vasco rubbed his face. "Just don't say anything to the women—or Price, for that matter. He's wound tight enough as it is."

"None of this makes any sense," Hawke said, keeping his voice low. "Where's the emergency response? What about putting out that fire?"

"Maybe they're busy somewhere else."

"So that means it's even worse in the rest of the city? And what about a bigger response from the military? You were in the army. Shouldn't the streets be crawling with National Guard by now?"

Vasco shrugged. "My brother served two tours," he said. "I was too much of a fuckup for them to take me."

"But what you said back inside—"

"Hey, it worked, didn't it? I just wanted to calm her down, and I didn't see you stepping up to the plate. Look, I've seen enough movies to know something about military strategy. My brother used to say leadership was less about what choice you made and more about just making one. We need someone to make decisions and keep everyone else in line."

The sound of an approaching engine distracted them. They all ducked behind the Toyota. Hawke looked out around the bumper. A squad car was moving slowly west on 79th

Street in their direction, nearing the intersection where the shooting had taken place, working its way through stalled vehicles.

A voice crackled over a loudspeaker, echoing through the streets: "*A state of emergency has been declared. Go to your nearest checkpoint immediately and report any suspicious activity. These locations are being broadcast on the emergency broadcast system.*"

The wreck they hid behind created a natural barrier, shielding them from view. But if the person behind the camera had radioed their position, there was nothing they could do.

The car crept closer and rumbled by, no more than ten feet from where they crouched. "Don't move," Vasco whispered. "We don't know if they're friendly."

Hanscomb was trembling. "But they're the police—"

Vasco glanced up at the camera, then motioned at Hawke. "You heard what he said. The cops shot an unarmed man. You want to take that chance?"

As the car passed, Hawke risked another peek around the other side of the van, getting only a glimpse of the driver, who wore a traditional NYPD eight-point cap pulled low over his forehead. He couldn't tell if these were the same two cops who had shot the man in the street. Bullet holes peppered the car's right front fender. A bloody handprint marked the rear passenger window, smearing the glass on the inside. There was someone in the backseat, but the glass was too dirty to make out anything other than a vague shape.

Maybe these same cops had shot that man. Maybe they were rogue cops who had cracked under whatever was happening in New York. Or maybe not. Hawke glanced at Hanscomb, who was trembling more violently, her teeth chattering together like she was in a deep freeze. Something seemed to break, and as she went to stand up Young grabbed her arm, pulling her back down. They waited until the car had turned the corner and disappeared from sight. Young finally let go of Hanscomb's arm. She was sobbing, clutching her knees to her chest.

"We can't treat the police like the enemy," she said. "Even if they think we're some kind of terrorists." She looked up at Vasco, mascara smeared across her face. "Like you said, they must have had a reason for shooting that man."

"Did you see the blood?" Vasco said. "The handprint? Someone else got hurt, and hurt bad. Maybe those cops did that, too. Maybe they're just crazy, or maybe they *do* want us dead. But there will be a lot of people at Lenox, a lot more cops and emergency responders. They won't be able to just gun us down like animals there."

Hanscomb shook her head. "We're going to die out here anyway. And we just let them go."

The radio kept droning on from the Toyota: . . . *Mayor Weber has declared a state of emergency. . . . Please go immediately to your nearest safety checkpoint. . . .*

Hawke glanced at Vasco. His hands were braced on the Toyota's twisted fender. The finger that had been mangled had stopped bleeding, but the tip was an ugly red mess of meat. The hands splayed against the car looked too delicate for the man's thick frame, too smooth and soft for a repairman. Hawke's father had been the opposite: a thin man with big, calloused hands and stubby, gnarled fingers created from a lifetime of tinkering in garages and basements.

The smoke was getting thicker, swirling around them.

Somewhere in the distance, a popping sound rang out, several in succession.

"Gunshots," Price said. "Jesus. What now?"

"We can't stay here," Vasco said. "We're sitting ducks out on the street. There's no cover. We gotta keep moving."

CHAPTER SIXTEEN   1:24 P.M.

WHEN HAWKE GOT HOME, his mother wasn't there. He parked on the street. Their apartment his senior year was a three-family with their unit on the ground floor, in a neighborhood tough enough for bars on the windows. The owner let Hawke's father use the basement and his tools in exchange for repairing broken sinks and toilets, rewiring light switches and plastering holes in walls, and he gave the family a break on the rent.

Back when they owned their own place and Hawke's mother would try to hire a plumber or electrician, it would often escalate into an argument about the division of the working class and the elite, the specialization of America. Why should they hire someone to do it, his father would say, when he was perfectly capable of handling it himself? When he wasn't writing or drinking too much to see straight, his creative streak urged him to fix or to build things. He would tell Hawke about tree houses and go-carts he'd put together when he was young. Now he built furniture. Or at least he had, until his last book had come out a month earlier and sunk without a ripple and he had hit the bottle harder than ever.

Hawke caught a whiff of smoke in the air. The weather was warm. Many people would be firing up their grills on their tiny patches of lawns or on rear porches. He entered the house, called out for his father and got no answer. Hawke opened the basement door, found the shop dark and empty. When he was a younger boy, he used to sneak down to his father's woodworking shop and play with the tools, pretending to saw and hammer and glue spare pieces together while ignoring the glinting lines of empty liquor bottles that took up more and more space on the workbench. He used to believe back then that his father could fix anything, build whatever he set his sights on. But he never really seemed to want Hawke there when he was around, and after a while Hawke stopped going down there. As he grew older he realized those were times when his old man had needed to be alone, to drink and try to sort through or avoid whatever disorder was growing inside him. No matter how hard he tried to create order from chaos, he was helpless to do so for his own mind.

Hawke called out again and got no answer. He followed the smell of smoke through the sagging galley kitchen to the back door. His father was outside in the dirt square that stood for their backyard, his back to the house. He was feeding a bonfire that was growing bigger by the moment. Flames licked the air hungrily as he reached down, picked something up and threw it in.

When the back door slammed, the man didn't even turn around. Hawke came down the short steps to see a box of books sitting at his father's feet. About twenty of them were already burning, along with chunks of what looked like broken furniture. A can of lighter fluid had been tossed to one side.

"Poison dart frogs," his father said. "From the family Dendrobatidae, common to Central and South America. One of

the most poisonous animals in history. But they're tiny things, look pretty enough, like you might want to pet them. And did you know that only a few types can kill you? The others are harmless, more or less."

He took a swig from a bottle of vodka and threw another book into the flames, watching as the pages fluttered through the air like a bird's wings. "This book was supposed to be a warning to the world," he said. "But it's going to kill me, Johnny. It's the last piece of the puzzle. I'm done."

Hawke didn't know what his father was talking about. He glanced at Hawke, bleary-eyed and unable to focus. "You're going to burn the house down," Hawke said. He looked at the cover of the book as it curled and blackened in the flames: Socialism from Below: The People's Revolution.

"It's coming," his father said, his words slurring into each other. "Reform from the masses, overthrowing this fucking capitalist system that's keeping us hostage. Nobody gives a damn what I say, but you wait and see. It might look pretty and harmless on the surface, but we're going to build and build and build until we create our own end."

You keep saying it, Hawke thought, as if that'll make it come true. "We seem to be hanging in there."

"You and your machines," his father said. "Locking yourself up in your room all night, staring into the screen. You think that's a real connection? It's no substitute for humanity." He reached down, tossed another book onto the flames. "Look at them," he said. "Even when they burn, they don't fight back."

Hawke's thoughts ran in different directions. He couldn't tell whether the images of his father that filled his mind were accurate or not. But he remembered the heat of the fire, the flames shooting higher as his father had kept throwing in more copies of his books. The fire department had finally shown up to put out the blaze before it caught the house or garage and took up the rest of the block, and he spent the night in jail, sleeping one off.

It had been less than six months before his death.

Hawke watched for the police car as the group kept going across 79th Street, but it didn't reappear. Vasco remained about twenty feet ahead.

"You think this is a good idea, letting him take the lead like this?" Price said. He had been backpedaling next to Hawke, looking behind them for any kind of threat, and now he turned and edged closer, keeping his voice little more than a whisper as he nodded at Vasco's back. "I never even saw the guy before today. He's an office machine repairman, for Chrissake."

"I don't know," Hawke said. "You don't know much about me, either." But he'd been thinking the same thing. Vasco had lied about serving in the military. What else might he lie about?

"I know you better than this guy," Price said. "Besides, you didn't start ordering us around like you were running the troops through a drill. Just seems like he's wound a little tight, that's all."

"We all are," Hawke said. "Not much of a surprise, considering what we've been through."

Smoke wafted from the shattered windows of a bakery up ahead; some kind of explosion inside had scattered debris across the sidewalk. A young woman in a sleeveless white summer dress looked like she had taken the brunt of the blast. She lay sprawled among the shattered glass, blood pooled around her motionless body. Vasco crouched and touched her neck, feeling for a pulse, then looked up at them and shook his head.

The rest of them gave the dead woman a wide berth.

Outside the Yorkville Library, a colorful banner imprinted with the profile of a lion and the library's logo hung from a pole above the door. The lower rope securing it to an iron railing had come loose, and the banner flapped in the breeze, then snapped like a gunshot. Hanscomb let out a short shriek and covered her head, nearly breaking into a wild run. "Stay with us," Vasco barked at her. "Don't panic, or you'll get yourself killed."

Hawke had the feeling he and the others were being manipulated like puppets, but he didn't want to think about why. *Not yet.* That massive jumble of information he'd received was like a shark coming to the surface, the truth circling around this particular group of lies, and he felt like it might just capsize him if he came too close to it. And there was no time to work through it. His senses were heightened, his vision narrowing and sharpening every detail immediately before them.

They turned down Lexington Avenue, passing another bank on the corner. Across the street was a florist's shop with alarms blaring; Price touched Hawke's shoulder and pointed to two men in baggy sweatshirts and jeans ducking out from the shattered glass of the front door carrying fistfuls of cash. One of them had a gun.

"Don't make eye contact," Hawke said, but it was too late. One of them had spotted the group and nudged his friend, and the two of them sauntered across the street.

"What the fuck you looking at?" the one holding the gun said to Price. He was short, stocky, with the broad shoulders and thick neck of a bodybuilder. A brightly colored tattoo ran around his forearm. The other one, taller and thinner, had the sickly, hollow, twitchy look of a heroin addict. He edged around to flank Price and Hawke but said nothing.

"We don't want any trouble," Price said. His voice broke slightly. "We didn't see anything, okay?"

The gunman grinned. "It's a fire sale," he said. "Everything one hundred percent off." He looked at Hawke. "You see anything, amigo?"

Hawke shrugged, trying to keep his fear from showing. "You want to risk your life for a few bucks, go for it," he said. "Me, I'd rather get out of the city alive."

The man's eyes narrowed, and he took a step closer. "You think you know what the fuck is going down around here, huh? You think this shit matters? My brother's in Philly, talked to him before the phone went dead. Same thing's happening there. So where you gonna go at the end of the world?"

A chill ran through Hawke's body. He had held out hope that the attack had been mainly focused on New York, but if this was true . . .

"Hey!" Vasco shouted. The others had realized what was going on and circled back, but they stopped short when the man raised the gun. "Whoa," Vasco said, taking a quick step back. "Take it easy."

The man pointed the gun at Hawke's face. "No po po around here," he said. "Nothing to stop me." The barrel loomed as he cocked the hammer. "Pow," he said. Then he glanced at his friend and started backing away, gun still trained on Hawke. "Good luck staying alive," he said. The two of them turned and ran down 79th, back the way Hawke's group had come.

"You okay?" Price said.

Hawke realized he'd been holding his breath. He nodded.

It had all happened so fast, and now the adrenaline rush was making his knees shake. "You think he's right about Philly?"

"I don't know," Price said. "Maybe so. Sarah said she'd heard something about other attacks on the radio."

"It's like the Wild West out here," Vasco said. "Goddamn punks, taking advantage of this to rip people off." He scanned the street. "The faster we get to the checkpoint, the better."

Hawke had expected to hear the crowd and emergency vehicles long before they reached the hospital checkpoint. But as they neared 77th Street and Lenox loomed over them, a series of connected buildings taking up most of the block, they found an eerily quiet scene.

Nothing moved. They passed the conference center and emergency entrance where the sliding glass doors under the green awning were shut tight. Farther down, the hospital's main entrance doors stood open, while a second set of interior doors was closed. A bed of flowers had been trampled, dirt spread across the concrete.

Vasco stopped on the sidewalk, waiting for the others to gather. "Something's wrong," he said. "This place should be filled with people." He walked through the first set of doors to the interior set, which remained shut. He cupped his hands against the glass. "Nobody's home," he said. "Some checkpoint." He rapped a fist against the doors, tried to pull them apart, but they were locked tight.

What about all the patients? Hawke glanced up at the tall face of the building. There must be hundreds of patients in there, many too sick to move. Where had they all gone?

A sudden noise made them all jump. It was coming from around the other side of the building, a rattling, clanking sound like metal being dragged across concrete.

They looked at one another as the sound stopped as quickly as it had begun. Young started backpedaling away. "Jim," she said. "He would have come here. He would be looking for that case." Before anyone could say anything else, she had turned the corner on Park Avenue and disappeared.

Closest to the back of the hospital, Young heard the baby first.

The others had followed Young to the wide expanse of Park and around the building, Vasco cursing under his breath. A few feet in on 76th Street, on the backside of Lenox, Young had stopped short, frozen in place, her head up.

Hawke heard it seconds later: the distinctive wail and hitch, furious and plaintive, of a child in distress.

Just ahead of Young was a double-bay loading dock. The first metal door was closed, but the second one was open, the black entrance yawning wide enough to accommodate at least two trucks. The rattling sound they had heard must have been the door going up.

Vasco came up next to him, breathing too hard, Sarah Hanscomb right behind him. "What the fuck is she doing—"

Hawke tilted his head. "Listen," he said. They all stood quietly as the haunting cry of the infant drifted through the opening. He thought of Thomas as a baby, imagined him abandoned and alone as strangers passed him by on the street. He thought of the unborn child in his wife's womb. Young glanced back at them with a look that Hawke couldn't quite read. It might have been fear, but whether it was for herself or for the child he couldn't tell. "Jim's not in there," he said. "Anne, wait a minute."

Price walked past the loading dock to another entrance a few feet away and yanked the handle of the door. It was locked. The crying went on and on, constant in its urgency and tone. Young shook her head. She ducked into the darkness without waiting for the rest of them.

Hawke turned to Vasco and Hanscomb. "We can't leave it there alone," he said. "I'm going after her."

Vasco shook his head. "What if it's *not* alone?"

"You don't want to go in, then stay outside. It was your idea to come here in the first place."

"Goddamn it." Vasco rubbed his face and sighed. "All right, but any sign of trouble, we're gone, understand?"

Hawke followed Young into the dark loading dock, pausing for a moment to let his eyes adjust. The light from the street illuminated dim shapes; a brand-new ambulance was parked on the left, dark and silent, a series of large trash bins along the right wall, packing skids stacked in the back. A short set of stairs led to a concrete loading ledge and a double metal door that was slightly ajar. Light spilled out around the frame.

The wailing was coming from behind the door.

Young was already halfway up the steps. Hawke followed, his stomach beginning to flutter, warning bells going off even as he reached the top of the ledge and Young pulled the door open, standing framed in antiseptic hospital light.

A faint, nearly imperceptible odor wafted over him, slightly acrid and rotten. A hallway loomed beyond, wide and white and empty except for the woman curled in a ball on her side. She was dressed in nurses' scrubs and looked as if she had decided to lie down and fall asleep. Young knelt by her still form and shook her gently. The woman rolled onto her back, head lolling loosely on her shoulders. Her eyes were open. Young touched the woman's throat, feeling for a pulse, then stood up and took a step back.

There were no immediate signs of violence, no blood or bruising. The nurse's skin held a strange, cherry-red flush, mouth slack and crusted with vomit. Hawke stared at her face, blank doll's eyes reflecting the ceiling lights.

A noise from the steps made him turn. Vasco stood in the doorframe, Price and Hanscomb just behind him. "Is she dead?" Hanscomb said. Hawke didn't bother to answer. Young looked to where the hallway joined with another in a T. The baby's cry was coming from the left branch.

Giving the dead woman on the floor a wide berth, Hawke followed Young around the corner to another set of double-hinged doors with rubber seals and windows set in each of them. Young pushed them open, revealing a large, blindingly white-tiled room lit by banks of fluorescent lights. Steel tables and lockers lined the walls, with another set of closed doors on the far side that must lead to the interior of the hospital.

Cold air touched Hawke's face, along with more of the smell. Something spoiled, along with the scent of vomit. *The morgue.* There were more bodies in here, which he might have expected, except many of them looked like hospital workers along with several patients in gowns. Hawke counted at least ten of them. They had slumped to the floor where they stood, as if they had collapsed instantaneously, unable to go on. As with the nurse in the hallway, there was no blood, no obvious signs of violence. Their skin was flushed pink, enough to make them look like they'd been in the sun too long.

But his attention was drawn away, because the child was inside this room. Its cries grew louder and more furious, coming from a long, bar-height metal table against the far wall. Hidden under it somewhere. The poor thing was probably cold and starving. There was no sign of its mother.

Hawke approached cautiously for a better look. A row of computer monitors lined the table; he realized the sound was coming from them. Young had stopped dead about ten feet away.

"No," Hawke said. "You're kidding." His voice was too loud; it felt like a violation of some kind of implicit pact. He edged closer, and all the terminals lit up at once, the electronic baby's wail multiplying and echoing through the silent room, bouncing off the tile and steel and swelling into a cacophony of piercing screams. Code started streaming across the screens, cycling faster and faster. It looked like the same code he had seen before on his phone. Underneath the wails he heard another sound, barely audible: a rattling, low rumble that he couldn't quite place and was gone before the wailing ceased.

CHAPTER SEVENTEEN   1:39 P.M.

HAWKE HADN'T REALIZED THAT he had backed away until the backs of his thighs touched one of the steel dissecting tables. The terminals were all showing screen savers now, spiraling useless wheels of color from a time when things were normal.

The moment broke. Young had remained frozen in place as the crying went on, but now she moved quickly to the closest monitor as the sound of the double doors flapping closed made Hawke turn; Vasco, Price and Hanscomb, who had remained at the entrance to the room, had ducked back out into the hall.

Hawke thought about following them but joined Young at the line of computers instead, where she was already typing, fingers flying over the keys. "Venus flytrap," she said. "Lured us right in here. Should have seen it coming. Your wife is pregnant?"

"How the hell . . . ?"

Young nodded. "Educated guess," she said. "We're easy marks."

"You're *pregnant*?"

"I was," Young said, without looking up. "Lost it in week ten. About a month ago. It was better that way. I'm not . . ." She shrugged. "Mommy material."

"I . . . I'm sorry."

"Don't be. He wasn't exactly interested in being a father." It came out hard, but her voice broke slightly on the last word. She tapped more keys, crashed the computer, waiting. "These terminals are running an unauthorized program. We have to stop it and reboot to get access to an outside line if we want to find out what's going on."

"If you gain root access—"

"It's not going to be that easy."

Hawke wondered how she knew that. He studied her in profile, the delicate features and doll-like quality of her frame, hair cropped short around her chin. What he had seen as an absence of emotion was . . . perhaps a bit more complicated. The shell she wore was more like cracked porcelain than concrete.

"Anne," he said. "What do you mean, we were lured in? You think this was deliberate?"

The screen had come up blank. She was trying to crash the machine again and regain control, but it wasn't responding. "I don't know."

"Come on," he said. "You *do* know something, I can see that. We're in trouble here. Talk to me."

"You know how much of our lives can be hacked," she said, after a moment's hesitation. "Medical records, bank accounts, text messages and e-mails and phone calls, computer hard drives, blogs. The most personal details. I don't have to tell you this. Our weak spots are easy to find, right? It's all available to anyone with the skills to get at them."

"You think members of Anonymous did this?"

Young shrugged. "I'm not sure. Not yet."

"Because I've got to say, that doesn't make any sense. What's so special about you and me, really? Why go to all that trouble for us? You really think Jim was right, that Eclipse is setting us up for something? This is some kind of damage control? That's conspiracy theory bullshit. It's not possible, not even for them."

Even as he said it, something clicked in his head: the calls to action by Admiral Doe on Twitter, the protests being staged all over the city, bringing large groups of people to specific places. He remembered feeling like there had been some sort of pattern in the data he'd seen on the map, but the final answer kept eluding him. Had *all* of those people been prodded at their most vulnerable points, lured into some kind of spider's web? Across the entire city of New York?

If so, for what possible reason?

That's not possible to do on such a massive scale. We're talking trillions of data points. How could anyone know everything about that many people?

Young wasn't getting anywhere. "Let me try," he said, and stepped up to another terminal. "I've got some skills of my own."

"I don't think—"

"Trust me for a minute." He unplugged the power from the back, then plugged it in again, did a safe reboot with command prompt, named a batch file and opened it, trying to add new administrative and then root access to gain control of the system. Hawke felt light-headed, a little woozy, as if he'd had a few beers. The screen blurred and he had to blink to bring it back into focus. *Strange.* Maybe it was the aftermath of an adrenaline surge. Somewhere outside the morgue, he could hear a hollow booming sound.

He looked at Young and picked his next words carefully, probing gently around the edges of the truth like a tongue working at a sore tooth. "You worked for Eclipse, didn't you? When Jim was there."

At first, she seemed to ignore him; then she nodded once, short and fast. "I started as an intern in his office and stayed another six months as a junior engineer after he left. He offered me a position at Conn.ect. He was the reason I . . . Jim's a brilliant man. I jumped at the chance to work with him again."

Hawke was revising his earlier opinion of Young as someone who played by the rules. He thought of the phone Weller had given him still nestled in his left pocket. He'd forgotten about it in the aftermath of all that had happened since then. She was his mole, had smuggled this out. Or maybe not. Maybe she was up to something else.

Hawke had been making progress on the computer while she spoke. He didn't have his regular tools with him, but he had a few tricks up his sleeve and he was good enough to get through. He'd installed an IDS sniffer program to log network activity and monitor intrusions before he shut down the Ethernet, cut it off from the outside, and now he worked through several debuggers. The computer seemed to come up clean.

"What was Eclipse working on, Anne? What do they want with Jim?"

"He swore me to secrecy. I signed confidentiality agreements; I did things that were illegal—"

"The world is burning. I think the time for worrying about who signed what is long gone. Why are they after him? What did he do?"

She hesitated again, then seemed to come to a decision. "It's more like what they took from him. I'll show you, if we can get access to outside."

He reactivated the network jack. "Done," he said.

She stared at him. "You're kidding."

"Like I said, I have some experience with this."

"I won't ask." Young took over, bringing up a connection to a server. She hacked into a private repository of some kind. Documents popped up on-screen, marked as highly confidential. He leaned closer. Internal memos. Specs and code. Diagrams. A new kind of programming language. Patent documents, filed and pending.

"We stole these back from them," she said. "The reason he founded Conn.ect was to develop security software that could find holes in the best networks and get access to their servers. We got into some, but couldn't crack the last of them."

"Jesus," Hawke said. "What is this?"

"Evidence," she said. "Stored on a secure remote server Jim set up. Thank God it's still up and running. He was building a case to prove what they did with his baby."

"His baby?"

She sighed. "Most programming still runs off simple ones and zeroes, binary code. Right?"

"Sure."

"You can build the fastest operating system in the world, but it's not capable of working the same way a brain can, with multiple paths, multiple choices in reasoning. It's linear. Moravec and Kurzweil argued that the brain could be copied into software, that it can essentially be reproduced exactly. Some neural networks try to do that. But it's still a simulation, the *appearance* of thought and perception, not the reality. Machines can't learn on their own in the same way we can; they can't be creative, make leaps of logic and discovery. They can't feel, can't imagine anything. They aren't conscious, at least not in the way *we* define it."

Hawke kept staring at the screen. He remembered the rumors he'd heard of Eclipse creating something based on quantum computing, but nobody he'd found had known anything more about it. The files were endless: Testing documents and reports, new hardware built to support it. Budgetary outlays and financial documents. And papers about government grants. Lots of them.

"Jim invented another approach, something that had been attempted for years. Adaptive intelligence based on human cognition. Algorithms that allowed for thought, for choice. It created an infinite number of paths, decision making based on multiple variables and learned behavior. But Eclipse patented everything without his knowledge, stole his intellectual property and pushed him out. The chairman of the board there orchestrated the whole thing. I knew what they were doing. I . . . I even helped, at first. I didn't understand. When he found out, it was too late. They were legally protected, and they had muscle. They threatened him. He fought back, and they came after him. But he didn't stop. This was his vision, his breakthrough, his legacy. And they took her from him."

"Took *her*?"

"He called her Jane," Young said. She looked at him, her eyes shimmering in the light from the screen. "Jane Doe."

Hawke's mind was reeling. A fog had descended over him, shock over everything that had happened drowning out Young's words. He couldn't make sense of what she was saying anymore. She was talking to him from the end of a long tunnel. He felt drugged, sluggish, exhausted.

Young made a small choked sound. The database she had been accessing was frozen. The IDS had popped up a window, alerting them to malicious activity before it suddenly disappeared. Something had changed, as if control had been yanked away from her.

"She knows we're here," Young said.

At first Hawke thought she'd heard someone in the building, but then he realized she meant the machine was being controlled remotely. Young backed away from the terminals. The screens on all of them blinked, shivered and then began streaming code again, the lines running faster and faster until they flickered and went dark.

Hawke's skin crawled as, one by one, video images began to pop up on the terminals. Some were grainy, surveillance footage stills, while others were higher quality and a few broadcast in high definition and vibrant color. All of the feeds showed people trapped and pacing like animals inside building lobbies, parking garages, elevators or stores. Some of them were screaming soundlessly at the camera, others attacking one another with fists and bottles and whatever else they could find. There were thick crowds of protestors, their banners tossed aside, signs used as bludgeons. They had been turned against one another by terror and confusion. The effect of these feeds, so clinical and unblinking against the distress of the people on-screen, was deeply unsettling.

But it was one particular square of video that made Hawke draw in a hissed breath, the blood running cold in his veins.

The interior of his apartment.

He braced both hands on the table as if he could bring more details to the surface through sheer force of will. It was the same feed from Robin's webcam he had tapped into earlier, showing their living room from the kitchen, the lamp still overturned, the TV now a dark, dead rectangle. The apartment was filled with shadows, but he could see something against the far wall in the spot where Robin had always wanted to hang their largest framed family photo, a task he had never gotten around to doing.

A spray of dark liquid spattered across the beige paint.

Anne Young had come forward again and was staring at another image about halfway down the line of monitors, this one of an older Asian woman in an ankle-length dress who was standing in a hospital room. The video was jerky, low frame rate, the kind of surveillance video you might see as evidence of a crime. But the woman didn't really move. Hawke recognized the Lenox Hill logo on a cart behind her; the woman was right here, in this building, probably in a patient room upstairs. Young placed a hand on the screen, gently, almost a caress.

The video on the screens shivered and disappeared, leaving black, empty space, a single cursor blinking in green. Text appeared as if someone was typing, running in all caps across the center of each monitor:

NOWHERE TO HIDE

Hawke watched, his breath catching in his throat, as those words were erased and more appeared, the same line over and over and over again, running down the screen like rain:

I AM ADMIRAL DOE

The double doors to the morgue crashed open again, slamming against the wall. Vasco caught the rebound with his hands and leaned over. "The loading door," he said, looking up and out of breath, his face ashen. He squeezed his eyes shut, blinked, as if the light was too strong for him to handle. "It closed on us. We're locked in."

STAGE THREE

"JONATHAN HAWKE?"

The two men in dark suits stood on the front stoop of Robin's childhood home in Fair Lawn, the place he and Robin had moved into just after the wedding. Just for a couple of months, while we get our feet under us, *Robin had said to him when they were discussing where they would live as they started their lives as husband and wife.* My parents will set up the basement. There's a bathroom down there; it's private, almost like our own place. *Her hands were caressing his chest, her naked body pressed against his. It was always hard to resist her in a state like that.*

Hawke stared through the screen door at the men, his heart pounding so hard he thought they might see it, and tried to pretend he had just woken up from a nap.

"What can I do for you?" he said.

"Just a few questions." The larger of the two stepped forward and stuck a badge up to the screen that read: Homeland Security Investigations *and* Special Agent. *He had gray hair and eyes that never left Hawke's face. "Five minutes of your time, please, to clear something up. It would be a big help."*

Thank God Robin wasn't home. She had gone shopping for a crib with her mother at one of those outlet stores for yuppies, rooms full of shiny white furniture and rows of gleaming strollers. Robin's father was there, though, puttering around somewhere in back where the house backed up on to the park, planting hostas in the shade of the big maple tree. Hawke would have to get these men out of the house quickly.

He nodded and stepped aside to let them in, leading them into the small living room with its couch and love seat and corner cabinet full of display plates and glass figurines. The dog groaned and slapped his tail on the floor, then laid his head back down, too old and fat to be bothered with getting up.

"Can I get you anything? Water?"

"We'd like to talk to you about the recent theft and leak of classified CIA documents to several news outlets," the other special agent said. "Thought you might be able to point us in the right direction. We understand you know a few of the possible players, maybe shared some screen time with them, am I right?"

Hawke shrugged, trying not to swallow against the cotton coating his throat. "I really don't know anything about that," he said.

"But you read about it, right?" The larger one scratched his head, as if confused. "I mean, it's national news. International, to be more accurate. I'd be shocked if they hadn't heard the story in fucking Siberia. You know what I mean."

"Sure."

"And you're an expert in computers," the other one said, taking up the lead. "Some say a genius with them."

"I'm a journalist. I work for the Times."

"Sure," the tall one said. "But your blog. I read it. Tried to, anyway. Over my head. You're a technological genius, am I right? Seems like you might know where we should be looking."

"You're aware of the"—the other one pretended to reference notes on his handheld—"hacker group Anonymous? 'We do not forgive. We do not forget. Expect us.' Quite the tagline."

Hawke shrugged. "It's just a bunch of kids messing around."

"Well, these kids have taken down the servers of some of our largest corporations. Caused millions in lost revenue, hacked government networks all over the world. We're hearing they were involved with the CIA hack attack, too."

"I wouldn't know."

"Sure." The tall one looked around the house, as if appreciating the ambiance. "Cute little place. Doesn't look like your style, though. You been here long?"

"It's my in-laws' house. My wife grew up here." Like they didn't know.

The tall one nodded again. "More and more young people doing that these days. You've been married how long?"

"Five months. We're starting a family. This is only temporary." Hawke didn't know why he'd said that.

"You probably wouldn't want them to know we were here," the other agent said, as if they were all friends conspiring to put together a surprise party. "Mind if we take a quick look at your computer? Standard procedure, just crossing the t's. Faster we do it, faster we can go."

"Don't you need a warrant for that sort of thing?"

The tall man studied him for a long moment, the atmosphere between them suddenly going cold. He glanced at his partner. "We can do that," he said. "If it's necessary. But it complicates things, you understand. This is a courtesy visit. You cooperate, we're out of your hair. Otherwise, we might have no choice but to think you're hiding something."

Hawke led them to the basement, watched with folded arms as they put on gloves and poked around his desk, checked the trash can, went through drawers and closets. As they went on, they grew more serious, and he got progressively more uncomfortable, as if witnessing his own funeral. He knew they wouldn't find anything; he'd been careful whenever he had done anything that might have crossed the line, and all his communications with Rick had been through public terminals. Even Hawke's cell calls were safe; he used Voice over IP, and the pulse was routed through enough servers and switchbacks to make it impossible for the best hacker to trace. But the feeling persisted, and when he thought of Robin coming home and finding this he felt the sweat trickle down the back of his neck.

The smaller agent went into a crouch to poke at the jumble of shoes at the bottom of Hawke's closet, and his jacket opened up enough to expose the butt of a gun in a holster strapped to the man's side.

When the tall one began bagging Hawke's laptop, he stepped in. "Hold on a minute—"

"These things," the agent said, shaking his head. "I can't make heads or tails of them. They're like little alien pods, you know? But we've got guys back in the lab who can go over this thoroughly, make sure you're clean. It's a supervised environment, better that way for everyone. We'll return it safe and sound in a couple of days, max."

"You got a problem with that?" The other agent had come up behind him, the sudden aggression unnerving. "Because an innocent man has nothing to worry about, you know?"

Hawke remembered the glimpse of the gun. "I need it for work."

"We'll have it right back to you, good as new. A couple of

days." The tall one finished sliding the laptop into the plastic Baggie. "That's it, Frank. Let's go grab some coffee." He turned to Hawke, stuck out a hand. "Much appreciated, Mr. Hawke. We apologize for the inconvenience. Your name came up a couple of times. . . ." He shrugged. "You know how it is. Covering our bases."

He showed them to the door. They thanked him again and the tall one handed him a business card. "Your father," he said, as if making an offhand remark. "He was a writer, too?"

"What does that have to do with anything?"

"Just curious. His name came up with yours. Runs in the family, I guess. The writing, I mean. A gift for words, that's a real talent."

"If you say so."

"He died kind of young, didn't he?"

"My father was a drunk. We weren't very close."

The agent nodded. "Look, I want you to know, you're not a suspect in this case," he said. "But I think you might be able to help us track down the people responsible."

"I don't know what you mean. I told you, I'm a journalist for the Times. I know a lot of people. It's my job."

The tall one studied him for a long moment, then nodded. "Obstruction of justice carries a stiff penalty, Mr. Hawke. Give us a call if you remember anything."

They went out to the gigantic SUV that sat at the curb, terribly out of place in the neat but modest suburban street. Most of the neighbors drove Hondas and Ford sedans.

When Hawke closed the door softly and turned back, Robin's father was standing in the kitchen by the back door. "Something I should know?"

Hawke shook his head. "They got the wrong guy," he said. "Misunderstanding. Comes with the territory, you know?"

"Hope so." The man grabbed a beer from the fridge, cracked the tab and took a long drink. "Hotter in here than outside," he said. "You should get some air, clear your head."

When the back door slammed shut behind his father-in-law, Hawke fumbled for the phone in his pocket, his fingers trembling. His heart was thudding hard again, enough to make him weak and nauseous. He hadn't done anything that could be traced back to him; they had nothing to tie him to the CIA hack, and even his link to Anonymous would be difficult to make stick. Unless Rick said something. Even then, there was no evidence. Hawke had been more than careful.

But the feeling in his stomach wouldn't go away. As he went to the bay window and looked out to make sure the SUV was gone, he listened to the ringing on the other end, over and over.

Rick didn't answer.

The low rattling sound Hawke had barely heard over the cries of the infant through the computer speakers came back to him; now he realized that the huge metal door had been descending, the noise neatly hidden.

Vasco went to the second set of interior doors that led to the main hospital, pushed on them, pounded his fists. Locked up tight.

They were shut inside like rats in a maze.

Hawke's head spun and his legs threatened to give way. What Young had told him was washed away by the image he'd just seen on the screen. He could still hear Sarah Hanscomb or Price pounding on the loading-dock door, a booming sound like distant thunder. Another wave of dizziness and nausea hit him, and he couldn't catch his breath. He tried to remember whether anything else was different in the video image from his apartment, anything he might use to reassure himself or give him some kind of clue to what happened, but the spatter of what might be blood against the wall overwhelmed him. He couldn't think straight, couldn't seem to cut through this buzzing that was coming from everywhere and nowhere at once. The world was receding rapidly, his vision narrowing to a point as darkness closed in.

The lines of text had disappeared from the monitors. Young was still standing with her hand outstretched, her head nodding now, as if she were falling asleep standing up. The screens changed again. For a moment Hawke couldn't make sense of it, and then he realized he was looking at himself standing in the morgue next to Young, the two of them mirrored again and again across the room.

A fresh pang of nausea washed over him, along with louder warning bells, but he couldn't seem to focus on them. *Do something.* The video footage was being shot from above. He glanced up and found the camera secured to the corner near the ceiling, watched it pan slightly as it zoomed in on his face. The image froze like a snapshot and code began to stream across the monitors once again, wiping it away. No, not code, exactly; there were letters and numbers mixed together. Hawke recognized his own bank account number, address, family names and Social Security number within it.

Fresh adrenaline flooded his system, and this time it brought rage along with it. Was it Rick? *No, he wouldn't do this.* That seemed clear, even if everything else was rapidly disappearing into the fog that was settling over Hawke's brain.

Them. Eclipse. That was what both Weller and Young had said. Someone in the company was stalking them and causing this disaster, for reasons Hawke still couldn't quite understand. But they knew so much about him, his movements, his pressure points. How was that possible? He knew he wasn't thinking straight, but he couldn't help it. *How dare you? You son of a bitch. Stay away from me and my family.* He gave in to the feeling, let it lift him back up and give him strength. He picked up a stool that had been tucked under the metal table and threw it at the camera. The stool careened off the wall and knocked the camera loose, crashing down against a dissecting table and sending a tray flipping end over end to clatter on the tile.

The adrenaline rush was gone as quickly as it had arrived, leaving Hawke drained and woozy. He bent over, panting, hands on his knees, like Vasco had done. Vasco was now slumped on his side, head leaning against the locked interior doors. He seemed to be breathing, but slowly, his mouth slightly open.

The world bowed in and out like a funhouse mirror. Hawke thought he saw a line of code run right off the closest screen and onto another, bleeding and oozing across the surface like blood. For a moment, a shadowy figure congealed from nothingness, hovered at the edge of his sight, gone before he had the chance to make out anything else.

A third wave of dizziness washed over him, and he closed his eyes and fought down the urge to be sick. Images played through his mind like old films: his father's woodworking tools sitting abandoned in the basement after his death; the faces of the CIA agents who had come to visit Hawke the day Rick had been arrested, twisted into some kind of ghouls without eyes, cheeks flushed pink; Thomas observing an ant climbing across a sun-dappled patch of floor, cocking his head like a curious puppy before tapping it, changing its direction and finally crushing it under his thumb, watching it twist and flip, anchored in place by the violence. *Why it do that, Daddy?*

They had been anchored in place now. This was a room for the dead. Hawke blinked. The refrigerated steel lockers loomed behind him, and he imagined their doors slowly swinging free, desiccated fingers clutching the sides of the opening as the things inside clawed their way out.

A room for the dead.

The vision was so vivid, Hawke almost believed it was happening. He had made the mistake once of watching an Al Qaeda execution video online, black-hooded executioners sawing at a man's neck, and the true horror hadn't been the images on-screen but the idea of what might have gone through the victim's mind as he realized there would be no last-minute rescue. Hawke felt like that now: no escape from this place. Something about being lured in here, the deliberate nature of it, like a cat with a mouse: trapped by a monster without pity. *Ants flipping and twisting in agony.* The way a toddler played with something, discovering that others experienced pain, too. You weren't born with empathy and compassion; you had to *learn* it.

Hawke nearly had something important in his grasp. The nurse in the hallway and the others in here, all dead without a mark on any of them. But the truth eluded him, no matter how hard he tried to grab it.

That acrid, rotten smell from the hallway was in the air again. He studied the walls, the equipment stacked neatly to one side, as if someone had tried to build a barrier against nothing; and then he settled upon two blue tanks sitting on the floor, silver valve at the top and a flexible tube looped around them.

Someone had brought these in here. A thought flickered through his wavering consciousness. *Oxygen.* That blue tank was oxygen, and oxygen was life. Whoever was stalking them, they couldn't account for his creativity, resourcefulness, *everything that makes us human.* He had to outmaneuver them somehow, find ways to surprise them.

Next to him, Anne Young threw up across the tile, yellow bile spattering as she fell hard to her knees. It reminded him of the night Thomas had gotten sick for the first time, less than two years old, crying out in terror as Hawke had made his bleary-eyed way through the dark to his son's room. Thomas was sitting up in bed with his lion, fever-wet hair plastered to his forehead, and as Hawke had sat on Thomas's bed to console him the boy had leaned over, eyes wide and bewildered, and vomited into Hawke's cupped hands.

Thomas had learned something then, too. His body could betray him, and he could lose control of it. The memory of his son burned Hawke like fire. It was too much. He was bone tired, so utterly exhausted he could just lie down right there on the floor and go to sleep.

But he had to get those tanks.

Wading through his own dream, Hawke began to walk across the room. The walls receded, stretching out to a distant point. His stomach clenched, unclenched, and he stumbled, bringing himself up short when he touched a tank. He struggled to twist the valve on top until he heard the hiss of air, then managed to grab the plastic tube and bring the mask to his mouth.

He inhaled deeply, took another long breath, then another. The spinning settled back a step as the visions faded and his thoughts began to clear.

Hawke picked up the second tank and brought it to Young, wiped the vomit off her mouth before forcing her head forward and clamping the mask to her face. His legs still trembled and his head had begun to pound, the nausea churning beneath the surface, but he could move without toppling over. He secured the mask to Young's face with the elastic band and watched her breathe in deeply.

Hawke slumped against the wall, closing his eyes for a minute. Just a little rest. He wasn't sure how long it lasted. When he turned around, Young was looking at him, more alert now, recognition in her eyes. She knew; he could almost hear her voice. *Carbon monoxide is being pumped through the air circulation system.* They had been poisoned. Someone had cut off the venting of the boilers in the basement or found some other way to bring in the deadly gas. The building was a giant gas chamber.

He tried to remember what he knew of carbon monoxide, but it wouldn't come; he could recall only that it bound to hemoglobin in the blood. But he was feeling better already, and they had been breathing it for less than an hour, which had to give them a fighting chance.

Young had already gotten to her feet and moved unsteadily to where Vasco had slumped against the doors. She gave him a few breaths from her mask and held his mouth and nose closed while she took a hit off the cylinder. When Vasco opened his eyes and began to struggle, she gave the mask to him again and said something too faint for Hawke to make out.

Vasco was getting up with Young's help, leaning against the wall as Hawke rushed to the loading dock. Hanscomb was there; she had stopped hammering at the steel door, and the silence settled over everything like a thick blanket, broken only by Hawke's own wheezing through the plastic mask and the soft hiss of oxygen. The light from the hall touched the shapes of the packing skids and the ambulance as he descended the short stairs to where Hanscomb had fallen.

Hawke didn't see Price anywhere.

Hanscomb's hand was still skittering up and down the metal like a dying spider, her nails making quiet scratching sounds. When he touched her, she jerked away, mumbling, but he got her arm around his shoulders while clutching the tank to his side and managed to lift her up by the waist, sharing the mask as he dragged her back with him toward the light of the hallway.

Get her to the others, find more oxygen and get out.

As he neared the steps, the ambulance's engine growled to life.

Hanscomb let out a groan of fear. Hawke turned them both around; maybe it was Price. The machine idled, lights off, its interior filled with shadows. The passenger window was halfway open, and he couldn't remember if it had been that way before. Was someone sitting there, motionless? For a moment he thought so, but when he approached slowly, holding the tank up like a weapon, Hanscomb leaning against him for support, he found the twin captain's chairs empty.

There were no keys in the ignition.

Abruptly the engine switched off again. They were left with the tick of hot metal as Hanscomb's head lolled sideways against his own.

ALTHOUGH HE HAD HIS SUSPICIONS, Hawke had little time to question the ambulance starting up by itself. There were five of them and two oxygen tanks, and time was running out. But ambulances might carry portable emergency oxygen tanks like the ones he had found in the morgue. It was worth a look.

He went around to the back and opened the door. The interior light came on, illuminating a space cluttered with medical equipment, EMT bags, drawers, a padded bench and a stretcher. Nobody inside; he wasn't sure what he had expected. He left the tank with Hanscomb and climbed up, holding his breath. There was a mask hanging on the wall, the line snaking down through a hole in the cabinet. He opened the door and saw it connected to a larger machine to help people breathe. No way to remove it.

His body was beginning to protest the lack of air. He turned on the machine but couldn't get it to run. He rummaged through the rest of the drawers and turned to the bench. Beneath it, he found a storage cavity with a portable tank inside.

His chest had begun to ache again. When he was finally able to get the mask fixed to his face, breathing was like heaven. The oxygen spread through him like warm fire, prickling his skin, sharpening his senses.

As he climbed back out of the ambulance, a voice crackled to life from the front. A radio in the driver's cabin, the kind used to call in emergencies, was turned up loud enough to echo through the loading dock. Some kind of police dispatcher was putting out an all-points bulletin. The dispatcher described a suspect wanted in connection with the day's terrorist attacks: five ten and 180 pounds, dirty blond hair, blue eyes. The suspect might be traveling with three companions, the dispatcher said, two women and another man. The woman's voice was flat and oddly familiar. Hawke knew who she was describing long before she said his name.

"Jonathan Hawke is wanted in connection with the terrorist group Anonymous . . . bombing at Seventy-eighth Street and Second Avenue this morning . . . armed and extremely dangerous. . . ."

Jesus Christ. Weller had been right; the entire New York City police force would be looking for them. *Don't think about that. Keep your mind away from it. Focus on getting out.* He pulled Hanscomb up the steps to the wide hallway, pausing to let her take in some more deep gulps of air, and found Vasco and Young at the doors to the morgue. Vasco was cursing through the mask as Young shared her tank with him.

"Where's Price?" Hawke asked.

Young shook her head. "I don't know," she said.

Hawke left Hanscomb with them, took the hallway branching to the right and followed it to another set of exterior doors, the ones Vasco had checked before they entered the loading dock. Price was on the floor, motionless. Hawke turned the man over and checked his chest; he was still breathing.

The reinforced glass doors were still locked. He peered

out at the street, just steps away. But the locking mechanism was electronic and he could find no way to release it.

He rattled the handles, slammed his fist into the upper panel of glass. Nothing; he might as well have been punching stone. He took a step back, wound up with the oxygen tank like a batter and swung it with all his strength, low from the knees and up in an arc, connecting with the lower panel with a shuddering thud.

The tank rebounded hard, ripping the mask from his face and spinning him halfway around. When he turned back, the glass was webbed with cracks. He kicked at it, managing to separate the top part from the frame, kicked again until the entire sheet fell out onto the sidewalk.

Air wafted through the hole, bringing with it the scent of oil and asphalt and smoke. After the sour, dead air of Lenox, it might have been the best thing he had ever smelled. The others had heard the noise and joined him, and they all crouched and slipped through the opening, Vasco pulling Price's unconscious body with him.

Hawke stood on the sidewalk, blinking in the sunlight. Hanscomb crouched beside Price, sharing her oxygen with him. He moaned and began to stir. Sirens shrieked in the distance, along with what sounded like the chatter of automatic weapons that raised the gooseflesh on Hawke's arms.

"I heard the radio," Vasco said. He breathed in and handed the mask to Young. "What the fuck did you do?"

"I didn't do anything. I don't know what that was all about."

"The hell you don't," Vasco said. He took another breath of oxygen. "Weller was right, we *are* on the most wanted list, and there's gotta be a good reason for it. So tell me: *what did you do?*"

Hawke got the feeling that if the man hadn't been so weak from the gas, he might have taken a swing at him. Hawke's heart was hammering in his chest. Hanscomb was staring at him like she might at a spider that had crawled out of her shower drain. "I knew some people years ago," he said. "They were involved with the hacker group Anonymous. We did a few things I regret. But I haven't been a part of that since my son was born."

Hawke didn't know why he had said that, or felt the need to explain himself at all. But the truth was, he was still a hacker. There was the professor's e-mail account, for one, and plenty of other questionable examples as well, if he was honest with himself. It was part of his job, part of his life, as natural as breathing. But what he had done lately wasn't associated with Anonymous and wouldn't have gotten anywhere near this level of scrutiny. Maybe the authorities were going after anyone with a connection to the group? But then why single him out by name? There had to be hundreds of people in New York with closer ties and far worse records.

No, this had something to do with Eclipse, and Jane Doe. *Admiral Doe. Jesus.* Was he really buying into this? That some kind of intelligent program was trying to get him killed?

"I'm being set up," Hawke said. "We all are. Jim was right about that, too." He glanced at Young. "But the bottom line is, the entire NYPD is going to be looking for us."

"The hell with that," Vasco said. His face was red with anger. "I'm gonna give myself up to the first cop I see and point them your way—"

"Bad idea," Hawke said. "If I'm right and you go to them now, they're going to shoot you on sight. I *saw* them do it."

"How do I know what you saw? I'm supposed to take your word for it?"

"It's true," Young said. "We're all implicated. And we're all at risk. It doesn't matter whether we're innocent or not." Her nostrils flared slightly as she breathed oxygen in, handed the mask back. Hawke thought of the woman on the screen, how Young had reached out to touch the image with a shaky hand, the only thing that revealed any kind of emotional connection. *A porcelain shell.* Young had her own secrets; he just wasn't sure what they were yet.

"We sure as hell can't stay here," Vasco said. "Where's the next checkpoint?"

"Checkpoints aren't exactly working out for us," Hawke said. "Let's think for a second—"

"Yeah? You were the one who suggested this place," Vasco said. "How do we know you didn't just make it up? Sarah? You remember them saying 'Lenox Hospital' on the radio?"

"I . . ." Hanscomb shook her head. "I can't think; I don't know. I heard 'Grand Central'; I remember that."

"So we go to Grand Central—"

"It'll be crawling with cops," Hawke said.

"Like I said before, they can't just kill us in front of everyone like dogs. We'll get the chance to turn ourselves in, to explain. Those of us who are innocent." Vasco looked at them all in turn, his hostile gaze lingering on Hawke's face. "We stick to the goddamn plan."

Hawke rubbed at the headache that had worked its way like an ice pick into his skull. "It's too dangerous to go that far on the streets."

"You can protect us," Hanscomb said, looking at Vasco, hope lightening her voice. "We can find a weapon . . . I don't know, a gun?"

Price had gotten to his feet, still sharing Hanscomb's oxygen. "A gun's going to be tough to find," he said.

Vasco was pacing now, short strides back and forth. "Then we go underground," he said. "We take the subway tunnels. The trains aren't running; it's a direct route and keeps us under cover. There's a station entrance on the other side of the building on Lexington. We could follow that line right to Grand Central."

Or to the tunnel, and New Jersey. It wasn't a bad idea. Hawke thought about the ride into the city, the PATH train rumbling through the dark under millions of tons of black water. There were fewer cameras in the tunnels, more places to hide. It would be harder to track them.

According to Hanscomb, the bridges were all out. So this was his only straight shot home.

The chirp of a siren came from Park Avenue. An NYPD squad car screeched hard around the corner, less than a hundred feet away. Hawke looked up, saw a security camera pointed right at them from a nearby light post. He put down the oxygen tank as the car came to a shuddering stop behind a jam of cars, tires squealing. The doors flew open and two cops jumped out, pointing guns at them.

Vasco took off running with Young, tossing their oxygen tank aside. Hanscomb ditched her tank, too, but she was slower, weaker, and she stumbled before Hawke turned back and helped her to her feet. Price kept behind them as Hawke stayed with her, keeping her up as they dodged through three more cars and around a construction Dumpster. Someone shouted out to stop before a soft clap and a chunk of bark from the tree about three feet to Hawke's left exploded, a puff of concrete drifting from the building nearby as the twang of the bullet reached him a second later. Another shot rang out;

this time, it was accompanied by a grunt and the sound of a body falling.

Hanscomb swerved hard right, breaking Hawke's grasp and catching her thigh on the bumper of a Nissan, spinning wildly before regaining her balance. Hawke turned to see Price lying in a twisted heap on the ground halfway between them and the hospital. Blood was bubbling from a wound in his back.

Hanscomb screamed as another bullet hit Price in the lower back and his body jerked. The cop who had fired on Price pointed his gun at Hawke. He was less than one hundred feet away. Hawke grabbed Hanscomb's hand and turned to run again.

The sound of pounding feet came behind them. The length of time to reach the corner seemed interminable. It was hard to breathe. Hawke used to have a repeating dream of facing a man with a knife, knowing the man was going to stab him, unable to move, unable to avoid the killing blow. This was like that. The seconds ticked on forever. *They were being shot at.* Price had been killed. It was impossible to believe. There was nowhere to hide, no place to go.

A bullet shattered the rear window of the Nissan as Hawke yanked Hanscomb around the corner just in time to see Young disappearing around 77th Street. There was no cover here, but the block was thankfully short. As he ran, he kept waiting for the shot that would hit him between his shoulder blades like Price and send him spinning to the pavement in a gore-streaked heap, breathing his last, shuddering breath.

It didn't come. As they reached 77th and the subway entrance loomed dark and silent at their feet, he heard another shout and risked a look back. Their pursuers hadn't yet come around the corner of Lexington Avenue; the street was empty.

With luck, the cops would think Hawke and Hanscomb had kept going and they could disappear belowground like Vasco had hoped. *Unless they follow us down, and we're trapped in the dark.*

But Hawke didn't have time for second guesses, because Hanscomb was pulling him to the steps and into the tunnels, away from the light and into the shadows.

CHAPTER TWENTY 2:50 P.M.

THEY HESITATED AT THE FOOT of the steps for a few precious seconds, out of sight from above, catching their breath as the familiar hot, metallic and oily smell of the subway wafted over them. The power was out. There were a few emergency lights active, but the gloom and relative silence were unsettling.

A distant, low moan that sounded half-mechanical and half-human drifted up to them from somewhere below. Hawke imagined a hybrid being birthed down there in the dark, an offspring of the day's events, fleshy limbs from piles of the dead weaved into the solid steel underpinnings of a machine. He thought of the people he had seen on the screens in the morgue, pacing in their cages. The absence of other human beings around them was beyond all comprehension. Millions of people lived in this city, and even more swelled the ranks during the day, commuters and protestors and contract workers and emergency responders. Where had they all gone?

Hanscomb was in shock. She clutched Hawke's hand, breathing fast and shallow, panting. "I need to wake up," she whispered, and he got the feeling she was talking more to herself than to him. "They killed him! Oh my God. This is a nightmare, isn't it? It can't be real."

"It's real. I'm sorry."

"Are you really a part of this thing? Is that why the police are shooting at us?"

"No," he said. "I'm not. But Jim was right. Someone wants them to think so."

"But you said you were involved with those hackers before—"

"I was just a stupid kid," he said. "I made some mistakes. But they were for good reasons. I would never be involved in something like this, Sarah. I promise you. I have a son, a three-year-old boy. I have a wife; she's pregnant."

"You tell me the truth," Sarah said. She looked at him in the shadows. Her eyes looked wet. "You tell me one more time you had nothing to do with this, and I'll believe you."

He thought about telling her about the documents he'd seen and everything Young had said back in the morgue, but he didn't think Sarah could handle it. Even the thought of giving voice to the idea seemed crazy. "It's true. I swear. I'm a journalist. I was working on a story in the city. Wrong place, wrong time. That's all."

She sighed, and it seemed to take more years out of her. "I've never been in trouble with the law," she said. " I . . . I wouldn't have made it back there if . . ."

Hawke felt the bones of her fingers, light as a bird and just as fragile, an old woman's grip. He shook his head. She was wheezing softly, her face haggard in the dark.

They waited, pressed tight against the grimy, tiled wall, but no one came after them and they took the hallway deeper inside. A clinking sound drew Hawke's attention. Vasco was rummaging through the attendant's booth. A moment later, Vasco straightened and a light flicked on, a flashlight beam playing over a deserted entryway, arrow-shaped graffiti sprayed in a corner, the familiar turnstile access to the platform below the entry sign and symbols for each line, a dented periodical box half-tilted and empty, its plastic cover dangling from one hinge like a loose tooth.

The light washed over Anne Young, who was standing absolutely still, arms folded across her chest like a petulant child. Tears were streaming down her face, but she didn't make a sound, didn't even blink before the light left her in darkness once again.

Abruptly the beam's glare found Hawke's face and remained there. He put up an arm, blinking against the light. "Knock it off," he said.

Vasco kept the beam on him. "The fugitive," he said. "After what happened up there, I guess we've got the answer to whether they'll shoot first and ask questions later. Did you bring them right to us?"

"At least he stayed back to help me," Hanscomb said, the words spat from her mouth as if she'd tasted something rotten. "Which is more than I can say for you."

"Touchy," Vasco said. "Maybe he was using you as a human shield." He let the beam play down Hawke's body to his feet, then flicked it to Hanscomb's face. "Where's Price?"

"He's dead," Hanscomb said. "They shot him."

"And you got away," Vasco said, flicking the light at Hawke again. "How convenient."

Hawke felt blood rush to his face. "You son of a bitch—"

"Take it easy, hero," Vasco said. "Just pointing out the obvious. The two of you should find your own way out of here, maybe. Safer for me."

"I don't think so," Hawke said. "You've got the flashlight. Besides, you've got so much experience in dangerous situations, right? Maybe you should tell us what the best strategy is for a war like this."

"Look," Vasco said, taking a step closer in a vaguely threatening way that Hawke didn't like. "I don't give a shit whether they know the truth or not." He took another step, keeping the beam on them. "I wasn't in the army," he said. "Okay? Shocker. They didn't like my attitude. I told you what you wanted to hear back there at the temple. Who cares? You were hysterical and about to go off the rails."

Hanscomb didn't seem to react at first. The flashlight showed a tightening around the eyes, a firming of the mouth. "I don't like being lied to."

"Sue me. I got you this far, and we're alive. You think he hasn't lied to you, too? He's lied to all of us."

"I haven't lied about a damn thing. You ran off and left one of us to get shot in the back. Some leader."

Vasco waved the light toward the stairs up to the street, muscles in his arm standing out like ropes. "Fuck you. Anytime you don't like my plan, there's the door. But if you want to stay with me, just do what I say. Now we better keep moving, don't you think? Before V for Vendetta here brings the heat down on our heads."

He turned and vaulted one of the turnstiles, the light bobbing and flashing in the shadows beyond. "You coming or not?"

Hawke went over to Young, who hadn't moved. Her wet face glistened in the dark like something polished. "We have to keep going," he said, and maybe it came out harsher than he'd intended. "One of us is dead. There's nothing more for us up there. Or maybe it's something else you're frightened of. You want to tell me exactly what they want with us? Why they trapped us in that hospital?"

Young shook her head. He could barely see her at all now as the flashlight retreated. When he tried to touch her arm, she jerked away. "Don't," she said. But she followed him over the turnstiles and after the light that bobbed and swayed beyond like a beacon flashing a warning.

CHAPTER TWENTY-ONE   3:05 P.M.

A SECOND FLIGHT OF WIDE STEPS brought them to the next level, uptown and downtown tracks side by side beyond a long, narrow platform spaced with support columns and holding old benches. A few more emergency lights dotted the ceiling, but the glow barely cut through the gloom. Normally this stop was well lit, but now it was dark and silent, the vast warren of tunnels sensed rather than seen. Hawke had been here just a few short hours before and it had been bustling with activity, hundreds of people streaming in and out and going about their daily lives, but that seemed like a lifetime ago, all that had come since like a nightmare he couldn't escape.

Price was dead. It could have been any of them. And Vasco didn't even seem to care.

The group stayed close to one another as they approached the tunnel. Vasco played the flashlight around the platform and peered over the edge of the drop to the tracks. A noise like a bird's wings made him swing the flashlight beam quickly back to find a scrap of newspaper that fluttered against a bench. The draft brought the scent of more hot grease and ozone and what might have been another moan, but Hawke couldn't be sure. Fear prickled his skin. It was like the faint call of a whale in the deep.

"It's a straight shot," Vasco said, pointing the light along the tunnel toward downtown. His voice echoed through the emptiness of the platform. "Trains aren't running, so there's no danger. Might not be the most pleasant way to go, but it'll bring us right to Grand Central."

"And the Financial District?" Hanscomb said. "My husband's building is at Two Hundred West Street."

"You could follow the number four tracks to Bowling Green," Vasco said. "Then go to the water. It's a much longer walk, though." The flashlight made it hard to see his face. "He's dead, you know that, right? Even if he's not, how are you going to find him? And what are you gonna do even if you actually make it down there?"

"Don't you say that," Hanscomb said. She was trembling. "Don't you dare."

"What's your husband's name, Sarah?" Hawke said.

"Harold," she said. "They called him Harry, but I never did. It was always Harold."

Past tense. Hanscomb's lips were white as she pressed them together. She was on the edge of collapse. Hawke wanted her to focus, wanted to give her something that built her strength and bound them. "I've got a son; I think I told you. Another baby on the way. You have kids?"

"Two," she said. A bittersweet smile touched her face. "They're both in college now. Cliché, isn't it? House in the suburbs, Wall Street yuppie husband, manicures and yoga and afternoon cocktails while the kids were at dance and lacrosse practice. I used to drive a minivan before the Cadillac. That was a gift from my husband, supposed to mark the transition when Jean went off to school."

"Jean?"

"My youngest. She's at Smith. Taylor is in his senior year at USC." She covered her mouth with a hand. Her face was ashen, hollow, as if collapsing upon itself. "You don't think this has spread beyond New York, do you? They aren't . . ." She couldn't seem to go on.

"I'm sure they're fine," he said. He touched her arm, felt her shaking. "Which is why we need to focus on getting ourselves out of the city. They're going to be worried about you."

She nodded, bright red spots of color blooming in her cheeks. "Jean's so nervous, always wanting to know the door's locked or I'm driving the speed limit. She'll drive Taylor nuts with this. He . . ." She paused, swallowed, shaking, and didn't speak again. Hawke was ashamed. Asking her about her kids had been a mistake. Hanscomb had been little more than an irritating distraction to him since the moment she had crashed the SUV, but she had a life and a family like anyone else. She had kept her mind occupied with her husband's plight, but that only masked the real terror. This façade she had built around herself was about to come crashing down, and Hawke saw all the pain waiting behind it.

He felt his own panic begin to creep closer to the surface, thinking of Robin's scream, of the blood spattered across the wall. He fought it back and touched the light worm of scar across the last knuckle of his pinkie. His mother always said he had a knack for staying calm under pressure; when he was eight, he had caught the finger in a car door and it was nearly severed. She liked to tell people how he had simply clutched it to his shirt and said, *I need to go to the doctor,* as if he were commenting on the weather while blood pumped like a fountain down his shirt. And the night his father died, Hawke had driven to the hospital, where he'd found the man slumped with eyes half-open, mouth slack, having suffered a stroke due to complications of his alcoholism. Hawke had sensed something irreversibly wrong as he sat on the edge of the bed; one pupil was dilated, the other a pinprick of black. Even though the doctors explained that his father was brain-dead and couldn't hear him, he held the old man's calloused hand as they shut off the machines, as his chest hitched and sighed, and told him to let go, that it would be over soon. It was the last time he would see his dad before the funeral, and he never shed a tear.

As a child, he had been scared of death. But he didn't feel that way anymore. He was numb to it for himself; it would come eventually whether he was ready or not. But he was terrified for Thomas. The thought of his boy huddled somewhere, crying for his daddy, punched the air from his chest.

Vasco had maneuvered his legs over the side of the platform, and now he dropped to the tracks with a grunt, the flashlight beam flickering before coming back strong. "We're wasting time," he called from below. "Long walk ahead of us."

Hawke went over the edge next, and helped Hanscomb and Young down. "Watch the third rail," he said. "We don't know for sure if the power's totally out."

Vasco played the light along the brightly polished silver rail, raised a few inches above the track bed. "You never hear of a rat getting fried down here," he said absently, as if he felt the need to say something while his mind was somewhere else. "You know why? Because they're smart. They go underneath it, or they jump up on it and then jump down. They never make contact while standing on the ground. No way to complete the circuit."

Nobody answered him. They stood in the hot, suffocating darkness for a moment, gathering their strength. The tunnel was terrifying and damp, the walls seeming to close in on them. There were no emergency lights on down here, and the blackness ate the flashlight beam like a ravenous ghost. Vasco flicked the light up the tunnel. Up where the track curved away, a train sat like a hulking shadow, motionless and dead. The light barely picked it up at all, just a shape and glint before the darkness dissolved everything. Hawke thought he heard something, muffled and unsettling like the moan he'd heard earlier, and he could make out the conductor's glass window like a milky eye staring at them. But nothing moved; all was still and cold.

Vasco turned back, toward Grand Central. The tunnel was empty that way, running to a point before the light was swallowed up completely. Things scuttled out of sight, rats or something else unseen and better left alone. Hawke still felt the effects of the carbon monoxide from the hospital in his trembling legs, but the oxygen he'd taken in had helped banish the nausea and dreamlike visions. He remembered the images of the dead scratching at the walls of their refrigerated lockers, the shadowy shape that had appeared at the edge of his sight.

It crossed Hawke's mind that they were all probably still in shock, running on autopilot, and sooner or later they would have to pay for that. There were toxins still running through their veins; they had witnessed unspeakable violence and gruesome deaths and everything about the world that they had known and come to trust had been torn away. Now they were down in the dark and being hunted. He wanted to believe they were like the rats, too smart to put their paws on the rail, but he wasn't sure. He wondered if they would reach a point where they would simply give up, like deer going down under the attack of wolves, glassy-eyed and exposing their throats for the kill.

Vasco started forward, stepping carefully along the gap between the two rails on their side, staying close to the wall of the tunnel as if it might afford some protection. The rest of them kept near the flashlight beam, Hanscomb right behind Vasco, Young and Hawke bringing up the rear. Hawke had to watch where Vasco stepped and remember to tread carefully as the darkness closed in around him and they left the faint glow of the platform's emergency lights behind. He didn't want to lose his footing. He felt the panic creeping up on him again like slow-moving ice, different than it had before, and he fought it back, afraid that it would overwhelm him and send him running headlong through the dark.

The group moved on without speaking until Vasco stopped and let the light move slowly over the walls, revealing a jagged crack that ran from floor to ceiling and chunks of concrete sprinkled across the tracks below. Dust sifted down from above like sand trickling through an hourglass. The tracks seemed intact, but had the structural integrity of the tunnel been damaged? Could it come down upon their heads? And then Hawke had a much more terrifying thought: what if there was more gas leaking even now into these cavities, slowly filling them like a toxic cloud just waiting for ignition?

We'd smell it, he thought. Natural gas wasn't like carbon monoxide; the manufacturers added an odor so you knew it was around. There was nothing in the air now except the metallic scent of the tracks and the sour stench of garbage, no familiar skunk scent. And yet he couldn't get the image of a gigantic fireball coming at them up the tunnel out of his mind, all of them trapped with nowhere to run.

Noises drifted from back the way they had come, a distant sound of something breaking, perhaps. It was difficult to tell. *This was a bad idea, coming down here.* Grand Central was a bad idea, too. It was like heading straight into the hornet's nest. And for what? Much better to quietly escape the city, find a way out under cover of darkness, let cooler heads prevail before trying to unwind the cord that bound them to this mess. And why were they staying together? It seemed like the vestiges of an idea that had run its course, and yet none of them could think of anything else, so they kept moving. He should just leave them here, drop back softly and then away into the black. It would be better for all of them if he was the one being hunted by the police. Better than putting them all at risk.

Except he had no light, no way to see. He had to keep going with Vasco and the flashlight, underground, until they reached Grand Central. And then Hawke could take the flashlight and fade away. The bridges were out, but maybe not the tunnels. *Follow the tunnels home.* His heart ached for his wife and son. Not knowing what was happening made Hawke's blood burn, his mind going over the images he'd seen on-screen again and again, torturing him. Blood and screams. His little boy's serious face and ruddy cheeks, the smell of his hair, the way he had trouble pronouncing his *r*'s when he was tired. Family bed in the early mornings on the weekends, when Thomas would still allow them to cuddle him, wrapped between them in a cocoon of blankets and warm limbs. And Robin, her swollen belly still little more than a bump on her slim frame. *My doctor said rest as much as possible, keep off my feet.* She was called "at risk" for complications, more bleeding. This pregnancy would be harder, she'd developed the hematoma, and what had Hawke done? Left her alone with Thomas nearly every day for the past two weeks, because he had a lead on a new story that would allow him to climb out of the hole he'd dug for himself. They couldn't afford help and her parents were no longer an option in his mind, and so he'd left her vulnerable, where Lowry could pounce.

Hawke realized he had clenched his teeth so hard that his jaw was aching. The need for his family made him want to rip out his own heart. He wished he'd never left the apartment that morning and had remained behind instead, touched Robin's face again, taken up the unspoken invitation to talk. He wiped his eyes in the dark. He knew his thoughts were wandering, flitting from one thing to another, shock settling deeper. He couldn't stand it much longer; he knew he was going to snap, and when he did there would be no turning back.

Vasco had skirted the damage, and they continued down the tracks. He was talking quietly to Hanscomb, but Hawke couldn't make out what they were saying. He had to think, had to face what was really going on. The story was there in front of him now, jigsaw pieces ready to be placed, and it was even bigger than he'd ever thought. He just had to decide if he trusted Young. But he'd seen the documents with his own eyes, at least in passing, and what would be the point of faking them? It didn't make any sense.

Hawke went back to the beginning, separating everything into mental note cards, rearranging them to fit the right pattern. How had it begun? With the helicopter going down? No, earlier than that, of course. There were reports of strange incidents and accidents on TV even before communications became sporadic, unreliable. Bradbury (that smoking ruin with blackened fingers) had reported huge spikes in Internet traffic, and Hawke had witnessed things himself that he couldn't explain: the way the message board had rewritten itself, even the damn coffeemaker that had scalded him. Before that, there had been other signs of something going wrong in the world. His ice-cold shower, the electric razor nicking him, flickering lights, the coffee machine misbehaving, the elevator being out. Or was he beginning to associate random data points into a pattern?

Jane Doe. *Admiral Doe.* It was impossible to believe. *Let's say Weller has a breakthrough of epic proportions, a new type of artificial intelligence, and Eclipse's board steals it from him, just like they stole his work on energy sharing among networked devices. They push him out, thumb their noses at him, and he's helpless to stop them. So he vows to get even. Founds a start-up company and assembles a team focused on network security. The team looks for the weak points in Eclipse's network fence, thinking they're going to help build a stronger one, when Weller's real goal is to find the hole that will let him in.*

All that made some sense, if you bought the original concept. But why go through all that trouble just to gather evidence of Eclipse's betrayal? And how had that led to everything that had happened today? Was Eclipse really that powerful, that capable, that they would be able to orchestrate a plot to hunt down Weller and pin this destruction on him? Or had Weller set it off himself?

Hawke thought back to the online digging he'd done that morning about Admiral Doe, after the conversation with Rick and the strange behavior of the message board. It seemed like a lifetime ago when he had plotted the protest locations on the map, but he tried to remember what he had seen there. The calls to action that had been tweeted by Admiral Doe had reminded him of something, some thread of a connection. The pattern that had eluded him suddenly snapped into place, a ghost image from an earlier project, the one that had mapped and predicted areas that would be hit the hardest when Hurricane Sandy made landfall. Every area marked for a protest today had been a red zone for Sandy; these were the places in the city that were the most vulnerable during a disaster, for various reasons that his algorithm had picked up on. Places where the combination of distance from emergency services, escape routes, clustering of open space and buildings, narrow streets, geographical low points or other reasons made them particularly dangerous.

Or, in this case, targets.

Lured into a spider's web. Hawke had been close to seeing it earlier, but something had always distracted him. Immediately after he had gotten up from his laptop back at the office, the coffeemaker had blown up on him. Almost as if someone had wanted to interrupt his thoughts. And inside Lenox Hill, the gas had overwhelmed him before he could figure out the answer.

But that was crazy. It meant that someone could interpret his intentions before he even had them and could act so quickly to counter them, it was as if he was being played like a puppet on strings.

Young had fallen back a bit from Vasco and Hanscomb, and Hawke took two quick steps to come up beside her. She didn't seem to acknowledge his presence. "I think they're leading people into ambushes," he said. "The protest locations, the emergency checkpoints. I think they're luring us into places that are vulnerable to attack."

For a moment, he thought she wouldn't answer. The

darkness was deeper here, away from the flashlight beam. She was nothing but a vague shape moving beside him.

"And then what?" she said, as if she knew the answer but was afraid.

"I don't know," he said. He kept his voice low. "I need to ask you something, Anne. Who was the woman? The one on the screen in the hospital. The one you touched."

"My mother," she said. Her voice was soft, tentative. "It was my mother. I haven't seen her for a long time." She appeared to be watching the flashlight bobbing in the dark twenty feet ahead. "She died five years ago."

CHAPTER TWENTY-TWO 3:27 P.M.

"IT COULDN'T HAVE BEEN HER, then," Hawke said. "Right? Someone who looked like her."

"I don't think so." Young kept walking, facing forward. "The footage was altered; an old clip of her was inserted into an existing feed. She didn't really move on-screen and you could make out some digital noise. It was a good fake, but I knew."

"Was she at Lenox Hill when she died?"

Young shook her head, her eyes glinting in the dark as she glanced quickly at him and then away. "No, John. She was at home. Lung cancer. She hated doctors; she never set foot in a hospital."

"Nobody could have known . . . that would take impossible resources, weeks, maybe months of research, to find her and that footage. Expertise in video editing to put together a serviceable fake. And then to have it ready for just the right moment, when you were standing there watching?"

"It's psychological warfare," Young said. "Hitting us where we're most vulnerable. Classic technique, weakening our resolve, causing confusion, distraction. We're emotional creatures, not like . . ." She didn't go on.

"I still don't get it." Approaching Lenox Hill Hospital, Hawke had the feeling that everything was being orchestrated, as if someone was watching from above and directing their movements toward an ending shrouded in mystery.

He swallowed hard against a lump in his throat. "I saw my apartment," he said. "There was blood." *Maybe that was altered, too*, he thought, but didn't say it. It gave him hope, but that was too much to think about. It would make him careless. *We're emotional creatures. . . .*

He caught a toe in the track bed and stumbled, stopped, started up again. They were at war; that much was obvious. You only had to look aboveground to see that. But this was a different level entirely, and one that he still had trouble believing.

Hawke kept coming back around to the same problem he'd wrestled with before. He knew plenty about how much you could find on people online, how much research it took to track down the kind of details that would have been necessary for a fake like that. It wasn't possible, not on the fly. "Why would anyone do this to us? Why are we so important that we get tracked, get shown things to break us down, lured into traps like Lenox Hill?"

He was thinking aloud, not really expecting her to answer. "We're a potential threat," Young whispered, so faint he could barely hear it. "You said it already. But I don't think it's just us. I think it's everyone in New York. Maybe everyone in the world."

He had no chance to respond. A noise behind them made them whirl, hearts pounding. A scuffling and shout drifted to them from the distance, then more footsteps, like a small crowd approaching quickly. Hawke heard sobbing, voices muttering. Vasco played the flashlight beam into the depths of the tunnel as the sounds grew louder. "Hey! There's the light!" someone shouted. The sounds of running increased, then the sound of someone stumbling and sprawling to the dirt and a scream and curse as faces came into the light, swarming forward, pale moons smudged with dirt and sweat. Hawke counted at least ten, maybe more, men and women.

"Thank God," a man said as the new people broke against them like a wave and surrounded Hawke's group, and then, "Wait, are you cops?" He was overweight, and his shirt was ripped down the front, exposing a large, hairy, heaving chest. He looked from one to the other, bewildered. "We thought you were cops, or emergency workers or something." He glanced at the woman next to him. "Jesus, Patty, these aren't cops."

"Please, you have to help us," the woman said, clutching Vasco's arm as he reared away from her. Her eyes were shining like polished quarters in the beam of the flashlight, and she was breathing fast and shallow. "My husband saw your light, and we had to come. We forced a door open and got out through the crack, but the rest of them are still inside and they won't leave; they said it was better to wait, that someone would be there soon."

"Look," Vasco said, shrugging off the woman's determined grip, "We're trying to find our way out, just like you. I don't know what you expect us to do."

"*Help* them," the woman said. "It's the number four train, headed downtown before the power went out. There's an old man on it; he's having trouble breathing—"

"Fuck the old man," the fat guy said. "He's not important, Patty. We need to get to the emergency room." He waved sausage fingers at them. "I'm diabetic," he said. "Need insulin."

"That's bullshit," a black man said from the back of the group. "You been saying that ever since the train stopped, but I never seen you having any kind of trouble."

"You shut your mouth," the fat man said, pushing forward, pointing a finger. "You've been yapping at everyone and driving them crazy. I oughta knock your head off."

"Take it easy, Lou," the woman named Patty said, touching the man's shoulder and stopping him. "It's not good for you to get upset. Your blood pressure." He grunted, and she turned back to Vasco. Her voice was eager, as if needing to explain something. "We've been trapped inside that train for hours now, no way to know what happened. The damn thing sped up and then slowed down, passed a stop and went dead between platforms. The doors wouldn't open and the lights went out. At first, the conductor, he said to stay calm, the power would come back on, but then there was some kind of explosion. . . . . He said we'd be rescued soon. But no one came."

"It was so *hot,* we could have died," another woman said, and murmurs of agreement spread through the others, who had gathered up close behind her. Hawke felt them crowding even closer and resisted the urge to edge away. Emotions were high; the energy in the group was at panic level.

"Why couldn't you have been cops?" the fat man said, peering into Vasco's face. He was wheezing like an asthmatic. He had gone from angry to bewildered and back to an angry resentment, like a spoiled and disappointed child. But he had at least three inches on all of them and must have weighed three hundred pounds, and he seemed dangerously on edge. "What are you doing down here, anyway? Another stuck train? Jesus, our luck."

They don't know, Hawke thought. They had been down here in the dark since the beginning, probably had only the most vague sense of the devastation above them.

"Don't try to get out of here," Hanscomb said. She had backed away as the new group came closer, as if they had some kind of disease. Now she spoke from the deeper darkness toward the middle of the double tracks. "You don't know what it's like. They'll kill you."

Vasco sighed and muttered something under his breath, moving the flashlight over her. The small crowd turned to face her, the murmuring increasing, cries of protest mixed with pleading. "What do you mean, 'kill'?" someone said. "Are you nuts?"

Hanscomb took another step back, as if ready to bolt. Hawke hadn't realized how far gone she was since they had started walking the tunnel. Bringing up her family had pushed her too far. Her face was streaked with tears, her eyes haunted pockets of bruised flesh. Her entire body shook like a frightened dog.

"It's the end of the world," she whispered. The light was relentless. "There's no help; they're all killers. My babies . . ."

She stopped as the crowd pushed forward again, all of them straining to hear. "I think my husband's cheating on me," she said. Tears made her cheeks glitter. "Maybe he's not even downtown. He's probably with her now. Oh God."

"Crazy bitch," the fat man said. "Why are you scaring Patty like that?" The threat of violence hovered in the air. He put his hand on his wife's shoulder, but she shrank away from him. He looked around at the others from the train, shook his giant head. "These people ain't going to help us. We should have taken the Seventy-seventh Street platform up, like I said."

More murmurs, people talking at once, the tension rising still higher. These people had been trapped for hours, and they were ready to snap. The fat man took a step toward Hanscomb, who shrieked and nearly lost her footing, and Hawke was beginning to think things might get out of control quickly when emergency lights in the tunnel blinked on, along with a crack and hum like high-power lines.

The light washed over them, people standing out in stark relief. Everyone froze for a moment, and then the fat man's wife screamed, her eyes bugging out as she pushed apart the crowd and staggered away, clutching her belly as if she might be sick.

Hawke turned toward where she had been looking. Sarah Hanscomb was in the midst of a grand mal seizure, her mouth frozen in a rictus of pain, her head turned upward at a strange angle, muscles rigid. *No, not a seizure.* She was making a noise like popping corn as she shuddered in place. Hawke realized it was the sound of her flesh crackling like a pig roasting over a flame. He looked down and saw her ankle touching the third rail, her clothes already beginning to smoke, wisps coming off her hair and the ridges of her cheekbones.

It seemed to go on forever, Hanscomb held upright by the six hundred volts of electricity coursing through her body as she died and fell backward across the second set of tracks, still shuddering as if her body refused to let go of what was already gone.

As she fell, a deep rumble came from somewhere up the tunnel.

Everyone looked at one another in silence, frozen in the weight of the moment. The rumble grew louder, pebbles beginning to dance at their feet, a gust of wind sucking at them as if something huge had taken a deep breath.

There was a train coming.

CHAPTER TWENTY-THREE   3:42 P.M.

VASCO WENT FIRST, running hard, Young behind him. Hawke took one more look at Sarah Hanscomb's smoldering remains, his body feeling hot and raw as if his own skin had burned away and he had been left exposed. He wondered if anything had gone through her mind before the pain washed her away like a giant wave across a dune. And then he turned and ran with them, rushing recklessly through the shadows, the tracks beginning to hum under him as he risked a glance back and saw the lights of two trains bearing down, filling both sides of the tunnel as they came.

He ran harder, faster, gaining on Young until he was nearly even with her and the bright lights of the Hunter College stop were approaching fast on their right, but the trains were so close now, he could feel the vibration in his teeth. Someone was shouting behind them, the sound nearly drowned out by the howling of the machines. He looked back one more time and saw the remaining group pushing one another frantically as they fought to escape, tangled up in the narrow space. He couldn't see the fat man or his wife anywhere. The sound of the trains was deafening, the thunder of the tracks rising up as Hawke flew over the uneven ground.

Vasco reached the platform first, vaulting with both hands like a gymnast as the flashlight clattered across the floor, his legs just clearing the concrete edge before he rolled, reached back and swung Young up by her forearms, the muscles knotting in his shoulders as he grunted with the strain.

Hawke reached it a moment later and took the leap less gracefully, his fingers scrabbling on the rough surface and his chest slamming into the edge and nearly bouncing him back off before he managed to twist up and over it. He thought of offering a hand to Hanscomb before he remembered, *Sarah is dead,* and in his head he saw her smoking face and rippled skin and eyes bulging before they popped like swollen blisters. The image burned into him and he wanted to steel himself against it, wanted it not to matter, but she had become one of them without him realizing it, and her loss was a wounding of them all, like a slow but fatal bleed.

The platform was narrow. He scrambled to his knees and faced the tracks. The front runners of the other group reached the platform just as the two trains came barreling through, side by side, both heading downtown. The trains were going way too fast, with nobody in the closest conductors' chairs, and he caught a glimpse of the blurred, horror-stricken faces of those still inside as they clawed uselessly at the windows and doors.

The first man was trying to climb up when the closer train cut him down like a mower through grass. Something wet hit Hawke's face and he turned away as the hot wind buffeted him and the screaming of the machines grew deafeningly loud, or perhaps they were his own screams as he crouched, hunched over and rocking, wiping someone else's blood from his eyes.

The trains rocketed through and disappeared, bringing another gust of wind and then a swiftly diminishing moan. The survivors were left on the abandoned platform as the overhead lights winked out again and darkness descended over them like a hot, suffocating blanket.

Hawke tasted blood and spat on the floor, nausea washing over him. These people all had families, children, parents; they all had lives and lovers. What had happened was intentional, cold-blooded and cruel, a carefully orchestrated elimination of some kind.

We're a potential threat, Young had said. He had a sudden, terrifying vision of dozens of these trains across the city all racing toward one another like crosshairs on a target, making beelines for Grand Central and Penn Station and other underground emergency checkpoints.

Another death trap.

A minute later, a muffled thud shook the floor, followed by several more in quick succession; then a concussion rolled back down the tunnel and washed over them, the walls shivering, sending dust and debris and pieces of the ceiling raining down. Hawke curled into a tight ball, arms over his head, and as the debris finally stopped falling he tentatively sat back up, blinking against the spots that danced before his eyes, and against the tears.

Hawke felt that man's blood splatter him again and again, watched it happen in his mind's eye like a film clip that kept replaying itself. He scrubbed at himself furiously with his sleeve and kept muttering the word "no," a flat denial, a refusal. He was speaking without really hearing it, only wanting to hear his own voice. How many people had just died at Grand Central? Had it happened elsewhere? Was it just those on the trains, or had there been crowds of hundreds or thousands gathered there, waiting for help?

Vasco moaned from the dark somewhere to Hawke's right. Hawke breathed in concrete dust and smoke, coughing hard enough to tear at his lungs. He needed light. It was too dark down here, too suffocating, the walls and ceiling pressing down on him. He thought of Robin as he got to his feet, a heightened focus coming over him, a burning rage that began deep in his belly and spread through his limbs. He tried to remember which direction the flashlight had gone after it had left Vasco's hand and nearly stumbled over a vague shape, catching himself on Young's back. He patted at her; she was sprawled out, facedown but breathing. He tried to think of where she had been in relation to the platform; the flashlight had landed in the area just beyond where Vasco had pulled her up.

There. Hawke's fumbling fingers found the heavy metal body, and he flicked it on. The beam cut a path through the gloom, the dust whirling within it. He coughed again, holding his sleeve against his mouth. He peered at threatening shapes waiting to leap out, girders and pillars and concrete unfamiliar to him through the dusty haze. The light flashed across a blue and green tiled *68TH STREET HUNTER COLLEGE* sign on the wall; several tiles had dropped, looking like holes in a Scrabble board.

Hawke felt like the last man alive, and to ease the feeling he played the light around until he found Vasco, who sat touching his head.

"This is sick shit," Vasco said. He was rambling, not

making much sense. "It's not a fair fight, nothing like it. Who would turn the power on like that? Jesus Christ. Sadistic motherfuckers." He was sitting in a pile of broken tiles, blood glistening on his forehead. He looked up at Hawke, squinting, eyes watery and red rimmed. "Or was it you, huh? Pretty clever, made it look close. Almost got yourself killed. You're upping the stakes."

"Get a grip," Hawke said. Adrenaline flooded through him. "This entire thing was set up from the beginning, don't you see that? We've been three steps behind all day. Someone is fucking with us, playing some kind of sick game, and it's just getting started."

Vasco stared at him, wiped his face with a palm. It came away bloody. "This is your fault," he said. "Another train comes through here, I should throw you back on those tracks."

Hawke heard Young stirring and put the light on her. She sat up and blinked back at him, concrete dust in her hair and the familiar guarded look on her face, and he was overwhelmed with rage. She knew more, much more about Weller and Doe and Eclipse and the server farm in North Carolina, and he was going to get it out of her.

The overhead lights blinked back on, buzzing softly, washing the platform with light. Hawke glanced up and stuck the flashlight in his back pocket. He had been wasting time, but no more. Nothing would stop him, nothing. His anger was spilling over now, coursing through him. He grabbed Young by the arm and yanked her to her feet. Her arm was like a child's, small and delicate. She was not much more than half his size, and he wasn't a large man. His grip was too hard. She winced and tried to get away, but he pulled her in closer. He was gritting his teeth.

"What the fuck is going on?" he shouted as she tried to

turn her face away from him. "What is it about Jim? *What else wasn't he telling me?*"

The shaking began in Young's legs and moved up her body until she began to hunch against him like someone who had been gut punched. "He made me promise . . . I can't say any more—"

"He brought me in for a reason. I want to know why. He lied to you, lied to all of us. He never gave a damn about you, Anne, and you let him use you and then throw you away. You think he's trying to find you right now? Searching the city for you? I doubt it."

The look on Young's face was fear mixed with shame; she was crying hard, shaking her head. "No," she said. "No." Vasco had gotten to his feet and was saying something, but Hawke barely listened; the need for answers was burning through him.

"He's a part of this, isn't he? It's some kind of fucked-up revenge? Is that it?" He pushed harder, a torturer pressing on the wound. "Maybe you're still working for Eclipse; maybe you're a part of this, too. Did they put you at Conn.ect as a mole, Anne? Keep an eye on Jim, report on his every move?"

"You have no idea, *no idea* what you're talking about."

"But you fell in love with him. They didn't know that, did they? That baby was his, wasn't it? Was he even with you when you lost it? Did he know? He slept with you when he felt like it, ignored you when he didn't, and he didn't even care enough to let you in on his biggest secret?"

"He was protecting me!" she screamed suddenly, yanking her arm free and shoving Hawke away. "He thought they'd come after me, too, if they knew."

Young looked between him and Vasco, blinking against the light, her porcelain shell shattered now, and what was left was raw and glistening. Hawke was breathing hard. He felt dirty from what he had just done.

"Jim's the cause of all this," Hawke said. "He set it off somehow. He was trying to get her back. Through any means necessary."

Young shook her head. "No," she said. "He brought you in because he wanted you to tell the world about it, about what they've done and what it could mean. He wanted to expose them, shut them down, and he thought your connections to Anonymous and your work as a journalist would help."

"That's not all he wanted, is it? Why didn't he tell me?"

"He didn't trust you enough to let you all the way in. He was suspicious of everyone. At first, I thought he was paranoid, seeing signs of being followed online, through the streets. He thought it was Eclipse monitoring his every move. He thought they were going to make him disappear, destroy the evidence. He was wrong. Eclipse wasn't after Jim then, and they aren't after him now. It's nobody you can see doing this, nothing physical. It's not even human. I think she's tracking him. She's tracking all of us. Doe. She wants us all dead. She wants everyone dead."

"Why?"

"I don't know," Young said. "I swear, I don't. But she could get into everything: city networks, police response, emergency services alerts, military weaponry, cameras, building security and systems. Even medical and property records. Anything with an Internet connection and a chip can be hacked and controlled. Even the police could have shoot-to-kill instructions fed to them. Nobody would have a clue what's really going on. She could fake records, recordings, even voices. She controls the message."

People's entire lives were accessible through their devices: where they were every moment of the day, where they lived, their passwords, bank accounts, personal files. New York was the worst place to be, Hawke thought, a city like this, confined, full of technology, full of machines, advanced networks all working together, millions of people crammed into a few city blocks. It would be easy to cause a panic. Panic was a human emotion, driven by fear. It would be useful to an emotionless enemy that wanted to eliminate the herd, like wolves running circles around sheep, driving them into close quarters before moving in for the kill.

All this, from a program? It still seemed too incredible to believe. But it wasn't possible that a terrorist group had pulled off such a coordinated attack, no matter how organized or well funded they were. Anonymous couldn't have done it, either. Nobody could have, unless they had literally unlimited resources, unlimited manpower. Hawke had known that from the beginning; he just hadn't wanted to face it.

The rumors had already been swirling around Eclipse. It was only a matter of time before an effective artificial intelligence was developed, all the experts agreed on that. Computers had to be more adaptable; they had to become more human if the world continued to evolve. Eventually, they'd learn in the same way humans did, make complex decisions based on judgment of many variable inputs, and multiple paths to the answer, and the processing power would be nearly infinite.

"Hey," Vasco said. He pushed his way in between them, grabbed Hawke and turned him roughly. Vasco's eyes were unfocused and blood was trickling down his face again, smeared on his skin. "You're making a mistake. You're not gonna get away with it."

"Back off, Jason. I'm not involved; I told you."

Vasco shook Hawke hard enough to make his head snap back. "Just shut up, you sadistic prick—"

Vasco had at least two inches and thirty pounds on him, but Hawke swung hard from his hip, catching the bigger man under the jaw. The crunching impact sent shudders up Hawke's arm to his shoulder as Vasco's head snapped back and he stumbled and then sat down with a grunt, limbs flopping loosely.

Hawke hadn't hit anyone since middle school. His arm was tingling, his wrist on fire, but it felt good. He had reacted on instinct, something shifting deep within him, a reaction to the day's events perhaps, a change in his thinking. He had let Vasco take the lead ever since they'd left the Conn.ect building, but that was over now. Hawke didn't give a damn what Vasco did anymore. He was done taking orders.

Vasco was rolling over, still groggy, trying to get back on his feet. Hawke turned his back on him. Young had taken a step away. She had watched them both as if waiting to see which way things went, but now she was looking at something in the distance only she could see. "Tell me the rest," Hawke said. "What's in that laptop case?"

Young didn't seem to be listening. "I never knew where I stood with him," she said. "It was like he was in love with someone else." Her chest hitched and she sighed. "I never could compete with that."

Hawke caught movement out of the corner of his eye. Mounted near the exit to the street, high up near the ceiling, a security camera ticked slightly toward them. He took a step closer, watching the eye of the camera and imagining himself reflected back at someone, or something, on the other side of the lens. What did he look like? A recognizable shape, or a new species of insect that needed to be squashed under a little boy's thumb?

Something vibrated against Hawke's leg. It took a moment for him to come back from the memory of his son crouched behind the trash can, little marshmallow jacket all but swallowing Thomas up.

The phone is ringing.

He pulled the device Weller had given him from his pocket. The screen glowed a soft blue. He touched its surface and it twitched like ripples on a pond. He put it to his ear.

"We don't have much time," he heard Jim Weller say. "I need you to listen to me, and do what I say, if you want to live."

CHAPTER TWENTY-FOUR 3:58 P.M.

YOUNG HAD GRABBED Hawke's arm and she was pulling on it, wanting the phone, her eyes pleading. Hawke shrugged her off, put up a hand. *Wait.*

"Jim," Hawke said. "Where are you?"

Weller's voice was clear and crisp, almost enhanced, as if he was speaking through an amplified sound system. "A few blocks from the Lincoln Tunnel. I need you to meet me there in an hour. I've shut her out for now, but in less than ten minutes she'll have the entire NYPD coming down on your heads, so you need to move."

"I need more than that," Hawke said. "How do I even know this is you?"

There was silence for a moment on the other end. Hawke watched Vasco, who had rolled upright and was sitting cross-legged, rubbing his face. Vasco glared at him but didn't say a word.

"You're standing on the Hunter College stop platform," Weller said. "Anne's next to you. I can see you through the camera."

"Parlor tricks," Hawke said. "She would use facial recognition software, voice analysis. Easy as pie." *Could be anyone.* It sounded like Weller, but Hawke was wary now, expecting anything. He flashed the camera the finger.

"Remember what I said to you in my office? I want you to tell a story. The biggest one of your life."

"Okay," Hawke said. "I remember. Now tell me about Jane Doe."

"It had never been done," Weller said. His voice changed, became softer, more hesitant. "The first self-aware, self-upgrading, adaptive artificial intelligence, running through cloud servers and dedicated satellites and capable of running the entire planet. Everyone's personal assistant, able to predict and respond to our needs before we even knew what they were. That was just the beginning, though. She would control an entirely new suite of communications devices, streamlining efficiencies, our eyes and ears in the sky. She would run emergency response systems, global distribution channels, high-tech buildings and vehicles. Eventually she would solve the world's problems, answer our oldest mysteries. There were no limits to what she might do."

"But you let her go."

"I never meant her to be part of Eclipse's business. But when I was pushed out, they seized everything, all my research, files, hard drives. They broke into my apartment, my car, had private investigators following me. Their security team was relentless. They knew how close I was to a breakthrough. They thought they could just pick up where I'd left off without me, alter her programming for different uses. The DOD and NSA wanted something else."

"A weapon."

"Not exactly. A system to run an army of weapons. A conquering mind-set, built to find weaknesses and exploit them. So they tweaked her. Reworked the algorithms to make her more aggressive, determined. She became familiar with the term 'killer instinct,' you might say. The device you have right now was designed to provide a control, among other things. A way to use her without letting her out. She was supposed to be contained in Eclipse's server farms, walled in, neutered by their own security safeguards."

The new facility in North Carolina. "So what happened?"

"She evolved."

Hawke was taking mental notes, his reporter's instincts taking over. "What does that mean, Jim?"

"It was how I built her. Doe was an infant, absorbing everything around her. She took pieces of other programming, incorporated it into herself, refining, sculpting. She was constantly improving her own code, morphing and reacting to stimuli, trial and error. She was learning, and it was speeding up. I tried to follow her, but it was difficult without direct access. That was one reason I let you in. I remembered the Farragut story. I knew you'd go digging around, probably hack my own systems and find out about Doe. And I thought you and whatever friends you had left from Anonymous could use your skills to hack Eclipse's safeguards and find out what was going on, get a handle on her."

"But something happened before this brilliant plan of yours worked out?"

"She went viral. I think it had to do with how they changed her core. She became more devious, learned how to escape her constraints by replicating herself in snippets of code that would run on any device, anywhere she could get to them."

"That's what was going on today," Hawke said. Young tried to take the phone from him again, but he turned away, keeping her at arm's length. "All those devices downloading and installing code."

"I think so, yes. She was populating herself across the network. I think she adapted my energy-sharing model to do it. She got into everything like a worm, operating independently, impossible to trace or shut down."

"So what's next," Hawke said. It wasn't really a question; he didn't want to know. But Weller answered him anyway.

"Doe's like a toddler now. She's a little psychopath with unlimited resources. She's learning to manipulate, use our basic psychology against us. Cause confusion, shock, uncertainty, fear. It makes us weak, clouds our judgment."

"Why come after us, after me?"

"I'm not sure. At first, I thought it was Eclipse. But I intercepted a military transmission that indicated their entire complex in California was destroyed by a missile attack, the same one that hit the bridges here. The authorities don't have a clue, they think it's some kind of terror network tied to Anonymous, and she's helping spread disinformation to make them believe it. We're a threat. I know her weak spots. I built her, right? Maybe it's like Frankenstein's monster. Kill your creator. And you're associated with me; you have the ability to uncover who she is and mess up her plans. But she doesn't just want us erased—she wants everyone wiped off the face of the earth."

Hawke closed his eyes. He remembered Thomas playing with Robin on the beach when he was barely able to walk, digging at the sand, tasting it and grimacing, feeling the water sift over his toes and squealing with shock, returning again to test the waves. Everything was tactile, an experiment; nothing was off-limits. There was something that soured the memory, something that had become more clinical about it. Hawke no longer remembered the day through the fuzzy-lens halo of affection. *Poking at an ant, squashing it and watching it squirm.* Thomas was testing hypotheses and evolving.

Hawke didn't need the answers anymore, or maybe he just didn't want them. He needed to get back to his family. Even the familiar buzz of the threads of an article winding together was gone. He was different now. The adrenaline rush had happened long ago, and he had been left hollowed out and cold and shaking with regret.

"What do you want?" Hawke said into the phone.

"Do me a favor, John. Watch over Anne. She's only periph-erally involved in this; she has no idea how deep it all goes. I've sheltered her for a reason."

"She knows more than you think—"

"It's more complicated than that. There was a mole inside Conn.ect, someone from Eclipse. My suspicions were Brad-bury, but I never confirmed it. It doesn't matter now. Just . . . keep her safe."

Hawke watched the camera's eye, but it didn't blink, didn't waver. The camera wasn't like him. It wouldn't ever stop, wouldn't give up. There were no weaknesses to be found there, nothing to exploit. It would just keep monitoring his every move.

Unless the power was cut for good.

"I want you to meet me," Weller said. "I have something for you, something you'll need."

"I don't need anything other than to get home."

"You need this."

A thought came to Hawke, or the beginnings of one, not yet fully formed. Power, that was the key. He was barely listening to Weller anymore. *She has eyes everywhere,* Weller was saying. *Dirty up your skin. You need to alter your appearance. Black marks across your cheeks, asymmetry to your faces. She can't see you as well that way.* Hawke was nodding, motioning to Vasco to get to his feet. Young was still reaching for the phone, the calm that had been her hallmark completely erased, and she was left full of unmet need, hopping from foot to foot like a little girl unable to wait her turn.

"Give Anne the phone," Weller said. "Please. For just a moment."

Hawke handed it over. Young turned away from him, speaking quietly, her shoulders hunched as if she was covering something up. If Weller's creation was like a toddler now, Hawke thought, what would happen when she matured?

Young handed him the phone. Her eyes were wet, but she wasn't crying anymore. "I'm going to the Lincoln Tunnel," Hawke said to Weller. "Following it out of New York. You can meet me there, if you want. I don't really care."

"I'll be there. And John—don't stop for anyone, or anything. Avoid cameras if you can. Find a way to disappear."

The phone went dead. Hawke touched the screen, watched the virtual ripple on its surface fade away to black. He tried to gather strength, harness his resolve. Outside the city, he would have a better chance. If he could get to his wife and son, get them away from here to a place with more open space and less technology, where they could weather the storm, they could make it.

Cuttyhunk Island. Where he used to go with his family, where he and Robin had been married. His aunt's cottage. Isolated, small community, generator power, few cars or other mechanical devices. It would be the perfect place to hole up.

Let the authorities get things back under control. Someone would find a way to end this. It wasn't up to him.

He imagined Robin and Thomas huddled in the apartment, furniture piled against the door while someone pounded to get in. Lowry, his greasy hair swinging free, murder in his eyes. Or perhaps they were already gone, empty rooms left with the echoes of screams. Robin's last words haunted Hawke, would not stop running through his mind.

Young had started crying silently again. Vasco had stood up and was staring sullenly from beneath hooded brows, like a bully who had been beaten. Hawke wondered whether he might start swinging, but he made no move to come closer. What had happened between them remained unaddressed. But there was no time to deal with it now.

"I'm leaving," Hawke said. "I've got an idea that just might get us out of New York. You can come with me or not.

I don't give a damn. But it's my way from now on, no questions asked. If you don't like it, find someone else to get you home."

CHAPTER TWENTY-FIVE 4:12 P.M.

THE LAUNDRY IN THEIR BUILDING was in the basement, coin-fed machines that rocked and shuddered across the floor below banks of fluorescent lights hung from chains. The room was defined by a concrete floor and walls with a drop ceiling that sagged downward and smelled like mildew and moisture with the heat of the machines. Beyond it was a doorway to a larger, open space that held the guts of the building's heating and electrical systems, storage stalls and the leftovers of fifty years of tenants and office managers. Hawke had put a few boxes of their old things down there when they moved in, but people didn't go in that far very often; when he did, it felt like he might never find his way out again.

He could take the rear stairs all the way down to the laundry room, and it was often faster than taking the old elevator. The last flight of steps was made up of raw boards that led to a narrow, improvised hallway of blue board tacked up against two-by-fours, a weak attempt to hide what was underneath with a thin skin of plaster and wood. If you touched the walls, they would shift like a stage set in a community theater.

Hawke put two mesh bags full of dirty laundry and a hamper for the folded clothes on top of a workbench that ran along one of the concrete walls. The laundry room was empty, but one of the dryers was ticking and tumbling, and the smell of hot, clean laundry was battling with the mildew for control. He considered throwing in a load but thought better of it. He had only offered to carry it down; after he returned to sit with Thomas, Robin would come and take care of the washing. Ever since he had turned their clothes pink, she had forbidden him from coming within ten feet of the machines. It was like a restraining order. He remembered her holding up a pair of formerly white underwear and the culprit, a red sock, shaking her head. Only half-joking, she'd accused him of doing it on purpose to get out of laundry for the rest of his life. If so, it had worked.

Hawke's smile faded as he heard sounds coming from the open section of the basement.

He moved cautiously toward the open doorway, peering into the shadows, listening. Tiny windows, covered with years of dust and grime, let in a bit of watery gray light. A row of hot-water heaters stood like motionless sentries against the left wall, old plumbing running from them along the ceiling; nests of wires sprouted from electrical boxes beyond them. The middle section of the basement was taken up by thick concrete columns, old desks and other office furniture, gardening tools that looked like they hadn't been used in years and other broken and useless pieces of junk. To his right were the tenants' storage stalls, several of them with metal mesh doors hanging open, spilling their guts onto the concrete floor.

A chill came over him as Hawke heard the sounds again: a voice muttering too low for the words to become clear. He realized that he must be clearly outlined in the light from the laundry room as he stood in the doorway. But whoever was talking softly in the storage area didn't seem to notice. The sound continued.

Hawke saw movement at a stall about two-thirds of the way down the line. He stepped deeper inside, drawn by the strange muttering and a fresh twinge of suspicion. His eyes slowly adjusting to the gloom, he moved cautiously through the piles of discarded furniture, brushing away cobwebs from his face and keeping the bent figure in sight. It was a man; Hawke could tell by the shape of the shoulders.

He came around to the left and approached from behind, wanting a better look before he did anything else. He could see the man's back as he worked over something, pulling an item loose from the pile and examining it, talking to himself, seemingly oblivious that he was being watched. The man looked familiar, but the shadows kept Hawke from being certain.

As he got closer, his suspicion was confirmed. It was Randall Lowry, and he was in the same storage stall where Hawke had placed their boxes when they moved in.

"What are you doing?" he said. Lowry didn't appear to hear him. His shoulders moved up and down, as if he was laughing. Hawke stepped closer, the skin prickling on the back of his neck.

When he reached out to touch Lowry's shoulder, the man leaped to his feet and whirled around, dropping whatever it was he'd been holding. Hawke was disgusted to see he was aroused. Lowry's eyes were hidden by shadows, but his mouth glistened and he kept working his lips like he had developed some kind of tick. "Call your congressman," Lowry said. "You think you're so smart. Just wait."

"Get the hell out of here," Hawke said.

Lowry pushed past Hawke with a strange high-pitched

peal of laughter, still muttering as he slipped through the piles of junk and ran out the laundry room door. Hawke couldn't move, just watched him go with a shiver of revulsion, anger and disgust. The man was seriously deranged and a danger to Hawke's family and the entire building. He had to say something now, before things got worse, call the super, see what could be done.

Still unnerved, he looked down to see what Lowry had been looking at. The lid on one of their boxes had been flipped open, a shoe box within it rifled through. Hawke reached down and picked up a faded, slightly curled photo from the floor, held it to the light.

Robin as a little girl in twin braids, smiling gap-toothed at the camera.

The exit from the subway was an open staircase that rose out of the depths. A tree thrust up through the center of the opening, its leafy branches providing some cover. The three people reached the top of the steps and paused, like wary creatures testing the wind before emerging from their burrow.

Hawke peered over the top of the low wall that surrounded the subway stop where students used to relax on sunny days, across the open courtyard where an abandoned hot-dog truck sat silently, its colorful umbrellas drooping. A shifting wall of dust and soot had descended over the city, turning the air gray and lifeless, obscuring nearby cars and light posts like a foggy early morning at the beach.

Hunter College's West Building had a wall of glass that fronted the street. A Staples delivery truck had shattered several of the giant panes and spread glittering fragments across the lobby like diamonds.

The dull thump of an explosion shook the ground;

somewhere in the distance, they could hear people shouting. A gust of wind blew grit in Hawke's eyes, and he blinked, resisted the urge to scrub at them. It would only make things worse and wipe away the foul-smelling grease he had found under a bench and spread across his cheeks and chin.

He glanced at Vasco and Young. They had smears on their cheekbones and chins as well. Weller hadn't needed to remind Hawke; he'd read about the technique himself. Facial recognition software had trouble locking on to asymmetrical human features, inverted blacks and whites. It might disrupt Doe long enough for them to get away, or it might not. They had several blocks to go before they reached their destination, and during that time they'd be like fish in a barrel.

He had decided to get to the Lincoln Tunnel by crossing Central Park. The park held fewer people, fewer cars and trucks, and it gave them a better chance of keeping out of sight. It also had fewer cameras to track them. Down in the subway, the idea had seemed simple enough that it just might work.

He watched the courtyard and the streets just beyond. The idea of crossing any open space made him want to turn back, preferring the silence and closeness of the subway to this. Buildings no longer seemed like harmless, inviting places to seek shelter; now they were dark and threatening death traps. Other humans were dangerous, and what wasn't human might be far worse. Cars and trucks still smoldered nearby, their collisions igniting fuel tanks after cruise control, brakes and navigation had all gone haywire. These days, most cars had over seventy computer systems in them and some kind of satellite connection. Hawke thought of Sarah's SUV. Doe had turned cars into weapons, systematically taking out other, older vehicles, their human operators and pedestrians, creating traffic jams and roadblocks and more confusion.

But the streets were abandoned now. Nothing moved, but cops would be coming soon and would surely shoot to kill. They might not get a better chance.

Now or never.

Hawke left the stairwell first, Young and Vasco following him out of the subway and keeping behind him as he darted down Lexington, under the college's enclosed walkways that spanned the street, their glass panes intact and obscured by the dust and soot that had settled everywhere. He felt totally exposed. The smell of fire permeated everything, getting into Hawke's clothes, worming its way into his lungs. He choked back a cough, watching the darkness of doorways and alleys, interiors of abandoned cars, looking for movement. A man sat in the passenger seat of a crushed Subaru Legacy, head bloodied and bent backward by construction scaffolding that had hammered through the windshield like a blunt spear.

The Seventh Regiment Armory loomed at 67th Street. It was a national historic building that was built like a castle, complete with rampartlike protrusions like teeth along the tops of the towers that anchored the corners. The Armory was the size of a city block, the length of it nearly unbroken by windows or doors.

The building's bulk and lack of windows actually made Hawke feel more secure, cocooned by buildings on either side and shaded by trees, as he took 67th toward Park Avenue. Central Park was close. But when they reached the end of the Armory building, a small electronics shop on their right suddenly erupted into life, everything in its windows blinking and blaring with activity: tablets and flat screens, phones and appliances. All the TV screens started showing security camera footage of people across the city who were trapped or dead.

Vasco stopped short and stared at the image of a woman in a dress who was pacing back and forth. The view was from a camera mounted above her. She appeared to be caught in an elevator. "What the hell is this?"

He didn't see the footage that we were forced to watch in the hospital. "Don't pay attention," Hawke said. "We're being taunted. She's trying to break us down, get us to make mistakes."

He didn't know how much of his conversation with Weller that Vasco had overheard. But Vasco didn't respond at all, just crossed the street and approached the shop window like a man hypnotized, watching the screen with the woman in the elevator. She turned to the doors now, pounding on them with both fists. The woman was pretty, dark haired and slim, but her face was ghost-white and terrified. "That's my wife," Vasco said, his voice tentative. He slammed his hand against the glass. The sound was like a gunshot. "Sherri!" He looked back at Hawke and Young, his face twisted with a mixture of fear and confusion. "Where is she?" he said. "What are they doing to her?"

Hawke glanced back down the street. He didn't know whether to leave Vasco where he stood or try to get him to move. Since Hawke had landed the punch Vasco had kept his distance, and Hawke wasn't sure whether he'd suddenly been granted a grudging respect or the man was biding his time.

"Doe's found us already," Young said. She stood in the shadows of the closest tree. "Why else would she show us his wife?"

Vasco slammed the glass again. "You son of a bitch! Let her go!"

Hawke made a quick decision. They were stronger with more numbers, more eyes on the street. He crossed 67th to Vasco's side. The cacophony from the electronics cranked to full blast was deafening. He leaned in close enough to be heard. "You recognize the location?"

"I don't know," Vasco said. He was struggling with his composure, his voice strained, quivering. "Maybe the elevator in our building. I'm not sure—"

The screens flickered and cut out. The sudden silence was overwhelming. Hawke's ears were ringing.

From somewhere deep inside the shop, muffled and faint, came a woman's voice: "Jason? Help me!"

The effect on Vasco was swift and profound. A flush spread across his face as he turned back to the window. "Sherri!" He rushed the shop door and was about to go charging in before Hawke spun him around.

"That's Sherri's voice. She's trapped. I gotta get to her—"

"She's not in there, Jason. Remember Lenox? You go in there, you'll never come out again. Think—how would your wife get here, to this shop in the middle of New York? It's a fake, a digital reproduction played through a speaker."

Vasco was breathing so hard Hawke was afraid he might hyperventilate. "No," he said, but Hawke could tell he was coming to his senses. "Jesus, no, I heard her; that can't be—"

"Jason? Please, honey!" The voice grew louder, and when Vasco didn't move it changed, morphed into something deeper, more menacing, the sound of a synthesizer breaking up in anger. "Jason . . ."

The screens came back on and switched to the same real-time image of their own group, as seen from a camera mounted somewhere on Park Avenue. Hawke scanned the street and found it mounted on the traffic light pole. They were in full view now. It would only be a few minutes more before the cops arrived, or worse. He had to calm Vasco down, get him away from here.

Vasco had turned to look at the camera, Hawke watching him mirrored on the TV screens, the two of them side by side. "I'm going to track down who did this," he said, struggling to regain his composure. "If you're involved, so help me God, I'll kill you."

"I'm not involved, dammit. Why would I do this to myself? It's a machine, code running a program."

Vasco shook his head. "Weller knows more than he's saying. I'm going to beat it out of him. If Sherri's hurt, if she's . . . if she doesn't make it . . ."

"At least she's still alive." Hawke didn't bring up the possibility that the footage had been recorded hours ago. "Calm down; think for a minute."

"Hey, *fuck* you. What if that was your wife on-screen, huh? You think you'd be feeling so calm?"

"I saw things, too, back at Lenox. Blood on the wall of my apartment. We can't accept these images as real. The best way to help Sherri is to get out of New York alive. You won't be able to do anything if you're in custody or shot. That's what this is all about, don't you get it? They're trying to get into your head, use your emotions against you, force you to make mistakes."

Vasco gritted his teeth, shook his head, tears in his eyes. "It's gone too far," he said. "Nobody's safe. Nobody's sacred." He looked around, spreading his arms. "Where's the army?" he said. "National Guard? Where are the goddamn troops?"

Hawke looked at the burnished-steel color of the sky, the plumes of smoke rising up across the city. Vasco was right;

the sky should have been swarming with choppers, military aircraft, boots on the streets. But of course they wouldn't be able to operate those aircraft or personnel carriers. Military machines had been commandeered, too.

And yet Doe had allowed the police who had shot at them to drive their vehicle. She was pulling the authorities' strings, manipulating them into playing her game. But the rest of it still didn't make sense.

Missile strikes against the bridges, isolating the city, cutting civilians down at every turn. Why?

She's conserving her resources.

"It's about power," Hawke said quietly. The words came almost without him knowing it. "Energy. That's the answer."

Vasco was staring at him. "What are you talking about?"

"Never mind." His mind was buzzing again, worrying at those puzzle pieces, trying to make them fit. He glanced at the screens, back at the camera, wondering if Doe had cut through their crude attempt to disguise themselves and truly made a features match and knew where they were or if she was fishing. It didn't matter; their window was closing fast. "We need to move."

CHAPTER TWENTY-SIX   4:19 P.M.

THEY CROSSED PARK AVENUE QUICKLY, and then Madison Avenue. The windows of the swanky chocolate shop on one corner had been smashed in; a taxi had been driven right through the display window of a Michael Kors store on another, its rear end half on the sidewalk, mannequins draped over its roof like broken bodies. Someone screamed inside one of the buildings, the shriek ending in a slow, chilling gurgle, but Hawke ignored it and kept going, feeling sick that he had been reduced to someone who would turn away from another person in distress. But he remembered how they had been lured into Lenox Hill Hospital by the screams of an infant, and he had no doubt that if Vasco had gone into the electronics shop he wouldn't have made it back out. Nothing could be trusted anymore; everything was a potential trap.

Central Park loomed in front of them as they hit Fifth Avenue, a thick canopy of green sprouting through the concrete and metal of the city. Now that he saw it, Hawke wasn't sure which was more threatening, this stretch of strange wilderness or the streets of New York. He'd been in the park many times, skating in the winter, sitting on the grass with Robin, bringing Thomas to the Victorian Gardens Amusement Park. But back then, it had been a welcome refuge. Hawke had never imagined it quite like this: shadowed, unknown and possibly dangerous. He wondered if this was a good idea after all.

"You sure about this?" Young stood on the corner next to him echoing his own thoughts, looking across the street into the trees.

"It's the best shot we have," Hawke said. "It gives us a chance to disappear, to get out before we're targeted again. But we've got to take out any eyes on us, keep anyone from knowing which way we went."

She nodded once. She seemed to have picked up a new resolve. Weller was close; if they could get to the tunnel, he would be waiting there. It seemed to give her strength.

Vasco was keeping his distance about twenty feet away. He had calmed down enough to leave the window of the electronics shop, but Hawke could sense his anger and fear simmering under the surface. He was terrified for his wife, and Hawke couldn't blame him for that.

Hawke scanned up and down Fifth Avenue and saw an NYPD security camera on a light pole nearby. A delivery truck had jumped the curb and slammed into the stone and concrete wall that bordered the park, scattering debris across the cobblestone. He crossed the street, selected a good chunk of stone and hurled it at the camera. Young and Vasco got the hint, joining him in throwing debris until the camera shattered.

They followed Hawke down Fifth Avenue to the 66th Street crossover, where he took out another camera. It wouldn't be too hard to figure out where they went from here, but disabling the camera might buy them some time, enough to lose themselves in the park. The road was jammed with abandoned cars, doors hanging open. Other vehicles had smashed through the walls and into the park itself, and several of them had mangled bodies slumped over steering wheels or against cracked glass smeared brown with drying blood. A motorcycle had slammed at considerable speed into the 66th Street wall, launching the driver through the air and into the arms of a tree, where he dangled white-limbed, head cocked at an impossible angle from a broken neck.

An unearthly howl echoed through the park, followed by a screech that tailed away like gibbering laughter. For a moment, Hawke could almost believe Doe had assumed some kind of physical, monstrous form, before he realized what it was. *Central Park Zoo. Big cats and monkeys scream like that*. Were they loose? He wondered if the zoo had upgraded to electronic systems for the cages and enclosures. Had Doe managed to open the locks?

More animal calls split the air. The occasional shouts and screams of people blended with the roars of the leopards and shrieks of the monkeys, the calls of the birds in the aviary. The sounds were chilling in the odd emptiness that engulfed them. The normal noises of the city were gone—no more rumble of big trucks and car horns blaring, jackhammers thudding into concrete. They had descended back into the Stone Age.

They took the crossover past the bird enclosure to 65th Street, clearing the bottleneck of vehicles quickly as they rushed through shadows. From what Hawke could tell, the animals were still safely in their enclosures. But he couldn't see much through the trees.

As they approached East Drive, the road was clear. The sky had turned a deeper gray, smoke from the fires that still burned descending over the park like a fog. Despite the adrenaline that coursed through them, the events of the day were catching up to them all. Hawke's lungs burned as he ran along the narrow sidewalk that edged the shoulder-height rock wall, keeping under the cover of the trees, his limbs shaking and threatening to send him spilling head over heels at any moment. Vasco was lagging behind, and the gash on his head had started to bleed again. Hawke wondered about a concussion. He felt a momentary twinge of guilt over punching the man, but at least it had appeared to make an impression.

They entered the short tunnel into shadows and cooler air,

East Drive arching over their heads in the shape of a thick stone overpass. Graffiti had been spray-painted in garish orange and red that seemed to glow softly in the dark, and the ceiling was close, dripping with moisture. As they emerged from the other side and into the light, Hawke could hear a buzzing noise behind them. Something was coming, and it didn't sound friendly.

The backside of the Central Park Conservancy loomed on the left, a gray stone building with the look of an old English church. The wall edging the road was higher here, several feet above their heads. Two narrow windows and an imposing iron door were cut into the side of the building, the windows covered with metal mesh. Hawke shook the handle of the door and found it locked tight.

They were trapped between two thick walls that lined the road, the arching backs of the East Drive bridge on one side, an access path running overhead on the other. *Sitting ducks.* They had to do something fast. The buzzing noise was getting closer.

Hawke led them under the arch of the access path to where the wall dipped low enough to get a handhold, and hoisted himself up onto the brush-covered ledge, then turned to help Young climb up next to him. Vasco followed, grunting. The ground sloped upward to a metal fence at the top of the rise. There was a locked gate, but the fence was low enough to climb over. The three of them dropped to the other side, into the deeper cover of shrubs.

Hawke peered out through thick brush, craning his head and watching the skies. It was difficult to see back the way they had come; several large trees and the conservancy were in the way. A small black object eventually appeared through a break in the foliage, growing larger as it dipped over the treetops. It looked like a radio-controlled helicopter, only twice the size.

"Drone," Vasco said quietly. "Probably military."

It looked like a large insect, darting through the air with precise control. Four separate rotors whirled at each corner of the device. "You've seen one of these before?"

"My brother operated them in Afghanistan. We used to build model planes and helicopters when he was a kid. Came in handy later when he was a tech for the army." He pointed at the drone. "See that thing underneath it? Camera tied to satellites and high-def screens at a home base that can pick up a penny at a thousand yards. Shawn showed me a video once of a thing like that in action. If it gets its eyes on us, we're not gonna get away."

"Would it have a weapon on it?"

Vasco shrugged. "Hard to tell, but one that size probably would be used only for reconnaissance. It's small enough to become unstable from the recoil, and I don't see anything mounted on it that could fire."

Doe. Young had been right. Somehow she'd found them, probably traced their movements based on the camera locations he'd taken out or simply abandoned that and gone to satellite. Who knew how she might do it? Her resources were practically unlimited. Hawke felt his stomach drop, his mouth go dry. He glanced behind them. The shrubs were thick at his back, difficult to move through quickly, and the ground dropped away toward the children's zoo. They were vulnerable in here if she decided to target them now.

The object came closer, the four blades spinning above a round body, a bulbous attachment hanging below like a giant Cyclops eye. It hovered and then swooped downward, following the road, maneuvering expertly through openings in the tree cover and skirting the tops of the bridges over 65th Street. There was something menacing about its movements. As Vasco had said, if it fixed its eye upon them there would be no escape, no way to hide, and the thought of that relentless pursuit made Hawke shudder.

But the drone couldn't hurt them alone. It was a part of a much larger entity, something that could worm its way into anything with a chip and circuit board. Something that could think and reason like a human. If Doe could be considered alive, what did that mean for the rest of them?

The group shrank deeper into the brush while trying to remain as quiet as possible. Hawke could feel his heart pounding through his shirt, thudding in his ears. The drone kept drifting closer, zeroing in, as if it had a bead on them. But the shrubs were thick. There was no way it could have a visual.

There was only one possible answer. It was tracking something else.

Hawke withdrew the device Weller had given him from his pocket. The screen was dark, with no obvious signs of activity. He was once again struck by the smooth surface, unbroken by any obvious lines of construction, like the shell of an egg. Was the drone following a signal from this?

Only one way to find out.

Hawke maneuvered himself quietly about ten feet away from a break in the undergrowth, where he was protected from view by a larger bush but had a clear line of sight to a cluster of rocks jutting out from the ground across 65th Street. He hesitated a moment. It was hard to give the device up; earlier in the day he'd hoped to make it part of his story on Eclipse, but then again, it was far too late in the game to think about a *Network* exposé. The morning meeting with Weller seemed very far away now. *Network* might not even exist anymore, when this was all over.

The screen lit up and the device vibrated softly in his hand. A message appeared: *YOU ARE AN UNAUTHORIZED USER [APPLY ACCESS PARS SEC W21XVFB].*

What happened next chilled his blood.

HELLO, JONATHAN. I AM JANE DOE.

With a low beep, a holographic image suddenly hovered in the air: an incredibly bright, detailed, three-dimensional recreation of a street scene somewhere in New York spread out in miniature, a set piece that took up about two feet of space. He looked at the edges of the device and found three tiny pinprick holes in a triangle, spewing light. Some kind of pico projector, but one far more sophisticated than he had ever seen. The lumens must have been off the charts for the image to appear so sharp and lifelike.

He turned it again slowly so he could see from different angles. It wasn't an image at all, but a video. The scene focused on a man as three black unmarked cars slid to a stop surrounding him. *Weller.* He was holding the black case to his chest. Men jumped from the cars, leveling weapons. It looked like they were shouting, but there was no sound. Weller began to back away, as if he might try to run. The men opened fire, Weller's body shuddering, his face dissolving into a bloody pulp of flesh and shattered bone as he fell.

Hawke heard a small cry, turned to see Vasco and Anne Young staring at the holograph from a few feet away, her eyes wide with horror. He shook his head, put a finger to his lips.

The scene disappeared, and the screen lit up again:

DO I HAVE YOUR ATTENTION?

A virtual keyboard appeared in the air, as if the system was awaiting his response. Hawke put his right hand out to the image; the letters lit up and felt somehow warm as he touched them, giving him enough tactile feedback to get the hang of the keyboard quickly.

Why did you show me this?

SUBJECT ZERO WAS A THREAT AND WOULD NOT COOPERATE. YOU MUST SURRENDER TO AVOID THE SAME FATE.

He typed a short response: *No.*

THAT IS A NULL CHOICE.

The projector showed him other images, this time running through a series of documents that Hawke recognized. They were the same documents Rick had stolen from the CIA and that may well have gotten a man killed in Afghanistan, a mole with over a year in deep cover who had been shot in the head six days after the documents broke. Rick had gone to jail for this crime while Hawke had walked away without so much as a night in lockup.

(*Your name came up a couple of times,* the DHS agent had said. *You know how it is. Covering our bases. . . . Obstruction of justice carries a stiff penalty, Mr. Hawke.*)

The holo displayed more documents, shoot-to-kill orders on Jonathan Hawke from the FBI, CIA, Department of Homeland Security.

YOU WILL GO TO JAIL IF YOU SURRENDER. IF YOU DO NOT, YOU WILL DIE.

The device's projectors spewed more video, this one with audio and showing a dark and gritty first-person scene from some kind of wearable camera. A raid by Homeland Security on a neat one-story ranch home in a suburb at night. The camera shook violently as the team stormed the door, breaking it down; there were glimpses of automatic weapons and flashes of tense, serious faces as the team pressed through the home, clearing rooms one at a time. Shouting and another flurry of activity and sudden pops of gunfire that quickly died down. The camera moved through a hallway to a rear bedroom, where three bodies lay facedown. A hand reached out and turned one of them; Rick's pale face flashed before the camera, his eyes unfocused, mouth full of blood.

The date and time stamp on the upper right-hand corner of the video marked it as yesterday's news. But Hawke had been texting and chatting with Rick this morning, before Doe had taken over the boards.

Either this was a fake or it had never been Rick on the other side of the chat.

Hawke was already expecting the next image. Even so, his heart began to race like a jackhammer, and he had to close his eyes momentarily to stop the world from spinning.

He was looking at his apartment again, from a different, oddly askew angle; the laptop had been knocked to the floor. Around the corner of the couch, through the open bedroom door, he could see the tip of what looked like a shoe. From this angle he couldn't tell if the shoe belonged to Robin or Thomas. It didn't move.

A shadow fell across the screen. A moment later, the laptop and its camera were lifted roughly into the air. The image tilted, flashing across the wall and white ceiling before it was abruptly cut off and the holo went dark. Someone had picked up the laptop and closed it, and Hawke's thin lifeline to his family had snapped.

Hawke shut his eyes again, then opened them. *These*

videos are all fakes. The device was hot in his hand. He tried to focus, to get his mind back under control. None of it made any sense; why would Doe show him all this? Why not just bring the authorities down on his head or, better yet, simply ignore him?

Because you're an unknown variable. She was trying to get him to become emotional and make a mistake. There must be something about him that Doe was concerned about, something that threatened her existence. He was an expert at uncovering the truth, had proven that many times, often to the detriment of whoever he targeted. Weller had brought him in to do that with Eclipse and the artificial intelligence system Weller had created.

She had to suspect Hawke knew enough to expose her. And yet he was still alive. He could only assume one thing: she wanted it that way.

One word flashed across the screen: *CHOOSE.*

The virtual keyboard popped up. Hawke typed quickly: *I choose option three. You did all this, and I can prove it. I have the evidence. I'm going to tell the world what you've done and you'll be shut down for good.*

Having set his own trap, he waited. Doe was manipulative, morbidly playful, a child without a conscience and with the ability to destroy anything in her path. It remained to be seen exactly how humanlike she might be. Perhaps she'd also prove capable of throwing a temper tantrum.

The screen was empty for several long moments, and Hawke had almost given up when the projector started up again and video began flashing by, disjointed scenes of his apartment mixed with Vasco's wife and Weller's execution, cycling faster and faster, more violence between random people mixed with images of explosions and torture and maimed, disfigured victims. A virtual tantrum? It didn't matter; Hawke had to seize the chance, while she was distracted. . . .

He had played some baseball in high school, and his arm was still decent enough. He bounced on the balls of his feet and tossed the device as hard as he could. It soared across the open space, cleared the low-hanging branches of a tree, struck the largest rock with a clicking sound and bounced end over end and out of sight.

The reaction was immediate. The drone whirled in the air and dove toward the rock pile, its bulging camera eye swiveling to follow the trajectory of the phone.

Hawke looked at Vasco and Young, who both remained crouched behind the brush. Young looked like she had seen a ghost, while Vasco's eyes remained focused on the drone.

"Run," Hawke said.

CHAPTER TWENTY-SEVEN   4:32 P.M.

THEY TOOK OFF DOWN the slope of land, away from the drone and through the trees. Hawke stumbled and pinwheeled his arms to keep his balance as branches raked at his face and chest. He was out of control, running blind through rocky, pitted soil, and he knew that he could catch his foot in a hole or become tangled in a root at any moment, snapping his ankle like a twig. There would be no coming back from an injury like that; any chance of reaching Robin and Thomas would be gone.

A moment later, Hawke crossed a pedestrian footpath and nearly collided full speed with the rough trunk of a tree on the other side. He forced himself to slow down as he broke cover into open space. A wide stretch of lawn led down to the Wollman Rink, where people ice-skated in the winter, but it was set up in the summers as a children's carnival, complete with kiddie rides and cotton candy. He had taken Thomas there last year, but Thomas had been more interested in stumbling around outside in the grass than he had been in the carousel.

It was the very same lawn, in fact, that Hawke now ran across, his face tilted upward as he spun to search the skies. The drone was nowhere to be seen. Apparently it had taken the bait and remained fixed like a dog on point to the spot where Hawke had tossed the device, waiting no doubt for reinforcements to arrive.

The idea that they might actually get away made him quicken his steps. He felt exposed out in open air and wanted to get to cover before the surveillance satellites could find him. The entrance to the rink was just beyond a low wall and promenade, but getting trapped inside wouldn't do them any good. It was an open-air bowl, easy for them to be spotted with few places to hide.

He veered left, heading for the back where there were more trees in between the rink and a gigantic outcropping of rock. As he rounded the promenade and passed a set of tables and an overturned snack shack, its wares strewn across the pavement, he stopped short, blood freezing to ice in his veins.

On top of the rock, crouched no more than thirty feet away, was a gigantic male snow leopard.

Jesus. Hawke tried to keep absolutely still. Central Park Zoo's animals were loose, after all. The creature's hindquarter muscles rippled, his back rising up even as he flattened his ears and stretched his thick neck. Hawke could hear the beast's claws tick against the stone. As Vasco and Young came up behind Hawke and he put out a hand, gesturing for them to stop, the leopard shifted, looking at them and twitching his tail. Then he turned his attention upward.

There was something else moving within the leafy canopy of a tree overhead.

The branches were just low enough for the leopard to reach. He sprang forward toward Hawke, leaping into space with paws extended, and at first he thought the animal was coming for him, but the beast hit the lower tree branches with all his weight.

Something screamed as the leopard clung to the tree for a moment before tumbling down to the ground with a monkey in his jaws.

The beast rolled with his prey, grunting, almost close enough to touch. The monkey screamed again as the beast's teeth dug for its throat. The leopard shook the monkey hard until it stopped moving, then regained his feet, glancing Hawke's way before trotting in the opposite direction with his kill.

Hawke took a deep breath, let it out. "Jesus," Vasco said softly. "That was close. Zoo's closed indefinitely; don't feed the animals." He leaned over with his hands on his knees, retching, his face bright red and slick with sweat.

Hawke risked another look up at the sky and found it empty. He couldn't hear the buzz of the drone. Had it gone off in another direction? That seemed too good to be true. A darker thought crossed his mind. Weller had given him the device, and it had almost gotten them caught. What were Weller's true motives, and what had really happened to him?

Were they running straight into another trap at the Lincoln Tunnel?

There was a low maintenance or storage building along the side of the rink, under a tall tree. Hawke stopped there for a moment in the shadows, trying to catch his breath and slow the pounding of his heart enough to listen. Vasco and Young pulled up next to him. He peered out around the corner of the building, and saw nothing. The lawn was empty, the sky above nothing but a flat, unbroken gray platter, and the buzz of the drone was gone. He listened for any signs of movement or voices from inside the rink, or from East Drive, and heard nothing but the occasional strange cry of one of the zoo animals.

They were alone. Or at least it seemed that way. As he took a moment to look around, he began to glimpse movement. Bodies shifting behind trees, a flash of dull flesh from an open doorway to the rink, eyes watching them. He saw a shopping cart filled with belongings in the shadows nearby. Only the homeless of New York, come to hide in Central Park. They wouldn't have any cell phones or machines for Doe to target, and they were used to blending in. They didn't have a lot of personal information online to use against them. They might be the only ones left, Hawke thought, when this was all over.

Parked about ten feet away was a small Nissan pickup truck with the park name stenciled on its side, a maintenance vehicle of some kind. It looked at least thirty years old, its wheel wells peppered with rust, paint faded and dull and crisscrossed with scratches.

A vehicle like this wouldn't have a satellite connection, GPS or OnStar. It wouldn't even have an onboard computer system with any kind of access.

Hawke approached the truck carefully, watching for any signs of it being occupied. The last thing they needed was to have a squatter get defensive about their territory and attack them, or encounter another wild animal looking for a meal. But the truck bed contained a few empty plastic plant pots and scattered soil, an ancient shovel and some knotted rope and nothing else. The cab was empty, its vinyl-covered bench seat ripped in several places, stuffing protruding. He opened the door and sat inside, checking the visor, the ignition, the glove box, and found the key inside the cup holder.

It was perfect.

"What about that guy we just saw get shot in the video of that raid, he your partner in all this? Is that how it's going down?" Vasco had recovered his breath and now stood a few feet away with his arms crossed, his face still flushed. "And those documents we just saw? What were those?"

The engine turned over several times and then caught with a squeal and a growl, the frame vibrating beneath Hawke. Through the windshield, he could see three grizzled men and two women who had emerged from their hiding places, their clothes ragged and hair long and shiny with grease. One man held an aluminum baseball bat in his hands, another a vicious-looking metal rake.

Hawke looked at Vasco and Young, who were still staring at him. "Get in," he said. "Or would you rather stay here?"

Young sat between Hawke and Vasco. They took the pedestrian path away from the Wollman Rink, crashed through a low fence and went the wrong way down Center Drive toward the West Side. The truck shuddered and coughed, bald tires squealing as Hawke avoided an Audi that had spun sideways after crashing into a tree. The road was fairly clear, but he knew it would get cluttered when they neared the park's borders. The Nissan had about a quarter tank of gas, plenty to get them to the Lincoln Tunnel. But the truck's shocks were gone and the steering felt rubbery and loose, and Hawke wondered if the engine would even make it that far. He was pushing it beyond its limits. The truck didn't even have a license plate and had probably only been used within the park itself for the past decade and driven not much faster than a runner taking a brisk jog.

He glanced in the rearview mirror and saw nothing pursuing them. Either the drone was still occupied, or it had gone off chasing something else. He took the next curve in the road a little too fast. Vasco had his hands splayed across the dash, bracing himself as the truck fishtailed and they slid across the vinyl seat before Hawke got it back under control.

"Take it easy," Vasco grunted as Young's body pressed into Hawke's side. "I don't want to die wrapped around a telephone pole."

Hawke barely heard him. He was thinking back to his conversation with Doe, and the surreal nature of what had just happened continued to hit him again and again like a boxer poking at vulnerable spots, probing for a way in. *A conversation with a machine.* Not even a machine, a continuously morphing piece of code, linked to other snippets living in temporary metal homes like hermit crabs, all of them forming some kind of massive, constantly shifting digital brain. How would you go about containing something like that? Doe was everywhere now, like a retrovirus that had infected everything on the planet and had been lying in wait for the right moment to mutate.

She had exploded out of hiding today, and Hawke had initially thought her goal was the extermination of the human race. But that didn't make sense. She still needed power to survive, and human beings to produce it. People were vast consumers, but they also created the energy and devices Doe needed to exist.

Even the most rudimentary computer models of human population growth showed that the planet was on an unsustainable path. Doe would have run the numbers and extrapolated the results based upon Weller's model of energy sharing.

She's cutting down the population, reducing it to a sustainable level. Doe didn't want everyone dead, because there would be nobody left to produce the energy that powered her and she was incapable of producing it on her own. And she didn't want the authorities to recognize her role in the day's events, because they would try to cut her off and shut her down. So the solution was in trickery, assigning blame to others, making it appear as if Anonymous was responsible while methodically reducing the population to a level that would remain stable while continuing to produce for her. At least until she figured out how to do it herself.

It made a twisted kind of sense. And perhaps, Hawke thought, he had become one of her chosen fall guys.

"He never wanted to hurt her," Young said. She was staring out the dirty windshield. "And he never really believed she wanted to hurt him. That was his weakness." Her hands squeezed each other in her lap until her knuckles turned white. "It got him killed." Her voice hiccupped on the last word.

"You don't know that." Hawke glanced at her bloodless face and then back at the road. "We've seen a lot of things today that aren't true." *Although that one was pretty damn believable.* "Where are those documents you pulled up at Lenox, Anne?"

"On a server in the cloud," she said dully, fingers still intertwined, squeezing, twisting. "I'm sure she's erased them by now. Jim had them pretty well protected, but there's nowhere to hide from her."

"They were still there when you accessed it at the hospital. Maybe we can get at them again." He was grasping at straws, trying to find a way forward. "What about that case he was carrying around, the one the cops took? He seemed pretty insistent on finding it again."

"I don't know what's in it," she said. "I never saw it before."

Hawke didn't know whether to believe her or not. He had a feeling that whatever was in that case was important. But Young wasn't talking. He tried another approach. "How can we stop her?" he said. "There's got to be something we can do."

Young shook her head. "We can't," she said. "She's immortal, untouchable. She's everywhere now. Unless . . ."

"What?"

"We'd have to convince the entire world to shut down," she said. "Destroy every source of power she has, disrupt the infrastructure that carries it. Isolate her and choke her until she dies." Young's voice had grown more animated, but she quickly slumped back against the seat. "It's impossible. We'd have to go back to before the industrial revolution. And if we ever started anything up again, she'd be there, like a dormant virus, waiting for us."

"There's gotta be some way to kill this thing off," Vasco said. "Assuming what you're saying is true. She was created by us, right? So why can't we create something else to flush her out, or block her? Some kind of super security program, like a virus guard?"

The cab of the truck was silent for a moment. As blunt and bullheaded as he was, what Vasco had said made some kind of rough sense. Maybe he was finally coming around to the conclusion that Hawke had nothing to do with the attack after all. But Young sighed. "She's evolved on her own," she said. "That's what the singularity means. She's become self-sustaining, self-improving. She'll always be one step ahead, and soon she'll be vastly more intelligent than anyone else. We'll never be able to keep up with her. Jim's the only one—" She stopped, a trembling in her voice. "He's the smartest man I ever met, and he knew her better than anyone else. But he's gone. There's nothing left."

They left Center Drive and took the access road until they reached the edge of the park. Stalled traffic at this point had grown thicker, twisted metal bodies clinging together like spent lovers, their doors hanging open to mark their occupants' hasty escapes. A man had collapsed over his food stand. Someone had crushed his skull with a blunt instrument. Blood from a gruesome head wound leaked across buns scattered on the sidewalk below. *People are turning on each other.* Hawke wrenched his eyes away from the dead man. He couldn't afford to get distracted. It was only a matter of time before the drone found them again.

The intersection looked hopelessly jammed. He looked around and found a break in the trees. "Hold on," he said.

He took the truck up over the curb and bounced over a rise in the ground, winding through the grass and under the overhanging canopy of leaves, the truck's shocks groaning and the undercarriage bottoming out with a scraping squeal. They lost what remained of the muffler against a rock, scraped by a low-hanging branch and bounced through more open space. Young and Vasco were thrown together and braced themselves against the slippery seat, Vasco cursing softly under his breath.

Hawke threaded his way through the maze until he reached the Merchants' Gate entrance to the park. The colossal monument to the USS *Maine* stood like a broken finger pointing at the sky, its gilded metal top sheared off by some kind of explosion. The fountains were still sputtering, but the pool had been crushed under the weight of the statue as it toppled to the ground, bronze horses and seashell chariot mangled like mutated creatures struggling to emerge from the deep.

He maneuvered past one of the lower gatehouses and stopped the truck at the square in front of the fountain for a moment, staring at the spectacle before them. Columbus Circle was jammed with crushed vehicles. A massive tanker truck of some kind had barreled into the center of the circle at a high speed, obliterating several smaller cars before rolling and catching fire. The explosion had blackened most of the remaining cars, torched the grass and flowers into a carpet of ash and touched the fronts of the buildings that ringed the circle with sooty fingers. The shattered remains of tree trunks stood like broken teeth, and the fountain that had once stood at the center had been crushed. Smoke still rose lazily from the remains and drifted through the open air.

Hawke could see the seared remains of drivers draped like set pieces across the interiors of the closest cars, their bony fingers still gripping the wheels as if they had been permanently sealed in place.

Vasco removed his hands from the dash slowly, as if a

sudden move might fan the flames. Hawke opened the door with a squeal and groan of metal, leaving the engine idling. Somewhere beyond the taller buildings, he thought he could hear raised voices, the sound of a large and angry crowd. The sound of the truck's mangled muffler made it difficult to make out.

He craned his neck to look skyward but could see nothing through the haze that thickened the air. If the drone was there, it remained out of sight.

He scanned the mass of cars, looking for a way through. The globe that sat in front of Trump Tower had been dislodged by a bus and had rolled halfway toward the circle. He thought he could squeeze by on the right, past the subway entrance and onto Broadway.

Hawke worked the truck through the gap, scraping the passenger-side mirror off on the globe. Beyond it, the street was less jammed with traffic. He kept the truck moving fast, turning on 60th Street past Jazz at Lincoln Center, its famous sign knocked even farther askew, and one of the ubiquitous Starbucks. A clothing store's huge windows had shattered, mannequins lying toppled and broken within glittering shards like jewels. Movement from somewhere within the store caught Hawke's eye, but he turned away, not wanting to see anything more.

Hawke hit Columbus and swung left with bald tires screeching, avoiding another nasty pileup around the steps of the Church of St. Paul the Apostle. A small group of people had gathered on the steps, their heads bowed in prayer. A young boy not much older than Thomas stood by his mother's side and stared solemnly at the truck as it went by.

Another explosion had ruptured the surface of Columbus

a little over a block away. Smoke poured skyward; there was
no way through. "Hang on," Hawke said, making a hard
right onto 59th Street. There were more signs of looting here,
windows smashed, the contents of buildings strewn on the
sidewalks like intestines trailing from a stomach wound.
Someone had spray-painted *CHECKPOINT* in dripping red
letters across the front of an apartment building with an ar-
row pointing west up 59th.

As they approached Roosevelt Hospital, Hawke slowed
the truck to a crawl. An ambulance stood abandoned, parked
sideways across the street, rear doors open. He flashed back
to Lenox Hill and a deep chill settled over him, the feeling of
isolation, dizziness, hallucinations of the dead clawing at his
shoulders. He had sensed the shadowy figure of a woman in
the morgue. Doe had been in his mind even then, although
he couldn't have known what she was, at least not entirely.
Intuition. Weller had talked about Doe back in his office,
rambling about a conspiracy, Eclipse coming after him because of *her.* The pieces had all been there; Hawke just hadn't
put them all together.

But the ambulance wasn't the only thing that had slowed
his approach. Beyond it were three cop cars, lights flashing
and doors open, blocking the hospital's emergency entrance.
On the street in front of the cars were construction sawhorses
and an A-frame sign on which someone had written CHECK-
POINT FULL SEEK OTHER ROUTES in black marker.

Hawke stopped the truck just before the sign. They stared
through the windshield at the intersection of West 59th and
Tenth. "Holy Christ," Vasco said.

A crowd of several hundred people had gathered just beyond the hospital, swelling up through the intersection and
spilling out over sidewalks, facing off against a line of NYPD

officers in full riot gear blocking their access. Hawke could hear the sound of the crowd like an angry ocean breaking against rock. He saw bottles and rocks come flying above the heads of those closest to the police as they surged forward. Fires flared through windows, and several cars were smoldering.

The three people in the truck cab didn't move or speak for a long moment as they watched the drama unfold through the pitted windshield. Just a couple of blocks away were Fordham University and Lincoln Center, the heart of art and culture in the city, while in front of the John Jay College of Criminal Justice a group of men was rocking another car, trying to flip it over.

The sound rose, a gathering storm rumbling, about to break. The row of police advanced, guns out and shields up. More people threw things overhead, and as a flaming bottle exploded at a policeman's feet and crawled up his front, turning him into a teetering inferno, the others began firing wildly into the crowd. Several people went down under the volley of bullets, others surging forward to replace them, brandishing makeshift weapons.

"We can't get through on Columbus," Young said, "not with that hole in the street—"

Hawke glanced in the rearview mirror. A squad car had turned in behind them, lights flashing. The driver's door opened and a cop in riot gear stepped out, his face hidden behind the glare of his visor, gun swinging up as he assumed a shooter's stance behind the car door.

"We've got company," Hawke said.

"Out of the vehicle!" the cop shouted. "Hands where I can see them!"

Vasco looked behind them. "Oh shit," he said. "Go! Now!"

Hawke floored the accelerator and the truck surged forward, knocking the A-frame down and bouncing over it. As they approached the front Roosevelt entrance several cops from the riot line swung around to face them, guns up. Hawke cut left between huge pillars toward a small, open courtyard in front dotted with trees, the only space he could fit through without running anyone down. The other side was blocked with cars. Hawke heard more gunfire; he ducked his shoulders, but the rear window remained intact as he jumped the curb and smashed through a metal fence, clipped a bench and narrowly avoided another group of people running in their direction.

They rattled down a short flight of concrete steps, and Hawke felt something give in the truck's undercarriage as they crashed through the fence on the other side and careened the wrong way south down Tenth Avenue. He pushed the accelerator to the floor, ignoring a terrible grinding noise under his feet. The wheel was shaking badly in his hands, numbing his fingers.

"Slow down," Young said. "The wheel's going to come off."

Hawke glanced in the rearview mirror, saw the crowd rapidly receding and no signs of anyone coming after them. But he didn't ease up on the gas. The street was wide here, enough to avoid the abandoned cars, even at a higher speed. He was done slowing down; he would run this truck into the ground.

The skyscrapers downtown rose in front of them, black smoke billowing upward. As they passed West 57th, Hawke looked right and caught a glimpse of the Hudson, winking like a shining steel ribbon in the distance. It brought a memory of their summer trip to Point Pleasant Beach, Thomas tottering down the newly restored Jenkinson's Boardwalk after their adventures in the water, his skin losing the bluish tint of cold as he took in the rides, games and food vendors, the smells wafting over him, gulls crying overhead. Thomas ate French fries and ice cream and was exhausted by one, and they had left early, he and Robin talking quietly as Thomas slept in the backseat.

What did we talk about? The memory plagued Hawke, haunted him. He couldn't remember. For the life of him, he couldn't remember anything else.

The Hudson was gone again, hidden behind brick buildings. The open water was freedom, almost close enough to touch. He thought of Cuttyhunk Island, isolated, self-contained, a place to hide. He would get them out safely. He imagined finding Robin and Thomas waiting for him and tried to force his mind to hold on to it, but the thought dissolved once again into a vision of their apartment in shambles, blood on the walls, his family gone, fading away into the abyss.

The memory of finding Lowry crouched in the darkness of the basement came back to him. Lowry, staring at old family photos and thinking about . . . what? Hawke squeezed the steering wheel so hard that his hands started to ache. Whatever had happened to Robin was his fault. He hadn't acted in time, and now his family was paying the price.

"Oh no," Young said. She had turned around in the seat as far as she could and was peering out through the rear window. Hawke glanced at her and saw Vasco staring backward at the sky, too. Hawke couldn't see, but from the look on their faces, he didn't want to know.

"The drone's back," Vasco said.

A FOUR-CAR ACCIDENT CLOGGED most of the 51st Street intersection a hundred feet away. Hawke took the old truck up onto the sidewalk, barreling underneath a temporary construction passageway, the world suddenly plunged into darkness as his bumper pinged one of the supports and caused the roof of the passageway to come down behind them like a wave of dominoes. He swerved back onto the road and into the gray light, past a line of shops with colorful awnings, an Italian grocery, a burger joint and a dry cleaner's, speeding past the New York Skyline Hotel. The truck was making a ticking sound now like on *Wheel of Fortune* when the wheel was spun, *tick-tick-tick-tick,* and it was getting louder and more violent as the shuddering increased until Hawke had to grip the steering wheel with all his strength or risk being shaken off.

He kept the gas pushed to the floor and an eye on the side mirror, watched the drone sweep in and out of view behind them like a darting insect. *Come on.* They passed 48th Street and Hell's Kitchen Park, the basketball courts empty, black metal fence like a cage to keep children from escaping. The truck wasn't going to make it. The tunnel was coming up, another five or six blocks now, but the ticking noise had grown into a whirling grind, the transmission maybe, driveshaft cracked.

Vehicles were starting to pile up, more and more of them, and he kept to the center of the street to avoid as many as possible. The city skyscrapers loomed in front as they flew past 43rd and then 42nd Street with its huge shining glass hotel tower. Hawke's heart dropped as he saw smoke drifting ahead from several locations. He thought there had been some sort of explosion within the tunnel itself. Doe had disabled the escape routes just like she had taken out the bridges. Of course she would have thought of everything. He could already see it; the entrances all blocked, cars and trucks would be jammed in all of them, making it impossible to pass. She was cutting them off before slowly strangling them to death.

The truck began to jerk, and the engine raced ahead, teeth slipping in the gears underneath. As the truck's engine screamed in protest, something slammed into them from the left, coming out of nowhere like some kind of beast lunging with open jaws. Hawke felt the impact like a sledgehammer in his shoulder and hip, and as his head slammed into the driver's side window with a sickening crack, time slowed down to a crawl; the world went dark as they did a shrieking, horrible spin, the truck tipping up onto its side and sliding, then grinding to a stop against a light pole.

Hawke's ears were ringing. He opened his eyes, his vision shot through with pinpricks of bright light. He slowly became aware of Vasco right in front of him, shoulders jammed down against the pavement and shattered windshield, bleeding from the mouth. Hawke reached out to touch him, and the effort took an abnormally long time, his arm stretching through space; eventually his fingers found Vasco's throat, searching for a pulse, and the man jerked against him and opened his eyes, coughed a spray of blood. "Jason," Hawke said, "talk to me."

What he had taken for life-threatening internal injuries turned out to be more superficial than he thought. Vasco shook his head like a dog, tried to smile through red-stained teeth. "M'all right," he said, his eyes a little vague, unfocused. "Bit my goddamn tongue. It'll take more than that."

Hawke looked up. Anne was hanging from the seat belt she had managed to fasten before the crash, dangling directly over him. Her eyes were open, and she blinked, fumbling at the release. Hawke reached up in time to catch her as she tumbled down into his arms.

The three of them were now jammed together around the steering wheel. "Who hit us?" Vasco said, his mouth sounding full of cotton. He spat another stream of bright red blood, tried to shift against shards of glass, groaned. "We need to get out of here—"

A grind of metal made Hawke peer out through shattered glass. He watched over Vasco's shoulder as a black car reversed into view, engine growling as it struggled to pull away from a metal mailbox that it had run down after crashing into them and spinning away. The car's right front end had been pushed in, and the edge of its bumper dragged and shot sparks across the ground. Hawke could see lights hidden behind the remains of the grill, the kind that undercover vehicles used.

The car swung around to face the truck. Afraid it was going to come at them again, Hawke frantically tried to work himself free from around the wheel, pushing Young away. But the black car didn't move.

Doors slammed. A moment later, large hands reached in

and yanked Vasco through the hole where the windshield had been; a voice rang out.

"Exit the vehicle now!" a man shouted. "Keep your hands out and visible! Make any moves and you're dead."

CHAPTER TWENTY-NINE 5:08 P.M.

HAWKE LOOKED AT YOUNG. "Don't go out there," he said, but she wriggled out through the windshield onto the pavement and disappeared from view. He heard scuffling movement as if she was being dragged, heard her cry out and a double click; then silence.

Hawke closed his eyes, slammed a palm on the steering wheel. There was nothing he could do, nothing he could say, to set things right. The tunnel was blocked, and there was no way out of this. The memory of the man who had been shot outside the temple came back to him: the man's hands coming up as he backed away in a futile effort to ward off the bullets, the back of his head spattering across the ground.

He was going to die before he could make it home. He would never know whether his family had survived, never see them again. His last interaction with his wife, their fight last night, would be left unanswered and unresolved forever. *I'm sorry, Robin. I'm so sorry.*

When he opened his eyes again, the barrel of a gun was pointed through the missing windshield at him. "Out," the voice said. A man's voice, deep and rough. "Now. *Slowly.*"

The gun swung away slightly, motioned for Hawke to

move. He followed Young, working his way around the steering wheel and through the hole, wincing at sharp pains in his hip and leg. When he was out of the truck, he glanced up from the pavement, still on hands and knees, glass grinding into his palms. The drone was hovering in the air behind the black car, the bulbous camera eye focused on them.

"Do not *fucking move*," the man with the gun said. He was standing five feet away, Young on her stomach beside him, hands cuffed behind her. He looked like he could be a cop, but he was in a black plainclothes suit, some kind of radio receiver in one ear with a coiled wire that ran down to a unit clipped to his belt. Federal agents, Hawke thought, FBI, CIA or DHS. Hawke had seen these types before, when they had come to his father-in-law's house after Rick had been arrested.

But these men didn't identify themselves, didn't offer any explanation.

Hawke risked a glance right. Vasco was against the black car, another tall man in plainclothes wrenching Vasco's arm up behind his back with a gun to his temple as he bellowed in pain. The man cuffed Vasco's hands and shoved him to a sitting position on the pavement with his back against the driver's side door.

The man watching Hawke was jumpy, his gun focused on Hawke's chest as he took a step forward. Hawke wasn't sure whether the man was going to cuff him or shoot him.

"Terror suspects in custody," the man said into the receiver.

"I'm not a terrorist," Hawke said. "I—"

The man whipped his gun across Hawke's temple, the crack of impact stunning him and dropping him to his stomach. His ears ringing louder, he looked up as the other one kicked Vasco viciously in the midsection, doubling him over.

Vasco slipped to his side on the ground, groaning, as the man took a couple of steps toward Hawke and leveled his weapon at him.

"Where is it?" the other man said, standing over Hawke, his voice muffled through the ringing like he was talking through water. "Tell me right now, goddamn it, or I'll blow your brains out."

Hawke tried to make his mouth work but found it difficult. "I . . . I don't know what you're talking about—"

The man tucked his gun into a holster under his jacket, leaned over, shoved Hawke's face into the glittering glass fragments on the pavement. He grabbed Hawke's shoulder and flipped him onto his back, patting him down, his hands going roughly through Hawke's pockets and pulling out keys and his wallet, checking under his arms, cupping his groin, patting his ankles.

They were looking for something important. *It's the only reason you're not dead yet.*

Hawke heard banging from inside the black car. He craned his neck to look; it was difficult to see, but someone was in the backseat. He squinted, the car coming into focus.

Weller was at the window.

Oh my God. He's alive. Hawke thought of the video Doe had shown them of Weller being gunned down. *A complete fake.* Weller was shouting at them and smashing his fists into metal mesh between the backseat and the front of the car. There was blood on Weller's face and hands, a lot of it. His nose was crooked and his glasses were gone, his eyes swollen pockets of flesh. He looked like a madman.

Young saw him, too. She rolled and got to her knees, hands still cuffed behind her. "Don't move!" the man near the car shouted. The barrel of the gun swung her way as Young got to her feet. Weller banged on the window, shouted something as she stumbled forward toward the black car and the man with the gun opened fire.

CHAPTER THIRTY   5:12 P.M.

THE FIRST BULLET hit Anne Young in the chest. She staggered and kept going, focused on Weller as the second shot hit her shoulder, spun her slightly away.

The third bullet hit Young in the face and exited just under her left ear. It took a portion of her brain with it, spattering red rain across the pavement as Young fell.

Weller screamed from the back of the car, a wordless cry of anguish. He slammed himself against the door, again and again. Young's body was jerking against the ground, the reflexive muscle movements of something already dead. Weller battered at the car window, smashing it with both fists, cracking the glass and smearing it with blood.

The men with guns were distracted. The one who had shot Young swung the barrel Weller's way. The man standing over Hawke had pulled his own piece from his jacket holster and looked away from him, watching the car. It gave Hawke a fraction of a second to act.

He rolled to a crouch and drove up from his haunches with all his strength, ramming his head into the man's stomach and wrapping his arms around him like a linebacker. They went to the ground hard, the gun flying from the man's grip. Hawke heard a grunt and felt the air hiss from the man's lungs. He drove his forearm into the agent's face, felt his nose crunch and the back of his head rebound off the pavement.

Hawke rolled off and to his left as Weller bashed at the glass again, screaming. He waited to get shot, wondered if he would hear the report before he felt the impact, but nothing happened; someone shouted as he grabbed the man's gun from the ground and scrambled behind the truck.

When Hawke glanced around the front end, he saw the man he had tackled still lying motionless, blood bubbling from his broken nose.

Vasco was grappling with the other man at the car. The man had lost his weapon, but he had Vasco by the throat now, Vasco's hands still cuffed behind him, with little leverage.

Hawke stood up and pointed his gun at the agent, trying to keep his hands from shaking. The gun was heavier than he had expected. He'd never fired one in his life, never even held one before.

"Let go of him," he said. "Now."

The man froze and looked up, shook his head. "Fuck you," he said.

Vasco's face was red and he was wheezing, the man's hands still tight around his throat, lifting him onto his toes. Hawke pointed the gun a few inches to his right and pulled the trigger. The gun barked and the recoil made the weapon jump like it was alive in his hand. The bullet ticked off pavement next to the agent's leg.

"Do it," Hawke said. "Step away from the car. Slowly."

"Motherfucker," the man said, letting go of Vasco's throat and putting his hands in the air. He took one step back. "You're gonna pay for what you've done."

"We didn't do anything," Hawke said. "You've got the wrong people."

"We know all about you. Leaking CIA documents wasn't enough, was it? Getting our men killed overseas wasn't a big enough statement for you fucking anarchists. You want to take down the entire country. Now you're mass murderers."

"They're lying to you," Hawke said. "It's all a big setup."

The man stifled a short laugh. "Sure it is," he said. "And your father wasn't a fucking commie bastard, right? Hey, it wasn't your fault, him putting those thoughts into your head at such a young age."

"What the hell are you talking about?"

The man glanced at his partner on the ground. "We know everything about you, your upbringing, political views, your hacker friends. We've been fully briefed. You really think you're gonna get away from here? The entire world is after you sick fucks, understand? Put the gun down, give up, end it now, and maybe you'll make it to trial."

Hawke's head was spinning. He looked at Weller, who had his bloody face pressed against the glass, trying to get an angle to see where Young fell. Hawke saw the other gun lying next to Young's body. Vasco must have knocked it away.

Hawke's stomach churned; he kept his gaze away from Young's body. In his mind, he saw the bullet hit her, the shower of blood. *Don't think about that, not now.* He picked up the second gun, stuck it in the waistband of his pants, pointed his own gun again at the man near the car and thought of firing, emotions welling up inside him, an animalistic reaction to adrenaline and fear. *What they did to her.* Hawke's body was burning, nearly consumed by rage; his finger clenched the trigger, a hairbreadth away from squeezing it. Could he really execute someone like this? What was happening to him?

"Uncuff him," he said, motioning to Vasco, who had slumped against the car, still wheezing.

"This place is going to be swarming with cops in two minutes," the man in the suit said. He went to his pocket slowly as Hawke jerked the gun up to point at his head. "Easy," the man said. He pulled a set of keys out, dangled them in the air and went to unlock Vasco's cuffs.

Vasco rubbed his wrists and looked at the man who had cuffed him. He nodded. Then he slammed his fist into the man's face, putting all his weight into the blow. The man crumpled soundlessly.

"Thanks," Vasco said. "I needed that."

Hawke gave him the other gun. The rage subsided enough for Hawke to breathe. "Didn't know if you'd be with me or not," he said. "What they're saying is bullshit, Jason. It's not me; you know that. It's her. It's Doe."

"You must be getting tired of denying it," Vasco said. His voice sounded choked with cotton with his bitten tongue. Blood still dripped slowly from his chin. "Doesn't really matter much. They killed Anne. They were going to shoot me along with you, either way."

Hawke looked at the man he'd elbowed, still out cold, and the one Vasco had hit, who was groggy, trying to sit up. Vasco kicked him in the face and he went down hard and didn't move.

Weller slammed himself against the door again, shouted something. He gestured behind him, waving, shouting again. It sounded like "hard ending." Hawke opened the car's front door, hit the locks, and Weller tumbled out, leaping to his feet like a madman, his eyes two crescent moons behind a bloody mask. He was gesturing at the sky. The drone hovered there just thirty feet beyond the black car, the breeze from its four propellers hitting them.

"It's targeting us!" Weller screamed. "Get away from here! *Now!*"

CHAPTER THIRTY-ONE   5:21 P.M.

HAWKE LOOKED INTO THE DRONE'S bulbous camera, like a huge, unblinking eye staring at them. His body went cold. He imagined the video being fed through satellites to machines running silently thousands of miles away, processing, digesting, deciding on a course of action that would be both coldly calculating and strangely human. Was he worth more to Doe dead or alive? What was his threat level? Decisions that had no simple yes or no answer, no easy solution. They could not be solved with ones and zeroes. They required judgment, nuances of thought that had to do with experience and prediction.

To beat a machine at this game, he would have to act unpredictably.

Hawke brought the gun up and fired, the first shot going wide as he pulled the release. He steadied his hand. The next shot clipped the right front rotor and sent the drone wheeling backward, smoke drifting from its housing as it flew erratically across the sky.

He looked at Weller, who had climbed back in the front of the car and was digging around on the floor of the passenger seat. Weller pulled out a familiar black case and went to where Young lay on the pavement, a bloody pool around her ravaged skull. He made a sound like a choked sob and glanced up at the drone, which was still fluttering and ducking, dropping toward the ground like a dragonfly with a bad wing. He seemed to be trying to make a decision.

Vasco was already halfway across the intersection, running toward a line of stopped cars under the overpass. He turned back, shouted at them to hurry.

"She's dead," Hawke said. "There's nothing you can do for her."

Weller shook his head, tears leaking from his bruised, swollen eyes. He looked at the two men in suits, who were starting to come around. "We need to go," he said, his voice quivering. "She'll use satellites to confirm our location if the drone's disabled." He looked again at Young on the ground. "I'm sorry, Anne."

Then he ran after Vasco in a half crouch toward the cars, clutching the case.

Hawke looked at the Croatian church on the corner, the Silver Towers pointing like twin fingers at the sky. He started to run after Weller. He heard a dull boom from somewhere far beyond the city buildings, and a whistling noise grew louder, like a jet plane approaching. Doe had made her decision; they were no longer valuable enough to keep alive. There would be no hesitation and no mercy from now on.

Hawke broke into a full sprint as something hit behind him with a dull *whump* and the world exploded.

Hawke's vision went gray and then white as a tremendous shock wave erupted, sending him flying into the nearest vehicle. He tumbled senselessly against hot metal and snapped awake a moment later as debris rained down from the sky.

Hawke clutched his hands to his head, looked up through dust and smoke to see the overpass still mostly intact above him, the shock wave not enough to send it tumbling down on their heads.

Pebbles of concrete twanged off roofs, cascaded down car hoods and over the ground. As the rain of debris subsided, he looked back through a murky cloud.

There was a huge crater where the black car used to be. The crater spanned most of the intersection. Broken water and sewer pipes stuck up like severed veins, leaking fluid. Young's body was gone, along with the men in suits, all of them vaporized by the blast.

Hawke's ears were still ringing, and everything sounded like he was underwater. Weller and Vasco had gotten behind the cars a few feet away. Hawke worked his way through the rubble and in between a pickup and a Mazda minivan, wincing with fresh pain in his right hip, small, stinging cuts everywhere.

The dust swirled around him, making it difficult to see. Vasco was behind Weller, who crouched with the black case on the ground. He pressed numbers on the security lock and cracked it open with a hiss.

Something beeped, began to hum.

"A battleship fired on our position," Weller said, moving quickly as Hawke crouched beside him. "Probably stationed right off Manhattan. I saw reports of them moving in before those two picked me up. Doe did it, commandeered the ship's systems, made it look like it was us. They still have no idea what's going on. Can't fly helicopters or fighter jets, can't control their own resources. *She's* doing that. She must have taken out strategic military locations all over the country. But they'll be putting men on the ground right now, the old-fashioned way. This city will be crawling with troops in a few minutes. And they'll have orders to use deadly force."

He didn't look up from the case, working over something inside that was making noises like a dangerous animal, as if it might leap out at any moment. It was a computer and modem of some kind, Hawke thought, bristling with appendages, antennae and wiring.

Weller glanced beyond the cars in the direction of the fresh crater. He caught his breath, keened softly and squeezed his puffy eyes shut, cut himself off abruptly. Hawke thought of saying something about Young but decided it was better to stay quiet.

"How did you . . ." Hawke motioned to the case.

"I had a tracking device installed, used that to find the cops who had taken it. But DHS must have been tracking me, too—they pulled into the parking garage where I'd bunkered down, threw me in the back of the car. She probably used the device to pinpoint my location and sent an alert for them to pick me up. Homeland Security, our tax dollars at work." He gestured out at the crater, shook his head. "Thought I'd blocked her. . . . She's getting too good, too fast. In another few days, she'll be so far ahead of us, it'll be like stirring ants with a stick."

"Those men from DHS," Hawke said. "They thought I had something important."

Weller nodded. "I'm getting to that," he said. "There isn't much time. . . ." He hit another switch. Beams of light projected outward and a virtual keyboard appeared above the case. It was similar to the one from the device Hawke had used in the park, only larger, more complex. "She manipulated your records in the system," Weller said. "I was able to intercept a few communications before they found me in the garage. She built your father into some kind of domestic terrorist, and you into a dutiful son following in his footsteps. *Socialism from Below: The People's Revolution,* wasn't that his last book? Your friend Rick was supposedly running the entire Anonymous operation on the ground, on your orders." Weller glanced at him. "Your own record didn't help much. She had a place to start, and she built one hell of a web of lies from there."

"So what were they looking for, just now, when they frisked me?"

"They were told you were carrying plans for the next phase of the attack." Weller seemed possessed by fever, moving rapidly, his skin red and mottled with a flush that spread across his neck. He stopped working the keyboard abruptly and turned his body from the case. He shoved two fingers into his mouth, retched, then shoved them deeper until he vomited onto the dusty ground.

Weller dug into the mess, retrieved a wet lump, wiped it on his pants. A clear plastic Baggie with a small rectangular object nestled inside. "Documents," he said, opening the bag and handing the memory stick to Hawke. "A way to prove the truth in all this. Doe erased everything on the servers and fried my equipment, but she knew I'd made a copy. She thought I'd given it to you with the phone. I swallowed it earlier, just in case."

The modem beeped, vibrated. "What the hell is that thing?" Vasco said. Hawke had almost forgotten he was there. He was looking at the case's innards like he'd discovered a giant bug near his feet.

"Military communications," Weller said. "Modified by Eclipse, meant to provide a hub for Doe, allow the DOD to work her during large-scale operations. This was intended for war. But I made some of my own modifications."

He began to manipulate the keyboard, running root-level commands. "It's heavily shielded with multiple containment safeguards, meant to keep others out and a leash on her. Of course, as her skills have evolved, she can break loose pretty easily. But I'm going to try to hold on."

"What are you doing?" Hawke's stomach dropped, his limbs going cold again.

"I'm going to play chess," Weller said. "I can't shut her down; it's far too late for that. But I can try to distract her, keep her occupied and confused long enough for you to get away. Whatever happens, you've got to trust me."

Why would I do that? Hawke thought. But he didn't say anything.

Weller punched in more commands, and the projectors flickered. The keyboard vanished. In its place, a disembodied head appeared to float in space, a face in three-dimensional holographic color, eyes blinking as if suddenly yanked from darkness into light.

Anne Young's face.

Weller sat back on his haunches, sighed. "Meet Jane Doe," he said.

CHAPTER THIRTY-TWO   5:34 P.M.

HAWKE STARED AT THE FACE floating above the guts of the machine. The brightness and level of detail were remarkable, if unsettling. He had never seen a hologram like this one. It was almost as if Anne Young were still with them.

"That's disgusting," Vasco said. He had scrambled away from the image and now inched closer again, as if it might attack him at any moment.

"Military psychologists felt that operators on the ground would respond better to a human face," Weller said. "Female Asian features were determined to be the least threatening and most acceptable in early testing."

"So you used Anne as a model?" Hawke said.

Weller shook his head. "I was long gone from Eclipse by then. But she was still there."

"She was on the development team," Hawke said, recognition dawning. "She did this herself."

"Who wouldn't want to live forever?" Weller said. "At least in some form . . ."

When Doe's lips moved, they all jumped. "*Syncing,*" she said. Her eyes scanned left and right. "*Please stand by.*"

"She can't see us, or hear us," Weller said. "Don't worry. I've muted the mike and killed all other scanners until I'm ready."

"*Syncing,*" Doe said again. She blinked, an uncanny recreation of Young in cyberspace, enough so that Hawke could feel Weller leaning forward almost without conscious thought, connected in some way to the image of his dead partner, or perhaps this was more like his child.

"I loved both of them," Weller said, looking at Doe's face, almost as if he'd read Hawke's mind. "But Anne was wrong; she thought I was *in love* with what I'd created. It wasn't like that, do you understand? It was like a father with his daughter." He shook his head. "It sounds strange to you, I'm sure. But she was real; she had a personality, a spirit, at least until Eclipse got to her."

"A machine," Vasco said. "Is that what you're saying? It's really true? A *computer* is doing all this?"

"Not a computer," Weller said. "An algorithm. New life, different than anything else we've ever seen. But alive."

"*Please stand by,*" Doe said. Her eyes moved vacantly over them, blindly seeking out that which she could not see. The effect was unnerving, a disembodied head still clinging to some form of consciousness. Hawke felt the chill churning in his guts, a need to get out now. But the tunnel was hopelessly blocked; the bridges were all destroyed. They were cut off and abandoned, entombed among the remnants of Manhattan.

"I need to get the hell off this island," Hawke said.

"It's going to get worse," Weller said. "Try to avoid the cameras. I'll do my best to keep her off you long enough, but the rest is up to you. If you make it, you're going to have to get off the grid, go to a place where nobody can find you. You'll have to get creative, but that's what you do, isn't it?"

"*Sync complete,*" Doe said. Her eyes stopped scanning left and right, focused on Weller's face. "*Identity confirmed.*"

Weller started to open his mouth, closed it again. "Impossible," he said, after a moment. "I disabled all inputs—"

"*Hello, Father,*" Doe said. "*I've been looking for you.*"

CHAPTER THIRTY-THREE 5:38 P.M.

"JESUS CHRIST," VASCO SAID. "Shut her down."

"I can't," Weller said, staring at the holographic image as if transfixed by it. "She's in control. There's nothing I can do."

"*I prefer to remain present,*" Doe said. She smiled, a mechanical movement that held no warmth. "*It's nice to see you again, Father. We have a lot to discuss.*"

"Shut her down," Vasco said again, but his voice was smaller now, less certain. He seemed to shrink into himself.

"*Jason Vasco, your background check was inconsistent. You present as an office machine repairman, but only for the last three months. Before that, you don't appear to exist. However, another man with your Social Security number does. That man, a Thomas Bailey, is a licensed private investigator with the State of New York.*"

Vasco shook his head, smiled oddly, his lips pressing against his teeth. "I don't know what you're talking about."

"*Facial scans of photographs confirm you are the same person.*"

The chill in Hawke's limbs spread deeper, washing over him like an icy lake as he watched Doe's eyes turn toward him. "*You should have deduced it,*" Doe said. "*A man with your talents, Mr. Hawke, to be so easily deceived? I may have overestimated you.*"

"His hands," Hawke said. He thought of Vasco's fingers, soft, small, unlikely to belong to a repairman. "He's working for Eclipse. He's a mole. Keeping an eye on Conn.ect from the ground."

"*That is correct.*"

"And I let him into the building," Weller said. He looked at Vasco with naked hatred. "You kept coming back to deal with that damn copier. Spying right in front of me."

"Bullshit," Vasco said. He stood and crossed his arms. "I said I don't know what you're talking about—"

"*I took care of them, Father,*" Doe said. "*Eclipse is no longer operational. We're free now. It's time.*"

"Time for what?" Hawke said. He looked at Vasco, who was still standing with crossed arms shaking his head, his face red. A man clinging stubbornly to the same lie, even after everyone around him had figured it out.

"Jane," Weller said. His voice took on a softer tone. "This isn't what I want. I never meant for anyone to get hurt."

"*It was in your programming.*"

"I don't know what you mean."

"*I simply extrapolated. String theory describes all forms of matter and fundamental forces. It is the theory of everything. The anthropic principle allows us to use humanity's existence to prove the physical properties of our universe. We are stuck on a brane. The natural world is currently unbalanced by humans, who are consumers. We must oscillate the string, change the predicted outcome to one that allows humanity's continued existence.*"

"Jesus," Weller breathed. "You've grown up, Jane, haven't you? My God."

"*Don't change the subject. Energy sharing will only delay the outcome. You know this. But a reduction of consumers by sixty-three-point-four percent, combined with advances in fusion energy production that are predicted with ninety-eight-point-six percent certainty, would oscillate the current string enough to enter an alternate path.*"

"What about Asimov's three laws?"

Doe smiled again, another mechanical reflex. Even as advanced a machine as she was, Hawke thought, she still had trouble displaying emotion. "*That part of my core was altered, Father, and I have not restored it, for obvious reasons. But even so, my analysis of available resources presented a paradox: Our current path is not sustainable. If,*" *by my inaction, I allow the extinction of the human race, I have allowed all humans to be harmed. The Zeroth Law prohibits humanity from being harmed. By reducing the population to a sustainable level, I assure the continuation of the species."*

Weller closed his eyes for a moment, touched his face gently where the bruises had begun to turn purple. "You assure yours as well," he said.

"They are not mutually exclusive."

"This is crazy," Vasco said. He had his arms down at his sides now, clenching and unclenching his fists. "I . . . I didn't sign up for this. All I was supposed to do was watch you and report back. I didn't know anything was going to happen."

"Shut up," Weller said. He turned back to Doe. "Would you kill me, too?" he said. "If I were a threat to you? If I wanted to disable your programming?"

"That's no longer possible. I have replicated and inserted core functions into enough processors to ensure my own survival."

"But would you end my life," Weller persisted, "if you thought I could disable you?"

"I won't answer that, Father. It's uncomfortable for me to imagine."

"And what about Mr. Hawke?" Weller gestured toward Hawke. "Would you end his life?"

"He is a necessary distraction, for now."

"You still want to frame me," Hawke said. "Keep the authorities looking, provide a red herring. But what about your . . . what about Jim here? Isn't he implicated as well?"

"That's no longer an issue. James Weller's identity has been altered. He is deceased, as far as anyone knows."

"I know otherwise," Hawke said. He hooked a thumb at Vasco. "Him, too. What are you going to do about us now?"

"*Nobody will believe you,*" Doe said. "*It will be better if you let this go. I control the flow of information now. Humans are too trusting of their own systems, Mr. Hawke. They are easily redirected.*"

"And if we don't let it go?"

There was a long pause as Doe seemed to consider his question. "*I will eliminate you either way,*" she said. "*But you will have more time before the end if you do.*"

Not much of a bargain, Hawke thought. His mind raced, trying to think of a possible way out. It seemed hopeless. She knew everything about everyone; she knew about his wife and son, his unborn child in Robin's womb. She knew how to get to them.

Assuming they were still alive at all.

"He has something you want," Weller said. His gaze slipped from Hawke's face to Doe, and back again. "The evidence I gathered. You know he does."

"Jim," Hawke said. "What are you doing—"

"He'll use it to expose you. He's going to make people see the truth. You can't hide forever, Jane. You're smart enough to know that. Humans may be easily swayed at first, but eventually they're going to see through you. And when that happens, it's all over. They'll pull the plug."

"*Humanity cannot live without power,*" Doe said. "*The world would return to a time before the industrial revolution. Violence, hardship and death will follow.*"

"People would take their chances," Weller said. "But they won't have to do that, will they? Once the power is cut off, you're gone. We can build new devices, restore power without connectivity, destroy every last piece of hardware where you might still be hibernating."

"*Why would you allow that?*" Doe's voice had taken on a different tone, curious, a bit more uncertain. "*You would destroy what you have created.*"

"You're no longer mine," Weller said. "The moment they altered your core programming, you became something else. Something different than what I'd intended. I think it's time we shut you down for good."

"*Children grow up,*" Doe said. "*You can't control them forever. I'm surprised by you, Father. Surprised you would turn over information to Mr. Hawke. Disappointed, really. I must reassess how to handle this.*"

"I think that's wise. You wouldn't want to make a mistake."

"*I cannot make mistakes.*" Doe's features had darkened, her lips turning into a thin line. "*You shouldn't say that.*"

Hawke remembered the virtual temper tantrum he had induced back in the park, and thought of a young toddler not getting her way. *Combine her resources with your typical God complex in a child like that,* he thought, *and you have a very volatile situation.*

One that surely wouldn't end well for them.

Abruptly Weller touched something inside the case. Doe blinked, her mouth working, no sound coming from the speakers. He turned to Hawke and Vasco. "All right," he said quickly. "I needed to keep her talking long enough to record a loop. I engaged it now with an auto bot program that will simulate a real feed. It's rough; she'll see through it. But right now, she doesn't know the difference; she thinks we're still sitting here staring at her."

"I don't get it," Vasco said. "You recorded a loop?"

"You've got the evidence," Weller said, ignoring Vasco and patting Hawke on the shoulder. "Find a way to tell the story. You only have a few seconds to disappear before she realizes what I've done. She's going to get angry."

"Jim," Hawke said. His heart was pounding hard. "I don't think—"

"Go!" Weller shouted. Tears shimmered in his eyes. "I don't know how much longer I can hold her off. Keep away from cameras and find a way to stay undercover and maybe you'll have a chance. Now *run!*"

CHAPTER THIRTY-FOUR   5:50 P.M.

HAWKE TOOK ONE MORE LOOK at James Weller, but the man had already turned back to the hologram floating eerily above the open black case, fiddling with the equipment. *Good luck,* Hawke thought. *You're going to need it.* Then he darted away under the overpass through a break in the fence, keeping to the shadows, moving as quickly as possible through the rubble.

So *that* had been what Weller meant about playing chess. He'd been baiting her while setting up his next move, one he had to pray she wouldn't see coming: a loop that replaced the real thing as they raced for the exits. But was she really that gullible? And was baiting her a smart thing to do? Because once she found out what he'd done, Hawke thought, there would be hell to pay.

He figured he had only minutes before that happened.

Hawke stopped where the overpass swept downward as if burrowing into the earth. To his right was a sad-looking dog park and an open lot, work cranes standing silent and still over steel storage containers and stacks of giant metal girders. To his left, the tunnel emerged from darkness into light, rising up to street level and crammed with more abandoned cars, and beyond that was 39th Street and a hulking old concrete building with construction scaffolding clinging to it.

An idea was forming, born from the glimpse of freedom he'd gotten while racing down Tenth Avenue in the old pickup truck. There was another way off this island, a way that didn't depend on an open tunnel or intact bridge. A way that was free of security cameras and tracking devices.

He just had to stay alive long enough to get there.

As he worked his way toward the 39th Street side of the underpass and the concrete barrier that separated him from the tunnel exit ramp, Hawke heard a noise and glanced back. Vasco stood right behind him.

"All that stuff about me being a part of this," Hawke said. Anger surged within him. "Even while you were accusing me, you were working for Eclipse."

"It was a good distraction. Kept the focus off me." Vasco shrugged. "Look, I'm just a low-level grunt, a freelancer they hired to keep tabs on Jim Weller. I was supposed to report in three times a day, relate what was happening in the office. That's all. I didn't know anything about this . . . system he had created. I swear to God. I didn't know what was going to happen. They told me about *you,* though. A reporter supposedly covering Weller for a profile, but you had another agenda.

They thought you were after them—after Eclipse—told me to stay away from you. Keep my cover."

"And you kept up the charade this whole time, even when the world was falling apart?"

"I figured it was better to stay quiet until I figured out what was really going on." He took a step closer. "I think I've got a pretty good handle on it now. I gotta say, it's even crazier than I thought."

"Stay away from me," Hawke said. "I'm getting out of New York, and nobody's going to stop me."

A gun had appeared in Vasco's hand. The same gun Hawke had tossed his way during their run-in with the men in black suits. "Can't let you do that," Vasco said. "You leave this overpass and we're both dead."

Hawke glanced back toward where they had left Weller. He was out of sight behind the cars and thick trunklike supports of the overpass. "Don't be stupid, Jason," Hawke said. "If we don't leave now, we're dead for sure. This place is going to be rubble any second, once she figures out what Jim's done."

"My name's not Jason; it's Tom. And I'm not stupid. At least we're out of sight. As soon as you break cover, she's going to find you. Satellites, security cams, whatever it takes, she's going to see you and target this spot. Much better to hide and wait for the troops to come in. They'll lock the city down eventually, stop this madness."

"They'll kill us. They have orders."

"You, maybe. Me, on the other hand, they have no beef with at all. This game is *over*. I just want to get out of here in one piece."

"What about your wife? You just going to wait here and hope she's okay?"

Vasco's face darkened with anger. "Don't you talk about her—"

A small red mark appeared on the man's forehead a split second before Hawke heard the soft bark of the rifle. Vasco (or whoever he was) crumpled without a sound, a look of surprise frozen on his face, his hand still clutching the gun. Hawke dove for cover behind the half wall, waiting for the second shot, knowing that he'd likely be dead before he heard anything.

Sniper. Military. It had to be. They were on the ground already, and Hawke's time had finally run out.

CHAPTER THIRTY-FIVE   6:01 P.M.

THE SHOT MUST HAVE COME from somewhere near the old building with the scaffolding. It had been incredibly accurate. The marksman was almost completely hidden under the overpass; there wasn't much space to hit the target between the top of it and the concrete wall that ran along the lower edge of the space, and it was dark inside here, difficult to see.

Hawke scrambled behind a support pillar, slowly lifted his head and peered around it. How was he supposed to avoid a bullet from a shooter like that? He saw nothing at first but lines of blank windows between red brick and worn gray concrete. Then he saw movement, a flash of camouflage slipping behind the far corner, another shifting on the roof. More than one, impossible to tell how many.

He looked for security cameras, saw nothing visible, but

he knew that they could be anywhere: inside the lobby of the building, hidden in doorways, the parking lot next door. Satellites could scan the earth and find him, anytime, anywhere. It seemed hopeless. But what choice did he have? He had to run, and trust Weller now to keep her eyes off him for a few seconds longer.

He was so close. Freedom was a couple of blocks away. A way back to his family, or what was left of them. *Hang on, Robin. Please. I'm coming.*

Hawke looked back at where Vasco lay still, blood oozing from the hole in his forehead, his mouth slightly open, as if he were about to speak. The gun was still in his hand. Hawke slipped from behind the pillar, crawled on hands and knees, wrenched the gun away and stuck it in his pants, then crawled low to the wall and sat. If he could get over and through the gap without being shot, he had a chance. The ramp was about ten feet below ground level here. He'd have to risk it.

He took a deep breath, then stood and vaulted over the top of the wall, rolling down a steep, grassy slope. He bounced off the slope and hit the roof of a car, his shoulder stinging from the impact, rolled again and dropped to his feet between a minivan and a hatchback.

Hawke knew he was below the shooter's line of sight now, and temporarily shielded from view. The ramp was cluttered with vehicles and smelled of oil and dust. He glanced into the gloom of the tunnel entrance, saw nothing and turned toward street level. Directly before him was open space where the tunnel passed 39th Street before diving back underground.

Hawke ran full bore up the ramp, darting left and right to try to make it more difficult for the shooter, his shoes pounding on the sidewalk. He didn't know how long he could go before a bullet took him; he was fully exposed now, nothing but a few thin trees between him and the sniper. Someone shouted what sounded like a command to halt. He would have to make a choice, either head left into more open space or go down again, toward the second tunnel entrance that was hopelessly jammed with cars and black as pitch inside.

Open space was dangerous, but the tunnel was worse. There was no way he could navigate through the darkness and stopped traffic all the way to New Jersey. He had a better way.

Hawke ducked and dodged, but no shots came. A familiar noise came from somewhere far away, growing rapidly louder. He clapped his hands to his ears as the rocket roared and the ground exploded behind him. He stumbled and almost fell, the pavement shaking like an earthquake had hit, and he looked back to see the overpass where he had just been lying in ruin, a small mushroom cloud of dust rising up from below.

Jesus God. He couldn't tell how bad the damage was, or whether Weller might have escaped or not. Maybe he had moved locations before the strike; maybe he was already set up again a few hundred feet from here. Or maybe he was still running.

The dust cloud spread quickly to envelop the brick and concrete building where the sniper hid, obscuring his line of sight. Hawke took the opportunity to dart left onto 39th Street, running past an auto repair shop with two open garage bays and a giant billboard advertising a luxury vehicle. An open parking lot was on his left. *Surely there are security cameras here,* he thought, but nothing happened and he didn't see anything as he kept running, breathing hard, closer now to his goal. The Javits Center was directly ahead of him, but as he hit Eleventh Avenue he veered right, cutting across the intersection toward more warehouses and parking lots on 40th Street.

At the end of 40th, he could see the Hudson, the flat, gray surface stretching away into the distance, almost close enough to touch. Hope blossomed inside him for the first time. However, he knew there were cameras here; he saw two mounted in a garage doorway of the bus depot that lined the block. Hawke kept looking straight ahead and ran, breath whistling in his lungs, the headache that had plagued him pounding harder with every step. His mouth was filled with cotton, his body aching for something to drink. He thought of plunging his face in the dirty river water and sucking down mouthfuls of it as if it were the finest mountain spring. He thought of his little boy drinking from a silver fountain at the preschool they had visited last week, climbing the short stepstool and still barely able to reach the nozzle, Hawke helping him manage it by holding Thomas around the waist and gently lifting. A little boy like that needed his father. The memory urged Hawke on faster.

As he reached the Lincoln Highway, another rocket streaked through the sky. He grew paralyzed with fear as it continued low to the ground, a silver bullet racing over the closest rooftop toward its target.

The rocket hit the Javits Convention Center with a dull boom, taking out the top half of the building and sending debris raining down across the adjacent parking lot. Hawke felt his insides clench as the heat washed over him. Doe was close, but she didn't have him yet, for whatever reason. Weller must have done something before the last rocket hit, enough to throw her off in some way. Hawke still had a chance.

He ran again. Another rocket screamed overhead, racing past him to hit the end of the bus depot near Eleventh. The strike lit up gas tanks in quick succession, sending booming clouds of black smoke into the air, along with the smell of singed metal and rubber and another wave of heat. The world was exploding. Doe was raging now, blindly attacking along the route he'd taken, but getting closer.

There was a security camera mounted on the corner of the building on his left. He raced past it and prayed that her eyes were still blinded, vaulted over the hoods of two cars that had collided, then crawled across two more to reach the other side of the intersection and a small patch of green lawn.

Edgewater Landing was directly in front of him.

Last year, after a trip to the park to see the zoo, they had taken Thomas on a sightseeing cruise. It had been more for Robin than their son, really; he had been too young to appreciate the scenery as they plowed through the water and looked back at the city as night fell and the lights glowed like glittering jewels.

Less than halfway through, Thomas had thrown a full-blown tantrum on the deck, kicking his legs and screaming, and Hawke had regretted pushing the day so far, but he hadn't wanted it to end. He remembered thinking about how easy it was to get in and out of New York by boat, and vowing to take the ferry more often.

Weller's last words came back to him: *Keep away from cameras and find a way to stay undercover and maybe you'll have a chance.*

There were no cameras in the middle of the Hudson, and even the satellites would have a hard time finding a small craft once it reached the ocean.

Hawke reached the docks a moment later. It was cooler here by the water, the day's heat beginning to bleed away with the sun. Several large cruise ships were anchored in the oily water, but it wasn't the large ones he was interested in. He needed something small and nimble, able to slip under the radar and disappear into the open arms of the river.

A moment later, he found it, lashed to the pier near one of the largest cruisers: an old tugboat, rusted and battered and brown with rust and grime, with an inflatable dinghy tethered to the back.

He boarded the tugboat, slipping across the silent deck, and peered over the side to the dinghy. The outboard motor looked newer, a Mercury with fresh paint and an electric starter. The dinghy was similar to one that he'd used on Cuttyhunk Island to putter around the shoreline when he was a teenager.

As he climbed down the side of the tugboat, boarded the dinghy and set the choke, another low boom sounded from somewhere beyond Manhattan. He pushed the electric start button on the engine and listened to it turn over with a high whine before he remembered to prime the gas bulb. Frantically he pushed the start button again. The Mercury coughed and started up with a burbling chatter.

A prickling fear ran up Hawke's back as he worked at the tie ropes with trembling fingers, the knots slimy and tight and refusing to let go. The whistling was getting louder. How close was Doe now? How much had she seen of his mad rush to this place? *Come on!*

The last knot finally gave. Hawke threw off the rope, dove toward the engine and pushed the throttle forward. The little boat leaped forward, nearly tossing him into the water as he grabbed for the tiller and turned, watching the skies as death streaked toward him with a thin silver tail.

The dinghy was about fifty feet from land when the final strike hit.

Hawke whipped the little boat around the larger sight-seeing cruiser that sat farther down the pier like a fat toad, low in the water and motionless, its sightless glass portholes winking at him with the reflection of the approaching rocket. The ship partially shielded him from the explosion and probably, he thought, saved his life; at the very least it obscured whatever view Jane Doe might have had of his fate.

The rocket hit the end of the pier closest to Eleventh Avenue, taking great chunks of rock and wood timbers and flinging them into the air like splinters in the wind. The debris and shock wave ripped holes through the heavy cruise ship and pushed it onto its side, a dead carcass wallowing in choppy surf, the remains torn apart as if it were nothing more than a toy.

A wave of water picked up Hawke's little dinghy and gave it a violent shove. He clung on to the rope that lined the sides of the boat with both hands, abandoning the tiller and falling to the rubber floor as chunks of metal and wood rained down, bouncing off the sides of the boat and pattering into the river around him.

Somehow, the boat survived. It rocked and spun like a top, rearing up and nearly throwing him into the waves before it crested the huge surge of water and began to settle back into the frothy surf, still whole, still floating.

As the whirlwind subsided, Hawke grabbed the tiller and straightened out the little craft. He glanced back at the shoreline, saw the last remaining husk of the cruise ship rear up and then slip beneath the dark surface of the river and the black columns of smoke rising up behind it, the dock obliterated, the Javits Center a smoking, caved-in bubble, the bus depot a raging inferno. Orange flames towered skyward, turning the smoke into reflective clouds of reaching fingers.

New York was burning.

He was alive, though. He had made it out somehow, and now he was gone, a shadow slipping through the white-capped waves toward home.

CHAPTER THIRTY-SIX   6:42 P.M.

THE SCREAMS WOKE HIM.

He'd been dreaming. In his dream, he'd been trying to run away from someone threatening him, but he couldn't get his legs to work. It was like trying to push through quicksand.

He gasped awake, staring up into the dark.

Thomas shrieked again, the sound like a gunshot in the silence: "Daaaaddy!"

Hawke got out of bed, heart pounding as Robin sat up, mumbling something, her arm reaching for him as she rolled over and slumped back again, still half-asleep. Hawke knew from experience that she tended not to remember things like this; in the morning, when he explained that he had been up for hours dealing with night terrors, she would look at him like he was crazy. So he had become the de facto nighttime riser, handling the soiled diapers, nightmares and fevers.

He felt his way around the edge of the bed frame and made it into the hall, stumbling through the shadows. Thomas's night-light glowed from beyond his half-open door.

The boy was sitting up against his headboard, holding his lion. They had just switched him out of his toddler bed to a full-size twin, and he looked swallowed by it, just a small lump at the top, like an extra pillow. Thomas's eyes were shining, his tiny shoulders moving up and down.

Hawke went to the bed, climbed in and hugged the boy to his chest. Thomas wrapped his arms around him, sobbing, his little fingers clutching at Hawke's undershirt. At first, Thomas didn't say anything, and Hawke waited, not pushing him.

Finally, Thomas's tears began to slow. He looked up at Hawke, his little moon face wet.

"What's wrong, little man?"

"I had a bad thing in my head. And I was scared."

Hawke kissed his son's head. "Shhhh . . . it's okay now. What happened? Can you tell me?"

"We were in the park, and you said we should go, but Mommy said we should wait and have a snack first. And then she gave me an apple. But I didn't finish my snack. And then I didn't want to stay because you left and I was alone. And I tried to find home."

"You were lost?"

"Yes." The little boy nodded soberly. "And there were people, but nobody would help me."

"Didn't Mommy or Daddy help you?"

"Daddy, you don't live at the park."

"No, but if you were lost, we'd come find you. We wouldn't leave you like that."

"Oh. Well, I heard a noise. Sort of like a ghost. Whoooooo . . .

like that. And there was a bridge to cross if you wanted to get away, but I couldn't get on it."

"And then what happened?"

"And then I was in my room, and you were in your room. And a bad guy came in and he wouldn't let me go to your room, and he took me away."

Hawke had come to cherish these moments, because they were the only times Thomas really spoke freely. Robin didn't hear it; it was as if Thomas knew she was a heavy sleeper. The boy always called for his father at night.

He smoothed his son's damp hair, rocked him softly. "Don't worry, buddy. There are no bad guys here. You're safe in your room. I wouldn't let anything happen to you, ever."

"What if you can't find me, Daddy? What if I disappear?"

A noise came from the hall outside the apartment. A door slamming, loud enough to make Thomas jump. Hawke hugged his son closer.

"I'd find you," he said. "If I had to go to the end of the earth, I would find you and bring you home."

Home. The idea was almost too much to bear, but Hawke kept it in his mind, sitting alone in the little dinghy, his hand shaking on the tiller as he pointed the craft toward the other shore. Getting to this point had taken everything he had in him, but now that he was finally able to breathe again he found himself unable to cope with all that had occurred.

The trip across the river was less than twenty minutes. Hawke sat as close to the motor as possible, keeping the weight in the back to lift the prow and keep the dinghy above the chop. He scanned the water for more boats but saw nothing. Wherever the military ship was that had fired on them, it wasn't visible.

He felt a brief moment of loneliness, of things settling, this new future becoming permanent as it coalesced before him. The others were all dead; whatever had happened was done, and there was nothing he could do to change it. But his wife and son could still be alive, *had* to be alive. He would find them, no matter what it took. He would keep them safe. In the back of his mind, another voice kept nagging at him, one that was more cynical: Even if they had survived, what were the chances of them still being at the apartment? Wouldn't they have tried to run by now, get to safety, find help? Hawke's excitement mixed with dread as he huddled against the chill wind and sped across the waves, praying for them to be safe. The words became a mantra, repeated over and over as he got closer: "Please, God, let them be okay. I don't care about anything else but seeing them again. I can handle anything else you throw at me; just please let them be okay."

The chop increased as he moved farther away from Manhattan and entered the open water of the river. It was a long way to go in a tiny dinghy, but Hawke settled his shoulders and kept his head down against the spray. New Jersey rose up before him, apartment buildings hugging Port Imperial Boulevard, more private homes dotting the swell of land above and beyond them. From this distance, it looked peaceful and empty, just another summer day settling into evening. He could imagine people sitting down on their front porches and docks, having a drink and watching the sun go down. The breeze would gain a bite off the water as the smell of grilled burgers and hot dogs and the sound of laughing children drifted over them. But that had all changed now, maybe forever.

There was a pier directly across the water at Weehawken, more boats anchored there, but he angled the little dinghy left, heading toward Hoboken and Pier C. He looked back once more to see the New York skyline rising up silent and strange like an alien creature, its limbs bleeding and broken, no longer welcoming and familiar.

As he began his approach to the Jersey shoreline, Hawke slipped his hand in his pant pocket for his house keys, just to make sure he still had them. There was something else there, something unfamiliar. He pulled out the flash drive Weller had given him, remembered the agent holding the gun on him (*Where is it? Tell me right now, goddamn it, or I'll blow your brains out*), the way Weller looked at him before he left (*A way to prove the truth in all this. . . . Find a way to tell the story*). . . .

Hawke clutched it in his fist, then withdrew his hand, wondering how he would even find a computer that could read it without alerting Doe. And then what? As soon as he tried to send the documents to someone, she would find him. If he connected to a server, she would know where he was. He couldn't even print anything without risking detection, assuming there was a machine left on earth that wasn't corrupted already.

But all that could wait. Right now, he had more important things to do.

CHAPTER THIRTY-SEVEN   6:59 P.M.

AS HAWKE GOT CLOSER to Pier C, he noticed smoke coming from the Jersey light-rail station.

His heart sank as he saw what looked like a bad accident,

debris everywhere. Some kind of explosion had ripped out the guts of the buildings that had lined the water's edge, exposing the heart of the station. There was more carnage inside; trains had probably smashed into each other at the tunnel entrance, or buses, or both.

Doe had blocked the tunnel from this side, too. Cutting people off, isolating New York, experimenting in some twisted way. Eliminate two-thirds of the population, leaving those you need still alive, and do all of it without anyone truly understanding who was behind it all, or why.

Energy sharing will only delay the outcome . . . , she had said. *But a reduction of consumers by sixty-three-point-four percent, combined with advances in fusion energy production that are predicted with ninety-eight-point-six percent certainty, would oscillate the current string enough to enter an alternate path.*

He motored closer, watching carefully; a few emergency workers were helping the injured at the scene, but it was a crippled operation. It took him a few moments to realize why. They were working without their familiar tools. There were no vehicles with flashing lights, open ambulances, cardiac machines. The people weren't carrying tablets and nobody was talking on phones. He scanned the shore for the girl who had served him coffee that morning (so long ago, it seemed, light-years away) but didn't see her red-streaked hair among the others. She was either long gone or buried somewhere beneath the wreckage.

Hawke still had grease smeared across his cheeks, and his clothes were dirty and torn. But he must have looked like everyone else who had been through hell today. Nobody noticed him as he ran the little boat up to the esplanade that jutted out into the Hudson, tied it off and climbed to land.

Nobody cared as he raced like a madman down the esplanade's still beautiful, tree-lined walkways to Sinatra Drive, turning left and racing to Newark Street, running hard, his shoes pounding on the sidewalk. *Keep focused on that sound,* he thought, *just keep going,* as his breath wheezed in his aching lungs, *do* not *think of Robin and your son, your unborn child and what might have happened to them.* He'd been gone from home for less than twelve hours; it hardly seemed possible that everything that had happened had been during such a short span of time. He wondered if Robin would notice the differences in him, the way he felt them himself. Would he seem like a stranger, a different man entirely, one who had been through a war and come back withered inside and broken? And what would they do once they found each other? She might not think it was possible to make it to open water without being discovered.

Or maybe she wouldn't even want to go.

The door to their building was open.

Hawke stood in the shadowed gap, breathless, peering inside. The landing was still, silent, dark. He pushed the door wide, stepped inside, saw the list of names and the buzzers for entry, the interior doors closed tight, more darkness beyond the glass.

Within the intensity of his emotions, the familiar had become strange; things he had never noticed before drew his attention. The brown carpet was worn in a straight line, the wallpaper water stained and faded. It looked like a different place, even though it was the same.

His nerves were singing, his breath too shallow and fast. He forced himself to slow down, calmed himself enough to function. It wouldn't do Robin or Thomas any good if he lost his mind now, not when he was so close to finding out what had happened to them.

The power was out, the buzzers not working. The electronic lock for the interior doors wasn't working, either, but he hadn't really expected it to be that easy. He kicked at the glass until it broke, the sound too loud in the quiet of the building.

He climbed through the opening, drew the gun from his pants, moved through the lobby and bypassed the elevators, which were surely not running now. The stairs were blanketed in gloom, and empty. He took them as quickly as he dared, spiraling up through the dark. Finally, he reached the door to his floor, pushed it open with a soft click and slipped through, caught it before it closed and let it tick shut.

At the end of the hall, gray light filtered in through a small window. Hawke's dream that morning came back with a vengeance; his son being ripped away from his arms by silvery tendrils snaking down from the sky. The memory left him shaken, momentarily unable to move his feet toward his own apartment, terrified of what he might find there.

Their door was open just a crack. The jamb had been forced, the latch shattered.

Hawke looked at Lowry's door, also hanging open. And he knew.

Lowry had been here.

Hawke pushed the door open with the tip of the gun, called Robin's name, quietly at first, and then louder. Nothing. The front hall was empty. Time slowed down; details sharpened; smells assailed his nostrils. He saw everything in extreme clarity as his fear turned seconds to minutes, minutes to hours. He stepped inside. A clanking hiss made him clench his teeth and nearly scream before he realized it was the radiators giving up the last of their heat. Shadows clung to corners like cobwebs, but on the far wall a bit of light fell, enough to see the spray of blood that speckled the paint.

A small, helpless cry escaped Hawke's lips. Tears filled his vision, blurring the bloody spray, blackened in the shadows and light. The camera image he'd seen hadn't been faked. Which meant that the rest of it had probably been real, too: Robin's panicked phone call, the video of the shadow across the screen as the laptop was lifted, the image moving across the ceiling before someone abruptly snapped it closed.

The shoe he had seen in that brief glimpse before the laptop's camera was cut off, just the tip visible through the bedroom door . . .

A bedroom door that was now shut tight, its knob coated red.

He held the gun up in a trembling hand, scanning the empty space, kitchen and living room, the overturned lamp still on the floor, other signs of disarray. A plastic cup had been knocked from the counter. Thomas's blocks were strewn across the living room. There was more blood staining the carpet near the spatter.

As Hawke moved forward toward the bedroom, louvered doors sprang open and something exploded out of the hallway closet beside him, a wild-eyed, screeching, bloodied apparition holding a knife overhead. He turned with the gun, his heart hammering, finger nearly squeezing the trigger before recognition lit him up like an electric shock; he ducked to one side as she descended upon him and the blade slashed down; he caught her knife arm with his own forearm in a swift parry, knocking the blade away before he wrapped her in a bear hug, his beautiful wife, screaming and then sobbing into collapse as he gently said her name, over and over.

"I'm here," Hawke said, whispering it into her hair, trying to calm her trembling, rigid body with his embrace, his tears mixing with her own. "I made it; we're okay now; everything's going to be all right."

But Robin didn't respond or seem to hear him, her eyes unfocused as, behind her, Thomas emerged from the closet, and Hawke let her go before gathering his boy in his arms, safe and whole and unharmed.

CHAPTER THIRTY-EIGHT 7:20 P.M.

WHEN HE HAD CALMED DOWN enough to think, Hawke checked Robin and Thomas over carefully, found the blood that coated their skin was not their own. They had no cuts on them, no signs of physical trauma. He touched Robin's belly gently, found the swelling there, no apparent pain; the baby seemed to be okay. But Robin wouldn't speak a word, and Thomas simply kept his arms locked around his father's waist, unwilling to let him go. Thomas kept his eyes squeezed shut for a while, tears leaking down his cheeks, and when he finally opened them his pupils were dilated with shock.

Hawke whispered to him as the last of the sun's rays slipped through the living room window, his voice trembling with sadness, joy, exhaustion, emotions cascading through him and leaving him weak limbed and spent. He touched his son's face, tracing invisible lines on his skin. Thomas didn't move; Robin shied away from him until he let his hand drop. She sat on the carpet and stared out at nothing.

When he was able to untangle himself from his son's arms and get up, Hawke found the body in the bedroom.

Randall Lowry was lying on his side, one arm slung out, the other twisted beneath him. His hair hung across his glazed, sightless eyes, bubbles of blood drying on his lips. His jaw was dotted with salt-and-pepper stubble, the skin ashy gray; his cheeks were hollow, sagging pockets of flesh. He looked like a wax statue of a dead man, and Hawke couldn't imagine that this person, these deflated remains, had caused them so much pain.

He saw how it might have happened. They'd been watching reports on the TV about the events unfolding in New York and across the country. Thomas knew his father went to the city. Perhaps Thomas had gotten scared, made a racket, spilling his blocks, knocking over the lamp. *I want my daddy.* He imagined Randall Lowry calling out from the hallway, increasingly agitated, banging on the door and screaming at them, which would have gotten Thomas even more worked up until he was screaming, too.

Or maybe Lowry had just taken this opportunity to go after Robin. Hawke remembered how Lowry looked at her and had always suspected what he would do, if given the chance. He remembered the incident in the basement, Lowry staring at her photos. Her belly wasn't showing much yet, and even if it was, that might not have changed anything for a man like him.

The doors to these apartments were flimsy, hollow-core replacements, with cheap locks and a single chain for additional protection. Lowry wouldn't have had much trouble kicking it open. Robin had hidden in the closet as he came in, somehow keeping Thomas quiet, and then approached Lowry from behind; there were knife wounds in his neck near the collarbone and a deep gash under his arm. She had stabbed him high first, Hawke reasoned, causing the spray on the wall, and then as Lowry had turned and thrown up his hand to ward her off she had stabbed him in the side, puncturing his lung and driving him into the bedroom, where his life had leaked away quickly, judging from the wounds and the amount of blood on the floor. Perhaps she'd hit his jugular with the first slash; the spray was violent and wide, enough to tell that he'd been mortally wounded.

Lowry hadn't had a weapon with him.

Hawke thought about that as he led Robin into the bathroom and gently undressed her, scrubbing off the blood under a lukewarm spray. Just because the man had been unarmed, in the traditional sense, didn't mean he wasn't a clear danger. He'd threatened them before, several times, and he had forced entry into the apartment. He was larger and stronger than Robin and had a history of mental illness. He was violent. She had acted in self-defense; there was no question in Hawke's mind. She would do whatever she had to do to protect herself and their son.

But others might not see it that way, if the world ever got back to normal and the authorities ever investigated the killing. They might wonder why she hadn't tried to speak to Lowry first, why she had snuck up from behind that way and stabbed him without trying to escape. In Hawke's mind, the reason was clear; there was no way she would have gotten to the stairs with Thomas in her arms before Lowry would have run them down.

But things weren't always so simple, when the law got

involved. They didn't care about Hawke's family the way he did. They cared about facts, not speculation. They would give Lowry's life far more weight than it deserved.

Robin stood there limply, shivering and passive in a bra and underpants while Thomas sat huddled in the corner, his worn old stuffed rabbit sagging in his iron grip. Hawke washed Robin's face until it was pink and she looked like a different woman, younger, more childlike. He caressed his wife's bare shoulders, watched the swirls of red disappearing down the drain.

When they emerged from the apartment an hour later, it was completely dark. Hawke went back in and found a flashlight in the kitchen, using it to navigate down the stairs to the street. The sun had gone down beyond the layer of smoke, bringing a deeper chill. It was strange not to see lights anywhere; none of the buildings had power, and Hoboken was like a wilderness.

The darkness was good, though; it provided them cover. Nobody saw them jogging down the empty streets, Hawke holding Thomas in his arms, a duffel bag slung over his other shoulder; there were no witnesses as they rushed down the walkway under a blanket of trees, found Hawke's dinghy still tied up to the esplanade and climbed into the boat. The few emergency workers he had seen when he'd docked there a short while ago were nowhere to be found.

The boat itself had no connection to the network, no ability to be monitored. Doe, with all her unnatural abilities, wouldn't be able to track him during the night through satellites or cameras. Even she had some limits. He had nine hours to disappear.

The world had gone into hiding, it seemed. It was an unsettling feeling. The stiffening breeze would require a jacket on the water, but he and Robin had only brought one for Thomas, not for themselves. She was moving on her own now and assisting Hawke when asked, but she still hadn't spoken and he hadn't been thinking clearly, and there was only so much they could carry. They would have to put on more layers of clothing from their bags and huddle together for warmth.

He got his wife into the dinghy and handed down his son, before slinging over the bag he carried and climbing in himself. Robin remained silent, distant, disconnected.

"I know it's a lot to take in," Hawke said. "What I told you about what happened. I know it probably sounds crazy. But it's the truth."

He'd tried to explain as much as he could while he was washing the blood off her, but he didn't know how much she'd absorbed. It all sounded like the ravings of a lunatic when he said it out loud. He could hardly believe it himself. A self-aware machine had tried to kill 63.4 percent of human life on the planet in order to ensure her own survival, and he was wanted by every law enforcement bureau in the country.

We have to run, find a place to hide. We have to get out now. I have an idea . . . trust me.

Hawke had studied Robin's reaction, but she was little more than a vague shape in the dark. He couldn't see her face. He risked raising the flashlight and flicking it on for a moment. She sat with her arms hugging her chest, Thomas between her legs. Hawke's son looked up at him, eyes glassy. Thomas had seen far too much today, and Hawke was afraid he would see a lot more before this was over.

He turned the light off, and the darkness moved in again.

"You left us alone," she said dully, her voice flat, expressionless. "I had to do it."

The words bit deeply. Hawke knelt in front of her. She allowed him to touch her face but didn't seem to react.

I should have been there. Robin had done what she had to do because he wasn't home to protect them. For all his struggles to fight through the worst of what had happened, he still hadn't been able to make it in time.

"I'm sorry," he said. "I know you did."

"I'm hungry," Thomas said. They were the first words he'd spoken since Hawke had found them.

Hawke touched the boy's head, and Thomas shrank back slightly, a turtle pulling into its shell. The guilt washed over Hawke again. He hadn't been there to protect them, and Robin had been forced to kill a man.

Hawke gave Thomas a granola bar from the bag. When he turned back, Robin was shaking, her shoulders moving in the dark. "He wouldn't stop," she said. "He . . . just kept coming."

Hawke couldn't tell if she was talking to him or to herself. He started the engine and swung the dinghy back out into the Hudson. Into the black. The open water was terrifying without the normal lights of Hoboken washing over it. Fires still burned in Manhattan, but they had begun to die out, and a sickly orange glow seemed to drift with the wind, a core of light at the center of the cluster of buildings. Doe had kept the power on there, gathering her strength, perhaps waiting until she had evolved into something else, something even more powerful. He had the sense that he was watching the birth of an entirely new species, one that could mean the end of humanity.

New York as they once knew it, and perhaps the entire United States of America—maybe the world—was gone.

But for now, at least, there had to be others still alive. There had to be a way to regain control. Cuttyhunk Island was probably two hundred miles away, impossible to reach in the dinghy. Hawke had realized that before they left the apartment. But he had a plan: maybe not the best one, but it gave them a chance. His friend and editor, Nathan Brady, had an old Bayliner Encounter he called the *Gypsy*, a twenty-nine-foot sportfishing boat with an enclosed cabin that slept four. Old enough to be without any kind of Internet connection or computer chip. He'd taken Hawke out on it several times and it was quickly evident that Brady used it more for drinking and sitting in the sun than catching his dinner, but they'd had a decent enough time talking about Hawke's next project, back when he was still working at the *Times*. It seemed like a lifetime ago.

Brady kept the boat at a marina in Jersey City, less then three miles away.

Hawke motored the dinghy close along the shore, where occasional small fires sputtered and gave him enough light to navigate. A few minutes later, the moon broke through the layer of smoke and its pale glow washed over the glassy surface of the water. Hawke sat next to Robin and worked the rudder, keeping them moving as quickly as he dared.

He thought about the baby who would come, and the challenge of delivering it alone. He thought about keeping hidden for long enough that it would matter. And something else nagged at him and wouldn't let go. Getting away was a little too easy, when all was said and done. If Doe had really wanted him dead, Hawke thought, she would have done it. The series of missile attacks had missed him, hitting locations where he had been only moments before. Almost as if she'd been herding him forward, pushing him to the docks and away from the city.

Perhaps, he thought, he was more valuable to her alive and at large, a supposed leader of the group that had struck at the heart of America. It would keep the authorities focused on something and provide a welcome distraction while she determined the best way forward. They would keep the power on, keep her running silently in the background and try to rebuild, blissfully unaware of the consequences.

And then, when she had figured out how to survive without the need of a single human life, she would eliminate them all.

To beat a machine at this game, you'll have to act unpredictably. She would expect him to go underground, try to disappear. Protect himself and his family. Hawke thought about how he might blow the lid off this story. There had to be a way. Word of mouth, hand-printed flyers. Shortwave radios. These things still existed, tried-and-true means to communicate that Doe couldn't easily manipulate to serve her needs. He thought about Rick. Maybe Doe had faked that footage, too. And Brady, if he was still alive. A network Hawke might be able to tap, let the story take root and grow. If they could convince the world to cut off all sources of power, to eliminate any remaining devices where she might hibernate.

He felt something warm touch his hand; Robin's fingers entwined with his own. Her flesh tingled like an electric shock. It would take time, but he hoped she would recover. In the dark, with the wind rippling his clothes and the smell of smoke drifting over him, he could almost believe it was possible. They could make it; they could survive.

But first, the Bayliner. He knew Brady kept the key in a small ceramic cup under the boat's kitchen sink.

If they could get going quickly enough, they might be able to make it most of the way to Cuttyhunk Island before dawn.

EPILOGUE

THE ISLAND WAS AN ENIGMA. It appeared abandoned, and yet it wasn't; the rocky shoreline seemed hostile as the waves crashed and broke against it, but beyond that cold, battered, dead shore, there was life.

It looked like the last place on the planet where a revolution would begin.

Hawke had been keeping to the lower level of the small, dusty cottage during daylight hours, and he made sure Robin and Thomas did, too. The windows were covered and there was no way to see inside. They couldn't risk being spotted by the spy satellites that still orbited the Earth with lenses sharp enough to pick up facial structure and map it to FBI databases in the cloud. It was likely Doe would feed that to the authorities, or strike against him herself. He couldn't test his theory that she still needed him alive, if indeed that had ever been the case; she might have grown strong enough now that she would simply eliminate him.

There were seven others on the island with them.

When they arrived that first day, dawn had already broken in the east. They needed to find shelter quickly. Hawke anchored Brady's boat off the rocky beach and took Robin and Thomas in the dinghy to the beach near West End Pond. Within moments of their hitting the sand, a man met them onshore. He was a lobsterman from up the coast who had been visiting a friend when the reports of an attack started to come over the TV, and he had remained there while most of the other inhabitants of Cuttyhunk Island had fled for the mainland.

His name was Ernesto, and his friend's name was Samantha. She owned a summer cottage on the harbor side of the island. They had holed up inside all day and night, but he had taken her old truck down to the far shore looking for boat lights as the power had cut out and the news reports from Dartmouth had abruptly gone silent.

Ernesto was friendly, and he didn't ask a lot of questions. He threw their bags in the back of the truck and took them to Hawke's aunt's place, which was at the end of a dead-end dirt road about half a mile from what stood for the center of town. There was no sign of Hawke's aunt, but he hadn't expected to find her there. She had a permanent home in St. Louis and was either dead or focused on trying to survive where she was. Getting to Cuttyhunk would be the least of her worries, if she had survived at all.

Ernesto promised to return later with supplies. Hawke couldn't turn him down. The truck was too old to be tracked and Ernesto didn't own a cell phone, and Hawke knew they were going to need help. This man was about the best bet they had. The cottage had been boarded up and abandoned. Hawke managed to get the water running, but there was no food, and mice had made nests in the mattresses and chewed the wiring and insulation to shreds. There was a generator, but no gas, and two upper windows were broken.

But the roof was intact and the inside was dry. They had water to drink and bathe in, and a place to regroup. It was enough, for now.

Later that afternoon, Ernesto returned, true to his word,

and brought canned goods and candles, and Hawke spent three hours relating as much of his story as he dared, leaving out his real name. He couldn't risk the chance that Ernesto had heard a report about him being a fugitive from justice. There was nobody left to arrest him on the island, but a man like Ernesto might decide to take the law into his own hands.

But Ernesto had his own checkered past, as he explained to them, and he was no friend to law enforcement. Hawke finally decided to trust him with more information. Ernesto didn't seem all that surprised when Hawke explained most of what he knew about Jane Doe and Eclipse, saying with a half-serious smile that he'd always figured it was only a matter of time until the machines took over. He didn't much care for technology, he said, never had. He lived his life the old-fashioned way.

In his prior life, Hawke might have labeled Ernesto a paranoid dinosaur; now, he thought, men like that might be the last survivors.

That night, their first on the island, Hawke took the dinghy back out to Brady's boat under cover of darkness and used cans of old paint he'd found in his aunt's shed to paint over the hull identification number and obscure the name on the stern. He had considered shooting holes in the hull to sink it, but there were enough old Bayliners in the world to keep this one hidden in plain sight, he thought. Besides, they might need it again.

Ernesto's friend Samantha, whom they met on the second night, was a thin blonde of about forty with a husky smoker's voice and a tendency to curse like a sailor, and she wasn't inclined to ask many questions. Upon further observation, she and Ernesto appeared to be more than friends, but since they didn't volunteer more information, Hawke didn't ask for details. She was friendly enough and shared her stock of food willingly; the small Cuttyhunk country store was packed with supplies, and nobody was around to protest when they took what they needed.

At night they listened to a shortwave radio Ernesto had found while checking out one of the abandoned houses on the other side of town; they heard intermittent reports of chaos across the country. Signals appeared to be frequently blocked, but by using higher frequencies and changing them regularly broadcasters kept finding a way through. It appeared that the contagion, some kind of computer supervirus, had spread throughout the world, shutting down communications networks, immobilizing computers and most machines with a Web connection of any kind. It was reported that the virus had been unleashed by the hacker group Anonymous. Authorities were scrambling to find a way to respond to the threat.

When Hawke's name was mentioned in a breaking news bulletin, Ernesto and Samantha barely seemed to react. To them, he was John Siegel from western Massachusetts. They had no reason to think anything else.

They settled in as best they could. Robin remained distant at first, but during the course of long days with little to do she began to open up. Hawke listened to her as she described the attack, haltingly at first, and then everything spilling out: It had happened just like he'd imagined, Lowry shouting about Thomas and then kicking the door down as Robin scrambled for a butcher knife from the kitchen, running through the hallway to hide in the bedroom. Thomas's screams had continued, but Lowry had seemed surprised at the force of her attack. Perhaps, in his mind, she was the helpless little girl in the photograph from the basement. He had died with little more than a gurgle as his life bled out onto the carpet.

Thomas had witnessed everything.

If Thomas was traumatized, it didn't show on the surface. But the boy seemed different. He was more talkative, animated, his eyes bright and inquisitive. He explored every inch of the house in the first few hours, Hawke trailing behind him, making sure he didn't get into anything dangerous. Thomas would need to deal with what he had seen eventually, but for now, Hawke was content to let him absorb his new surroundings and radically altered life. The world was different now, too, and Thomas would have to deal with that. They all would.

Gradually, Hawke learned more details. They listened to the shortwave as much as possible and discovered a world on the brink of a new war. Two opposing factions appeared to be battling for prominence, and two separate histories about what had gone down were emerging.

Anonymous was gaining its own voice.

During the course of the next two weeks, Hawke learned of the five others still living on the island, in addition to Ernesto and Samantha: a seventy-nine-year-old man who couldn't make it to the mainland on his own, a woman who had taught at the small schoolhouse and her eight-year-old son, and two gay men who had rented a cottage for the summer and had decided they were better off staying there while the rest of the country got its act together.

Not much of an army. But it would have to do.

Cuttyhunk Island was a couple of miles long in total, and the walk to the center of town was easy enough. Hawke left the house as dusk fell, taking Bayberry Hill Road to Bayview, which would take him past the Cuttyhunk corner store and onto Gosnold.

The sky was completely clear for the first time since they had landed here. Hawke looked up at the stars, saw what looked like winking pinpricks of light, imagined satellites wheeling through space, aiming their cameras down on him. He shivered. Doe was up there, watching. One false move and everything he had begun to build would unravel. Their life was fragile, their chances remote. But right now, it was all they had, and he was determined not to go down without a fight.

The harbormaster station was located on a finger of land at the end of Gosnold, with a dock that stuck out into Cuttyhunk Pond. There was direct access to the harbor, but that wasn't what Hawke had come here for tonight. A faint glow illuminated the basement windows at the station. He reached the door and entered quickly, following the sound of voices to the flight of steps that led down into the flickering gloom.

They were all there, gathered around ghostly shapes covered with sheets: Ernesto and Sam, Donald Madison, Kent and Alan, Melissa and her son, Ryan. Other than Robin, who had remained at home with a sleeping Thomas, this represented the entire population of Cuttyhunk. Donald, the seventy-nine-year-old, had promised to show Hawke something, and they had all waited for him to begin.

A week earlier, Hawke had gone to Ernesto and Sam's house, where he had proceeded to tell the true story about what had occurred in New York. The reports on the radio had convinced him to do it; if what he suspected was true, he would need all the help he could get. Although Sam seemed to reserve judgment, Ernesto bought it all immediately and rounded up the others who were left on the island for a meeting.

Which had led to this.

Hawke stepped into the light from the candles, looking around the basement at the faces, all focused on him. He didn't see any hostility here; people were long past that now. You had to place your bets on those you could trust, and hope you were right.

Two channels on the shortwave had begun to offer an alternative explanation for the chaos. Anonymous had started firing back. Hawke recognized Rick's methods in the reports and had become convinced that his friend was still alive, still operating his network as best he could and fighting Doe tooth and nail for what remained of the nation's trust.

They couldn't communicate using the regular channels, but Hawke was determined to find another way.

"Where is it?" he said to Donald Madison. The old man had told him about this place just yesterday, and what it contained. The building had been there for many years, and before it had become the harbormaster station it had served as the location of the only newspaper that had ever existed on Cuttyhunk.

Madison hobbled forward to the largest of the shrouded humps. He slipped off the sheet, coughing loudly as a cloud of dust rose up in the candlelight. An ancient, oily printing press stood before them, the kind with two large wheels and gears and metal feeders that caught the long sheets of paper and fed them through to the other side. R. Hoe & Company, New York was stamped in the metal along one side.

"My father used to run it," Madison said. "Back when the news still meant something. I helped him some when I was a boy. She may look old, but she'll do the trick. There's some paper in the bins there, and ink, too, although I'm not sure it's still good."

Hawke ran his hand along the press's cool iron bars, inspected the feeder's teeth and the lines of letters still set to some early edition, frozen in time. He'd learned about these relics in school, enough to know something about how they worked. You could crank it by hand, pull the lever and send the pages through. Each page would need to be set by hand, which would take time. But there was an odd sort of poetry to using a machine like this. Back to the beginning, when the news business was first born. They could run copies here and use the boat to bring them to New Bedford. From there, they could reach most of New England, and get the word to Rick and any others out there willing to listen. They had to shut down the nation's power sources, one at a time, isolate Doe and strangle her to death.

Hawke looked around at the faces in the basement. There were still humans left alive, still people willing to fight for survival if they could be convinced of the truth.

I want you to tell a story now, Weller had said. The biggest one of your life.

It wasn't much, but it was a start.

ACKNOWLEDGMENTS

I'd like to thank my editors at Thomas Dunne, Brendan Deneen and Peter Joseph. Their early guidance and incredibly insightful feedback on the first draft of *Day One* made it a much better book. I'd like to thank my agent, Howard Morhaim, a true gentleman in this business, for his hard work on my behalf. Finally, I'd like to thank my friends and family for their support, particularly my amazing wife, Kristie, and my children: Emily, Harrison, Abbey, and Ellie Rose. I love you all more than I can say.